Reignited Passions

Reignited Passions

JOHAN MIDDELTHON

StoryTerrace

CONTENTS

Chapter One
NOW
Jennifer

I loosen my grip on the paddle and size up our opponents. Everything rides on this game. If we win, we progress in the tournament, and finally get our chance at those golden tickets. If not…

All the off-court worries I've been staving off come rushing back. Mia's frantic call during our break, and the knot in my gut every time I think about Mom. She hasn't seemed entirely herself, lately—not the energetic, go-getter woman who raised me.

Plus, there are still the latent questions about our son. Is he doing okay? Is he still mad at us?

Worse, was there anything else we'd missed about our kids' lives? What if—

Across the net, the couple we're playing exchange eager grins. They're at least a decade younger than us, and they've been gaining steadily for the last few rallies. They obviously know they're on a verge of a win.

But they haven't beaten us yet.

My old competitive instincts kick in, the ones I've honed ever since my soccer era in college. I'd forgotten them for a long time, but in the past few months, they've resurfaced with a vengeance, all thanks to this.

To us.

I take a deep breath and shake out the knots in my shoulders, then glance over at my husband. He doesn't notice. He's watching our opponents, brow furrowed.

"Bash?" I call.

Sebastian—Bash—cuts me a glance and nods. Then his eyes go straight back to the game. I examine his profile for a moment: the familiar cut of his jaw and curve of his mouth. The faint stubble, visible because he didn't shave this morning, since we were running late.

Memories rise, unbidden. Our bodies, slick with shower water, pressed hard against one another. His hands on my hips, my waist, ripping my shirt off with abandon. And yesterday afternoon, on the hiking trail, my God—

"Yours!" Sebastian shouts, and I snap back to attention just as the ball bounces right in front of me. I manage to get the edge of my paddle on it, send it flying back over the net. Way too easy, though, right down the center. It bounces, and the girl opposite me volleys it back.

Bash and I toe the edge of the kitchen. The ball sails his way, and Bash returns it. Another one comes toward me, and I do the same.

When it returns the next time, it straddles the center line. Bash doesn't say anything, so on instinct, I swing my paddle around for a backhand hit.

I crack something a hell of a lot harder than a standard

issue Franklin X40. Bash swears, and we both freeze. I hit his paddle, not the ball. The latter dribbles right past us, rolling out of bounds. Fuck. Another point for them. One more and they win.

"Jen." Bash looks at me, but I turn away before he can say another word.

I stomp over to the ball, scoop it up and pop it over the net for their next serve. Focus. I can't get distracted. Not by our off-court problems, and certainly not by fantasizing about my own husband.

Things have changed so much for us, so quickly. Just a few months ago, our whole lives were different. Not great, necessarily—I was drowning in work back then, completely hating everything about it, and we hadn't had sex in... well, a shocking amount of time.

Now, though, I've still not fully adjusted to the new us. The fresh sparks that trail our interactions, the way every nerve ending in my body feels fired up, alight with desire. It's confusing. Good confusing, usually, but there's an undercurrent of worry. Will we lose it again? And so soon after we recaptured it, too.

"Jennifer." Sebastian again, more urgent now. "Last point."

"I know," I snap, irritated now. "I'm aware of the stakes here." My gaze travels past our opponents, to the other nets at our club. I spot a few familiar faces, friends of ours.

There are a few enemies, too. Crys in particular draws

my eye—she's been strutting around the place all afternoon like she owns it. Tall and immaculately styled, with stark blonde highlights, she's the type of person who knows how to make everyone around her feel small.

She catches me looking and her lip curls in a familiar sneer. I force my gaze away.

She and her equally asinine husband don't matter. Just me and Bash. Just the game.

"Ten, nine, one," calls their server as he positions the ball. Ten points to them, nine to us. They're in the lead, but we can still pull this out of the fire.

No way I'm letting them get the winning point. Not today. My blood sings. We can do this.

He serves, straight at me, and I raise my paddle and charge.

Chapter Two
THEN
Sebastian

"We're going to be late!" I yell up the staircase.

"Do you have to be so loud?" Jennifer mutters, brushing past me on her way to the kitchen.

"I wouldn't need to if our children would remember what time they start school." I direct the latter upstairs too, and I'm rewarded by thundering footsteps. Logan stomps downstairs first, hair a mess, jeans hanging halfway down his ass. "Oh hell no." I point at his waist. "We buy you clothing that actually fits for a reason."

"But everyone wears them like this," he says, hurrying by me into the kitchen.

Jennifer puts a pot of coffee on, then roots through the fridge. "Who ate the last yogurt?"

"Mom," Mia hollers from somewhere in the stratosphere, to judge by her volume. She inherited that from me. "I can't find my tablet."

"Would you tell your daughter to stop screaming and ask me when she has a question?" Jennifer shoots me a pointed look.

"Sure thing, if you tell your son to stop dressing like he's in a 90s boy band."

Jennifer releases a long-suffering sigh and waves at Logan. "You heard your father."

"But Mom—"

"No buts. You're running late already."

Grumbling, Logan wrestles his jeans up to a normal height while I jog upstairs. Mia's in her bedroom, looking like the eye of a tornado. "I can't find it!" she wails, in what I recognize as a precursor to a meltdown.

"Okay. Deep breath." I wait for her to take one. "Where was the last place you remember seeing it?"

She exhales through her nose, annoyed. "If I remembered, it wouldn't be lost!"

"All right, we'll do it the old-fashioned way." We dig through her bedroom, starting with the various purses and bags she takes to school, then shifting to the bed, where she thinks I don't know she sneaks her tablet after dark to browse social media.

Half an hour search, another argument about breakfast, and two last-second purse changes, and we're finally all in the car. I drive our usual route—dropping Logan and Mia at school before I drop Jennifer at her office. In the parking lot, we pause to write late slips for them both, since we don't get to the lot until half an hour past first bell.

As we watch them stride off into the building, Jennifer worries at her lower lip. "They're going to get in trouble if we keep doing this."

"I'm sure the school understands," I say.

Jennifer shoots me a look. "Did you know Logan skipped two assignments last week? He just never turned them in."

My brow furrows. "Are you sure? That doesn't sound like him."

"His teacher called. I texted you about it."

Now that she mentions it, I vaguely recall a message about his teacher reaching out. "I didn't realize it was that serious."

Jen exhales through her nose. "Color me shocked." She glances down at her phone. "Anyway, the same teacher called again last night. He didn't do the extra credit she assigned either."

I grimace, starting the car again. "I'll talk to him about it."

"Uh huh." Jennifer scowls out the window as we turn toward her office. The roads are empty at this hour, and still slick from last night's freeze. I slow down, navigating carefully. A couple blocks later, Jen mutters, "Course, if you'd talked to him the first time I asked, maybe he'd already be caught up by now."

I tighten my grip on the wheel. Do not respond. I recognize that tone. Whatever I say will only dig the hole she's determined to toss me in deeper.

Sometimes it's hard to believe where we've ended up. It seems like just yesterday we were kids ourselves, baby-faced freshmen at UNC Chapel Hill. Jennifer's whole family went to UNC, all the way back to her great-grandfather. As for me, I was the first generation to go to college—and the only reason I could afford it was thanks to the soccer scholarship I won.

Back in those days, adulthood seemed a million years away. All we needed to worry about was the present: winning the big game, getting a decent enough grade to pass (since sports scholarships alone couldn't sustain you if you fell too far behind)… and each other, of course.

I steal another sidelong glance at my wife. The years have aged us both, but her more gracefully than me. Aside from a few crow's feet and laugh lines, she looks the same as the day we met. From the first time I saw her on the sidelines of a soccer match, sandwiched among a cluster of other girls, I couldn't get her out of my mind. The other girls wore the same jerseys and painted their faces in school colors just like Jen. But unlike the others, who seemed more preoccupied with drinking the beers they'd smuggled into the stadium and making eyes at all the guys, Jen was laser-focused on the game.

Her eyes tracked every play, intent. I found myself checking the sidelines to ensure she was still looking. When I scored my first goal that game, my eyes went right to hers. She caught them and grinned, and it seemed like that smile was all for me.

Now, I find myself trying to remember the last time I saw that smile. A genuine, unguarded one.

Nothing comes to mind, which only makes me feel worse.

It's just because the kids are at a tough age. Mia's sixteen going on thirty, exactly the same kind of snarky know-it-all I was at her age. Logan, on the other hand, is a broody, introverted fifteen. He worries me. At least when Mia acts out, everyone knows about it. But Logan... He takes after Jen, a mystery more often than not.

"Drop me here," Jennifer says, startling me from my reverie.

"You don't want to go to the office?" I stop on a corner, several blocks away. Outside, a sparse smattering of flurries has begun to fall. They aren't sticking, just melting into the cold sidewalk, but still. Not exactly an inviting scene. I reach into the backseat to search for an umbrella.

"It's fine. I could use the walk. See you later." She pops the door and hops out before I locate an umbrella. Before either of us can go in for a kiss, either.

If I can't remember the last time I saw her smile, I really can't remember the last time we did more than give each other chaste pecks on the lips. To say this is a contrast from our early days would be the understatement of the century. Back when we first got together, we couldn't keep our hands off each other.

"Call me if you need me to pick anything up on the way home," I say. She slams the door, her only response a curt nod.

I idle on the side of the road, watching her stride up the street. Memories flit through my mind, torturing me. That time we snuck onto the roof of her dormitory with a bottle of fizz. The taste of that too-sweet wine on her lips. The even better taste of Jen herself, when she let me lay her flat on the rooftop and peel off her layers. I can still feel her belly contracting as I ran my tongue over her smooth skin—the jut of her hip, the soft fuzz at her navel. The soft sounds she made when I moved lower, ran my tongue between the folds of her thighs, spurred me on. God, she tasted so good.

She sounded so good, too—until her cries grew too loud, and half the lights in the dormitory below flicked on. We had to hide behind one of the chimneys on the roof until people stopped looking for long enough that we could actually sneak back inside.

The whole time, Jen took it upon herself to torture me as revenge. Her hands slid into my jeans, worked at me, her grip firm and soft at the same time, her thumb flicking over the head of my cock in that way only she's ever done.

I stiffen now, just remembering it, and I drag my palms off the wheel to wipe them on my jeans. Get it together, Bash. We're not teenagers anymore. As for the life we imagined, well, imagination tends to skim over the tough parts. I figure this is just what life is—you start out fun and uninhibited and free, and slowly, you add responsibility and weights, until all your best moments are in the past.

At least we get to keep the memories.

I turn toward my own office, per se. Unlike Jen, I've never been one for desk jobs or numbers. So I was thrilled when we settled here in Lake Heather, just outside of Charlotte. Not only is this the perfect location for an outdoors-lover like me—two hours from the mountains, three hours from the beach, close enough to a major city for anything we need, and right on a lake for day-to-day distractions—but it was just my luck that when we moved here, the town was in dire need of a full-time firefighter. There was a volunteer squad, but most of the full-timers had retired before I got here, so they scooped me right up.

Since then, we've hired a whole roster. Work at the firehouse suits my disposition—I'm pretty shit at boring tasks, but throw me into any emergency and I'll get the job done.

Of course, I prefer the non-emergency days, for everyone's sakes. I park outside the firehouse and scan the horizon. The clouds from earlier have cleared up. It's still cold—always is, in February—but now the world turns blue as far as the eye can see. The sun winks off the lake, just visible from up here, a bright sheen between the winter trees.

Whatever else is going on in my life—however stressful the daily grind becomes—I'm glad we get to slog through it here. Anytime I feel too unbalanced, I just need to bring myself back to the same old touchstones that've always saved me: bright sun, fresh air, exercise to get the blood pumping.

Doing my best to leave this morning's sniping behind, I stride into the firehouse with a broad, if somewhat forced, grin on my face.

Chapter Three

Jennifer

Columns of excel spreadsheets march behind my eyelids on the ride home. Ellen, my best friend at the office, always drops me off in the evenings, so Sebastian doesn't have to come out of his way. Today, she must sense something of my mood, because she keeps shooting me worried looks from the corner of her eye.

"What?" I finally demand, unable to stand the staring.

"Nothing, nothing." Ellen turns on a blinker, steering left toward my street. "You just seem a little tense, that's all. Something happen with Bash?"

My shoulders, already tense, feel like the knots are growing knots of their own. "What do you mean?" I reply, a little more harshly than I mean to.

"Well, just, you guys have had a few tiffs lately. Right?"

I scrunch my nose and stare out the window. I forgot that I mentioned our last argument to Ellen. And the one before that. Normally, I'm better about keeping our issues to myself. Why, I don't know. Maybe it's a holdover from our college years, and the reaction from the circle of friends I used to hang out with when we started dating. They judged him pretty harshly once they found out he was a scholarship student, not a legacy like them.

Like us. I was a legacy too, which is how I got to know most of those girls. Daughters of my parents' friends. For a couple years, I tried to make those friendships work—constantly defending Bash and justifying our relationship. Then, thank God, I finally woke up and realized they were the problems, not him.

I know better now—and Ellen's nothing like those girls. But still, it's second nature for me to hide any issues we have. "It's nothing serious," I hear myself saying. "We've just both been under a lot of pressure lately. There's the kids, and then everything at work…"

"What's wrong at the firehouse?" Ellen asks.

I shake my head. "Oh, no. Nothing. I mean, the usual, I guess." It can get pretty intense when there's a bad fire. But we've been lucky the past few years. Nothing since that terrible conflagration three summers ago, the wildfire that injured two of Sebastian's close friends and killed a guy from another firehouse a few townships over. I still have nightmares about it.

So does Bash, though he'll never admit it.

"But I've got a lot of new clients lately," I ramble, distracting myself. "I mean, don't get me wrong, I'm grateful. We need the money. But it's been a lot to deal with, and we've barely even started tax season. It's only going to get worse from here on out, and something's going on with Logan."

"Being a teenager?" Ellen suggests. "God knows I was a wreck my entire high school career."

"I don't remember that," I say, and she gives my arm a playful shove.

"You were too busy being 'Little Miss Soccer Champion' to notice your nerdy friends' plights. But don't worry, we all grew out of it. Logan will too."

"Maybe." I worry at my lower lip, not entirely convinced.

From the corner of my eye, I notice Ellen studying me more closely. "When was the last time you did something for yourself?" she asks.

"I splurged on a croissant just this morning," I say. "Not to mention those new shoes last weekend, and the new laptop after my old piece of crap crashed—"

"Doesn't count," she interjects. "I mean like, a spa day or something. Get a massage. Or maybe a facial."

I sigh internally. She and I used to take semi-regular spa trips, just like my mother and I did when I was growing up. Some of my fondest memories were of melting into the massage table as a skilled, and way-too-strong-for-her-size girl bludgeoned the knots from my back muscles. But... "After tax season," I say. "I just don't have time for it right now."

Or the spare cash, what with all the kids' extracurricular activities. Since when did going on a band trip cost this much money? Not to mention the fees for Mia's volleyball team and the costume budget we need to contribute to for Logan's part in the spring musical production.

It feels like everything's getting busier and more expensive at once, which doesn't exactly leave a lot of room for me time.

"Sounds to me like you need it now more than ever, though," Ellen says, and I shrug as she pulls into our driveway.

"Don't worry about me. I'll be fine." I grin and lean in for a quick hug. "See you tomorrow?"

"It's your turn to grab the coffees, remember?" she calls as I hop out of the car. I acknowledge her with a backward wave and trudge up to the house.

It used to be bustling by the time I got home. Back in the day, when the kids were small, Sebastian would arrange his schedule to be home for them after school, either going in during the day or in the evenings after I got there. Once the kids were old enough not to need a sitter, Mia used to get home first and make snacks for her and Logan. I'd come in to a trashed kitchen, more often than not, but delicious-smelling treats on the table and my kids watching TV together in the living room, or filming whatever the latest social media video trend was with each other.

These days, Mia stays late at school for volleyball practice, while Logan is at theater practice right up until dinnertime. By the time they get home, I'm lucky if I get one full hour with them, before they have to run upstairs to cram their homework into the remaining hours of the day before bedtime.

As for Sebastian, well, his schedule these days is all over the place, so it's anyone's guess when we'll see each other. Looks like tonight is one of the not nights.

Sighing, I turn on all the lights and start some music, just to make the place feel a little less empty. In the kitchen,

I heat up the lasagna we ordered from a local Italian spot a few nights ago. I love Bash's cooking, and so do the kids—I did not inherit my mother's kitchen talent, alas, though I do make a mean salad. But lately, I've been resorting to takeout more and more often. Neither of us have time to prepare anything more than the most basic dinners.

The lasagna just finishes reheating when someone turns a key in the front door.

"Logan?" I call.

"Just me," Mia shouts back.

I pull out two plates, frowning. "Where's your brother?" Usually he gets home before her.

"He texted to say theater's running late again."

That's the third time this week. I wonder if this might have anything to do with the assignments he missed last week. I make a mental note to talk to the theater director about it—you can't keep kids his age at school so long that they don't have time to finish their class assignments. Theater's fun, but it's an artistic outlet, not a career. "What about your father?"

"How should I know?" Mia plows into the kitchen, nose already in her cell phone. I can't blame her too much—I know they don't allow them during school, and her coach is pretty strict about the girls checking their phones at practice, too.

Still, my chest tightens with regret. I can already tell how dinner's going to go—just the two of us, her scrolling online, me chewing in silence and watching the clock.

I check my phone to see if Bash texted. Nothing. I debate messaging him, but then our tiff this morning in the car rears up again, and I pocket my phone, defiant. If he doesn't want to keep me in the loop about his life, I'm not going to go around chasing him.

Mia and I eat, as predicted, in relative silence. She pulls faces at her phone, in response to whatever her friends send her, while I study the lines on her forehead, around her mouth. Did I have that many lines when I was her age? Things feel so much heavier for her generation. I wonder if it's the phones, or something greater than them, if they're merely a symptom of the direction the wider world is headed. More connected, but more frantic at the same time, all of us rushing, rushing, rushing toward a destination we can't even see.

Oh, I'm definitely in a mood tonight.

After dinner, Mia helps me wash and dry the dishes. I ask about school, and she gives me one-word answers. Good, fine, okay. After a while, I relent and let her scurry upstairs to spend what free time she has with her cell phone, that one true love. As for me, I plop down on the living room couch and do the same thing—scrolling through social media posts of old high school friends, intermingled with advertisements.

Everyone always seems so happy online. Here's a friend hiking the Appalachian trail, and another one posing by a fishing boat with her family. There's a friend bragging about the multi-course dinner she cooked her family, and another friend advertising some sort of new workout brand gear. She looks great, which makes me think about the last time I went to the gym. Two weeks ago. Is it even worth still paying for my membership?

Ignoring the unpleasant twist in my gut, the sense of missing something, I shut off my phone and turn on the TV instead. But nothing's on—just reality crap and even crappier remakes of classic old movies.

Logan gets home around nine, dropped off by a friend from the Drama Club. The moment he walks through the door, I ask what the hell his theater director is playing at.

"It's just for this week," he says. "There's one scene we're really stuck on. The director says once we nail it, we can go back to the usual schedule next week."

I frown. "That's it. I'm calling the school."

"Mom, don't." A pleading tone enters his voice. "It's just one week. It was so hard for me to get this part; I don't want to lose it."

I relent, though not without a worried press of my lips. "Fine, but if you're late on another assignment, we're going to the principal about this. Understand?"

He hitches his bag higher on his shoulder and nods. "I know. I won't be. Promise."

After that exchange, I can't concentrate on anything on TV. I wind up going to bed early, taking an extra-long shower in my attempt to make up for what Ellen pointed out has been my very severe lack of anything resembling a spa day in months. Afterward, I collapse face-first into bed, on the verge of sleep when I finally hear the garage door open and Sebastian stomping inside. I listen to the clatter of plates and the buzz of the microwave as he helps himself to our leftovers.

I shut my eyes, determined to doze off before he gets here. But my anxiety brain won't let me sleep. I'm still awake, still circling the drain of all the same worries as usual, when Sebastian finally pads into our bedroom on tiptoe. I can tell he's trying not to wake me, which should be sweet. Instead, it annoys me further.

He dodges me all day, and now he's trying to sneak in without me realizing?

"There you are," I say, voice a little more acrid than I intended.

He flinches, which gives me a vicious surge of pleasure that I immediately regret. "Sorry. Didn't mean to wake you."

"You didn't. I've been awake." I roll over, facing him as he roots through the drawers for a change of clothes. "I'm sorry. About earlier."

His eyes jump up. Find mine across the darkened room, just for a split second. "Me too. I know things have been tough for you lately."

"For all of us," I counter.

He doesn't argue. We study one another across the dark expanse of our bedroom. I remember when we first came to look at this house together. Mia was only a year old, but we knew Logan was on the way, and our old two-bedroom apartment in uptown Charlotte wasn't going to cut it anymore. We wanted more space, somewhere close enough that we could drive into the city often (or so we imagined), but with nature in our backyard, a lake at our fingertips.

Walking through this house, hand in hand, I remember how we both paused on the threshold of this bedroom, our eyes wide. We'd never lived anywhere with this much space—even in our Charlotte apartment, we'd been forced to buy a queen-sized bed, since otherwise we wouldn't have been able to fit a decent sized wardrobe.

Here, though, we have space for a king size bed and then some. I remember Sebastian leaning over, one hand around my waist, his breath tickling my neck as he whispered, "The things I'll do to you in this bedroom." We offered on the house that same day, waited on tenterhooks for a week to find out whether the bid had been accepted. And all the while, we traded vivid imaginings of what this bedroom would hold for us. What our whole future would hold.

Now here we are, and, well…

"It's not what we imagined," I whisper. "Is it?"

For all our communication struggles of late, I don't need to explain this one. Sebastian eyes me for a long, quiet moment, studying my face. Whatever he sees there, he must not like, because the muscles around his eyes tense, his jaw going tight with what can only be displeasure. "No," he admits, voice soft in the dark. "I suppose it isn't."

With that, he pads into the bathroom, leaving me alone

again. I roll back over, face to the wall, and shut my eyes. The next time he pads into the room, fresh from the shower and smelling like the woodsy soap I love, I pretend I'm already asleep.

Chapter Four
Sebastian

For late February, it's surprisingly warm today. There's still patches of snow lingering on the grass outside the firehouse, but for the most part, it's melted off the big driveway out front, where the trucks pull in and out.

This is a good thing, the guys say, because we finally have enough space for a court.

"What do you mean, a court?" I ask. "A court for what?"

Brian, our resident old-timer, surprises me by answering first. "Pickleball." He points as Jim and Ryan, two of the younger guys, sketch a big square box onto the pavement out front with chalk. Another couple of guys hang a low net between two traffic cones, before Jim and Ryan add more lines—a smaller box on either side of the net, and then a central line dividing each side of the court into two halves.

"Like tennis?" I ask, because that's what it looks like.

Brian shakes his head, his eyes twinkling. "You'll see. I'm surprised you've never played before. My grandkids forced me to start playing last fall; now I can't get enough of it."

I'm more of a pickup basketball game man myself—that's our usual go-to in the summer months. But the side of the firehouse, where we bolted our basketball hoop so it's out of the way of any potentially damageable equipment, is still frozen over, so I'm willing to try something new today.

It's warm enough out to go jacketless, as long as you keep your blood flowing. That should concern me, but right about now, I'll take whatever pleasure I can from the warmth. God knows there's not been enough of it to go around at home. I think back to yet another strained breakfast this morning, both Logan and Mia in low spirits—Mia because she got a bad grade on a math test, and Logan because he's stressed about his part in the spring musical being given to an understudy if he can't nail his lines.

As for Jen, we haven't had a real conversation in days. Not since she looked at me across the wide expanse of our bedroom, eyes glowing in the dark like some wild creature's, and murmured, It's not what we imagined.

I'm aware, of course. I was there when we did our imagining, back at UNC in our youthful, high-on-first-love days. And afterward, when we coasted through the pitfalls of starting out in our careers, finding our footing, navigating young adulthood together and figuring out if this really was the type of love that, as we hoped, would stand the test of time.

We passed all those early tests with flying colors. Everything seemed effortless with her—any fight we ran into, we could always unfurl if we worked hard enough. And always, underlying it all, was the heat between us. The kind of passion I couldn't imagine ever fading.

Now...

My shoulders slump. Maybe this happens to everyone, eventually. Or maybe... Maybe this isn't what we thought. I hate to even think it, but someone has to ask the question. What are we doing? Where do we go from here? Does it get better again, and if so, how the hell do we get there?

"Bash!" one of the guys calls, and I startle back to the here and now. They've got the court all finished, and Jim's handing out lightweight paddles. They remind me of Ping-Pong paddles, except they're narrower and a bit longer, made of what looks like fiberglass in the middle with wooden handles. They feel lighter than I expect, and I give one an experimental swing, earning me a laugh from Brian.

"Come on." He gestures to me. "You can be on my team while you learn the ropes."

We pair up across from Jim and Ryan, who exchange eager grins. They talk me through the basic rules—it does sound kind of like tennis, batting a ball back and forth across the net, except with a few added rules. The section in the middle, seven feet to either side of the net, is called the kitchen, and nobody can be standing in it when they hit the ball. Also, on the first hit, the ball has to bounce twice—once on the server's side of the net, and once on your side before you hit it back to the other team. After that, you can volley back and forth like tennis, although once we get started, it reminds me more of a giant ping pong game.

Brian explains that he's responsible for his half of the court, while I'm in charge of mine. We have a few clumsy collisions at first, where I stumble into balls he should've gone for and vice versa. But it doesn't take long before I find my footing, returning more and more of Jim and Ryan's shots, even the tricky ones.

When Jim sails a winning hit over our net, I feel a genuine flash of disappointment. "Can we go again?" I ask. "Think I'm getting the hang of it now."

Ryan laughs. "Oh, someone's hooked."

I don't know about that, but I'm eager to redeem my loss as soon as possible. And it feels good to be moving, drinking in the winter air, clad only in a T-shirt because, for a game this simple to get a hang of, you sure do work up a sweat once you get going.

We're setting up for round two when the bell goes off, the claxon call ripping us away from the court. Jim tears down the net as Ryan races inside to start the truck and I grab our gear. We move faster than we normally do, maybe because we were already up and moving, our blood pumping, before the call came in. Usually this time of year, we'd be lounging around inside on our phones or watching the crappy little TV in back, and it'd take us longer to spring into motion.

We roar out of the firehouse, sirens blazing, in record time. By the time we reach the address, a residential block a fifteen-minute speed-drive away, there's a fire blazing on the rooftop. Luckily, it doesn't look like there's much other damage—we whip the hose out while Brian goes to talk to the family who called us, now huddled on the front lawn—a mother and two terrified-looking toddlers wrapped around her legs, accompanied by a sheepish-looking older teen.

I don't get the full story until after Jim and I have doused the roof, which doesn't take long. Looks like the fire originated on the roof itself, or in the attic just beneath. Hopefully it won't damage too much of the rest of the house—though the spray from the hose might do some water damage in the rooms directly below.

Brian comes over, shaking his head, though I can tell he's suppressing amusement by the tight lines around his mouth. He juts one thumb over his shoulder at the older teen, whose mother has rounded on him now, whispering furiously. "Kid thought it would be a good idea to set off a firework in his backyard. Landed right on the roof. Burned a hole through the tile and some of the insulation, but looks like we got here just in time. Would've spread otherwise."

The team trades backslaps all around, as I go to check in with the spooked mother.

"I had no idea it was an illegal one," she's babbling. "His father bought it on a trip a few weekends ago; I thought it was just one of those little box fireworks that shoots sparks from the ground."

I wave off her worry. "No harm done." Then I look past her at the boy, a year or two younger than Logan, I'd wager. "But don't let us catch you using anything like that again, hear me? You put your mother and your sisters in real danger."

The boy, wide-eyed, nods at me with such terror-stricken sincerity that I feel certain he really has learned his lesson. Plus, I'm sure his mother will ground him from now until kingdom come.

I offer his mother a few murmured tips on how to spot which fireworks are the dangerous, rocket-launching kind—something I've become sadly familiar with in my line of work—and then I trudge back to the fire truck, shoulders held high. A sense of pride washes over me, like it always does on a job well done—anytime a bigger crisis gets averted, and no one gets hurt.

To judge by their smiles, the guys are all in a similar mood. Our spirits remain high the whole ride back to the station, where we take it upon ourselves to set up the court again. This time, I help Jim redraw the lines, which got a little smudged when we drove the fire truck straight over them.

In our second game, I do a hell of a lot better. I manage a couple of seriously epic overhead shots, firing them straight down the center line between Jim and Ryan so fast they both miss the rebound. Brian and I high-five when we win this round, beaming. Across our makeshift net, Ryan shakes his head. "No wonder they call you Bash, with an arm like that."

I laugh. But deep down, an idea is forming. Only half-baked at the moment, a flicker of an idea. But I can't help thinking about how fast we got ourselves together at the ringing of the bell today. How much more in sync we seemed, like a real team. My gaze drops to the paddle in my hand, and I wonder if there might be a connection between the heated games we were playing and the ease of that reliance on one another.

In the coming week, as we play a few more pickup games at the firehouse, always between rounds and during downtime, of course, I notice it happening more and more. When we get called to jobs, Brian and I switch positions, teaming up where normally I'd run with Jim or Ryan instead. The other two pair off more easily as well, all of us relying on our game partners as naturally as if it were preordained.

It all gets me thinking, harder than usual.

If only that kind of camaraderie carried off the courts all the time. There are so many other areas of my life where I could use this same level of synchronicity. I wish my kids and I could pick up this natural ease together. Or, of course, that I could find it in the most important area of my life of all…

But then I shake my head, dragging myself back down to earth. There's no way I'd be able to talk Jen into playing a game, let alone some new and popular game like this. She barely has enough time to keep her head above water lately.

And I get it. I've been working longer hours at the firehouse, volunteering for extra shifts to try to make up the difference in cash we need, now that our mortgage rate has spiked higher than we anticipated. In the past couple weeks, I've tried to pick up more of the slack at home, checking in on the kids, talking to Logan about his missed assignments. He hasn't missed any more, not since his teacher called to speak to us, but he's still getting stuck late some nights at rehearsal and struggling to keep up with his coursework. Then there's Mia and her schedule, already so hectic that I wonder how she has time to sleep, let alone get all her homework finished.

Times are tough all around, and only feel like they're growing tougher by the day, time siphoning down the drain, so fast I can hardly track where it's all going.

Still, I can't help but think about what a boon it was to get to blow off steam like this with friends. And how, if only we could make time for it, something like this might be exactly what Jennifer needs...

What both of us need, my mind points out. Because for better or worse, she and I are in this mess called life together.

Chapter Five

Jennifer

"Just play one game with me," Sebastian pleads, one day in the middle of March. He's ambushed me in my home office, which is so covered in stacks of client files and excel printouts that it looks like some kind of mad hoarders nest, or one of those rooms in crime dramas where the detective tacks up all the clues on the walls to try to trace connections between them.

I feel that way sometimes, like a detective ferreting out my clients' best options. It's not always easy—some of my older clients don't understand everything they can write off under tax law, while some of my young and hot shot clients with huge incomes try to write off way more than they ought to—the types of write-offs that could get me into trouble as an accountant, unless I catch them and head them off at the pass.

To be honest, Sebastian's sudden interruption irritates me even more than usual. But I suppress my urge to snap at him—that's the job stress talking, not my actual feelings. Still, it takes me a minute to pull myself out of work mode, and another few seconds to take deep breaths and stop from rejecting him outright.

"Pickleball?" I repeat, thinking back to what he just

said—a long, rambling story about some new game he's started playing with the guys at the station. Not gonna lie, that part irks me a bit too—he has so much downtime at work, while I feel like I'm constantly drowning.

But then I remind myself that's not fair. He might have downtime, but when Sebastian needs to be on, he's far more on than I ever have to be. He's the one running headlong into danger with only a flimsy fire suit and a helmet between him and sudden death. The thought of that poor man from the neighboring firehouse, only a few years older than Bash, makes my chest cinch tight. I have no idea what I'd do if I lost Sebastian, much less in such a horrifying way.

Throat tight, I force a smile as I close the current file I've been working on and rotate in my home office chair to face him.

"Yeah," Sebastian's saying. "It's a new sport. The guys introduced me to it at the firehouse, but apparently there's all kinds of local clubs and tournaments around. Anyway, Ryan was telling me he plays a doubles game with his wife at the Riverbend Pickleball Club; it's pretty close to here, but there are also lots of local community courts that we could play on as well. Ryan's coach, June, has an open slot, if we want to take a lesson—"

"I don't know," I interrupt, my patience straining. The unfinished file looms large at the back of my mind, like a pulsing, animated thing. Only a little over a month left, I can't help thinking, my usual countdown to tax deadline day a blaring red exclamation mark in my mind. "I'm pretty busy…"

"I know, Jen." Sebastian steps further into the office, then pulls over a spare chair, dropping down so he's at eye level with me. His honey brown eyes burn bright and eager, boring into mine. There was a time when I used to think I could fall into those eyes. Drown in them.

Now, my throat tightens, because I can't remember the last time I looked close enough to see the little starburst pattern around his irises, the gold mark in one corner.

"When was the last time we had a real date night? Something just for us."

I purse my lips. But I can't think of a good comeback, because I don't remember. Last year, maybe? What did we do for our anniversary? I don't even know. How did we get this way? I ask myself, not for the first time this month—or year, really.

"You really want to spend our first date night in ages playing some random game?" I ask.

Sebastian's smile widens. I can tell I've played right into his hand; that this is exactly what he expected me to ask. "Remember how we met?"

How could I forget? Cheering him on from the sidelines, the hottest hotshot player on our college soccer team. He caught my eye a few times, but I didn't think he actually noticed me—why would he, with all those other screaming fangirls to choose from?

But then he came to my game, a couple weeks later. The women's soccer team always had a way lower turnout than the men's—college life reflecting the major leagues, unfortunately. Aside from the women on the other sports teams, who usually turned out when they could to support one another, and a few die-hard fans, our games usually barely filled the first few rows of stadium seats.

But that week, Sebastian turned up with half the men's' team in tow, a big banner strung between them, faces painted the way the girls painted theirs at our games. My heart leapt when I spotted the number painted on Sebastian's cheek—mine.

To this day, it remains one of the most romantic gestures I could imagine a college-age boy pulling off for a girl he barely even knew yet.

"Of course," I say. "But this is different. I don't even know how to play pickleboard."

"Pickleball," he corrects gently. "And you don't need to know in advance. Trust me, it's pretty easy to pick up. Only took me a couple of rounds with the guys before I got the hang of it, and that's why Ryan recommended this coach. She could help us with the finer points, really get a good game going."

He looks so eager, so excited. For a second, I'm catapulted back to our college days. I remember Sebastian at that game, cheering every time I scored or successfully foiled another player's attempt at a goal. After the game, he bounded up to the fence line, and I jogged over to meet him, heart racing, all the way up in my throat, adrenaline surging through me. Some of that was the usual post-win adrenaline rush, but the rest was all him.

Those dark eyes of his bored into mine, made my stomach roil and my blood run so hot I was grateful that I was fresh off the field and stinking of sweat, if only because it would excuse the red hot flush in my cheeks.

When I reached the fence line (careful to linger a couple feet back just in case I really did smell from all that running), Sebastian suddenly flushed too, his face a careful balance of forced confidence and hope. "Good game, Simons. Bet you could give me a few pointers," he said, in that low, sultry voice that I've never been able to get enough of.

I'd never been good at flirting, but something about Sebastian's approach—his obvious interest—gave me the confidence to grin. "Bet I could."

"I'd love that." His eyes smoldered. Pinned me in place. "Meet you on the field sometime?"

My pulse fluttered at the base of my throat, thrummed in my extremities. "Tomorrow night, same time?" I asked, one eyebrow cocked in a way that I hoped made me look cool and not confused.

"It's a date," he said, thereby ensuring that I would not sleep a wink all night.

He's wearing that same expression again now. Confident, but hopeful, and both of those a front over the nervous teenager beneath. Like he desperately hopes he can talk me into this, but if he can't, he'll try his hardest to hide his defeat. It makes my heart hurt to see my husband bracing himself like that against me now, as if we don't have a lifetime of shared trust between us, as if we're those nervous teenagers again, neither of us sure how far we can push the other.

Then again, is it any wonder? I realize that, in addition to not knowing when was the last time we had a date night or any time to ourselves, I also can't remember when was the last time we did more than give each other brief, almost perfunctory kisses.

And even then... God, when was the last time we actually fucked? We had sex... I don't even know, last year sometime? In the fall, for certain. But it was lights off, all business. He knows exactly how to make me cum at this point, and fast, but that was pretty much the extent of it—one quickie, both of us eager to finish so we could get to sleep early enough for a decent night's rest.

I can't remember the last time I felt butterflies around him. Or the last time I caught him staring at me the way he used to, savoring every inch of flesh I bared as I undressed. Maybe he's not into me anymore. Not like that.

Maybe this is normal, maybe all couples lose it eventually, and I should just be content with the memories we have...

But now here he is, looking at me like his nervous nineteen-year-old self again, and I feel the first spark of hope in I-don't-know-how-long.

As much as everything I said is true—I am busy, I do have a ton of work to be getting on with, and I don't at all think I have time to pick up some new hobby—I cannot bring myself to let my husband down. Not when he's looking at me like this.

I swallow hard around a sudden lump in my throat. "One lesson?" I ask.

His eyes widen, his smile going so big that I immediately realize he expected me to say no. That only makes me feel even worse. "That's all. We don't have to commit to anything more, not unless we like it. And if you think you can find time for more, of course. It'll just be a fun new thing to try, no pressure."

I take a deep breath, both intimidated and flattered by his obvious nervousness. Who knew that I could still make my husband nervous after all this time? "All right," I say. "Let me check my schedule for days, but I could probably squeeze one in."

He whoops and leans in for a hug. Laughing, I wrap my arms around him, but he pulls back far too quickly, leaving my chest feeling strangely empty.

Chapter Six
Sebastian

June comes highly recommended by both Ryan and Maria, which makes me hopeful that this lesson might not be a complete disaster. But watching Jennifer's face as we walk up to the new pickleball courts just installed at our town park where June teaches some of her lessons, I'm about fifty-fifty on whether this will turn out well or crash and burn. She looks apprehensive, if not downright nervous, which isn't like her at all.

The Jen I met in college was adventurous, always up for trying something new. Early on in our dating life, I invited her on a college-run ski trip to one of the nearby mountains, and she eagerly accepted. I didn't realize she didn't know how to ski until we got there and she asked me what size skis she should get for a newbie.

She told me she'd rather I just teach her, instead of taking a class, so we tumbled down the bunny hill a few times, Jen getting more confident with each pass. Before long, she was whizzing circles around me, eager to experience the lift and test out her newfound skills on an actual slope. The whole lift ride up, she leaned against me—I assumed due to nerves at first. Turns out she was vibrating with excitement at the height, the winter wonderland spread beneath our feet.

Me, I was just plain nervous about the girl I was starting to really like, her lithe body pressed firmly against my side, cheeks flushed with exertion and excitement at once.

And then, later that night, before the bus came to bring us all back to campus, there was the hot tub Jen figured out how to sneak into, at a private ski-in ski-out cabin halfway down one of the green runs, lights all off, the occupants clearly not coming home anytime soon...

No, Jen is not the shrinking violet type. So I'm confused by my wife's obvious hesitation as we enter the gate of the dozen outdoor courts. Most are already occupied, and I take a second to examine the scene.

The court layouts look pretty similar to the makeshift ones the guys at the firehouse and I have been chalking out for ourselves over the past few weeks: a net in the center, another line seven feet from either side of the net demarcating the edge of the kitchen, and a fifteen foot "service area" behind that, divided by the center line into the right and left service areas.

My gaze wanders to the games already in progress. Most people are playing doubles, and of those teams, most are mixed gender. I wonder how many are couples, like us, versus friends or family members. There's one pair near the doors who are obviously mother and son, and another pair of women further in who look like twins.

As we're staring around, me fascinated and Jen still with that uncharacteristic apprehension on her face, a redhead around our age appears, hair only slightly graying around the temples, tied up in a neat bun. She grins from ear to ear, sticking out a hand at Jen. "You must be Ryan and Maria's friends. I'm June."

"Jennifer." Jen shakes, and shuffles aside to let me do the same.

June grips my hand so tight I'm surprised I can still feel my fingers when she lets go. She doesn't seem to have done it on purpose, since she's all smiles as she points at the far wall. "We'll be over here."

As we trail after her, Jennifer and I exchange glances, both of us theatrically shaking out our fingertips. We smirk, and some of the worry in my chest eases. I've missed this—the little knowing looks we always used to exchange, understanding without words exactly what the other was thinking.

It doesn't last long, though. Jennifer's features cloud once more as we reach our court, and June hands us each a paddle. "It's so light." Jen gives it an experimental swing, the same way I did when the guys first showed me one. "How fast can you hit the ball with one of these?"

"This isn't tennis, don't worry," June says. "Pickleball is less about power and speed, more about strategy and finesse." She gestures to the court directly next to ours, where a couple who must be at least eighty are facing off against a pair young enough to be their grandkids. "That's why the sport has become so popular, if you ask me. Almost anyone can master it, with the right lessons. It doesn't matter how old you are, or how in shape. What really matters in this game is your attention to detail, and your communication."

Jennifer and I snag eyes again, involuntarily. This time, she seems less amused, her mouth a little twist of concern.

For once, I understand why. Our communication hasn't exactly been our strong suit of late. But then I think about the firehouse, and how much faster and more efficiently me and the boys work as a team when we've been out on the makeshift court playing pickup games beforehand. Who knows? Maybe the game will have the same effect for us.

A man can dream.

June must notice the looks we're exchanging, because she pauses, tapping her own paddle against her thigh. "Before we start, I just want to clarify: my goal is to get you two up to speed with the rules, playing, and having fun above all. There are lots of competitions out there—and lots of competitive people—but if you ask me, going into the game with a winner-take-all mindset is a surefire way to lose, and frustrate the hell out of yourself in the process. If you're not having fun by the end of this lesson, tell me, because that means we're doing something wrong. That's our number one goal, got it?"

Jennifer shakes out her shoulders, a little of the tension flowing out. "Got it."

I smile and nod my assent as well.

"Great." June claps her hands. "Now, Jennifer, can I get you across the net from Sebastian? Usually, of course, you'll be playing on the same side in a doubles game, but for now, just to get the hang of things, I want to demonstrate to you both at once…"

Our first half an hour of lessons involves getting a feel for the paddles, the weight of the balls we use, the positions of our feet on the court. June is thorough, calm, and patient, which I can tell helps alleviate some of Jennifer's dubiousness. By the end of the lesson, we're both moving with relative confidence—I bounce one over the net on a serve and Jen waits for it to hit on her side before batting it back over. We volley back and forth, both our toes right up to the edge of the kitchen, from where June assures us we can return the most hits and take full advantage of the court's layout.

When June blows the whistle to indicate the end of the hour and our first official lesson, I catch a brief glimpse of genuine disappointment flash across Jennifer's features, before she schools her face back into forced indifference.

But I know what I saw. I stifle a grin of my own as we thank June, pack up our bags—the lesson we paid for came with a set of our very own paddles, as well as a ball that looks different from the whiffle we've been using as a makeshift one at the firehouse. I study it as we stride out to our car, waiting until we're back in our seats and on the road home before I tentatively clear my throat.

"Well?" I ask.

From the corner of my eye, I catch Jennifer pressing her lips together, suppressing that smile again. "I had fun," she finally admits.

See? But I resist the urge to gloat, knowing how she'll

react. Instead, I nod, gaze fixed on the road. "Me too. I wouldn't mind doing that again."

She scratches the back of her neck, gaze wandering to her purse, tucked on the floor of the passenger seat. I know what she's really looking at—her phone, the jam-packed calendar it contains. "I wouldn't either, but…"

"I know you've got a busy schedule," I hastily assure her. "But if, say, we just wanted to try one lesson a week…"

She hesitates. That's how I know she's seriously tempted—if Jen doesn't want to do something, she'll let you know straight out of the gate.

"We can work around your schedule, and the kids'. Whenever we're all free. I talked to June; she's got a few regular clients during the weekdays, but that's fine; we'd be more interested in a weeknight or a weekend anyway, right?"

Jennifer worries at her lower lip. "I suppose… I mean, we could try it for a couple of weeks? See how it goes?"

I manage not to let out a victory shout, but I can't help grinning. "Of course. No pressure, no commitment. Let's just see how it goes." My mind darts back to our lesson with June, the opening speech. "What'd she tell us? The most important thing is to have fun. So, let's keep is low stress, and just… well. Have fun."

Jennifer smiles, too, turning to study my profile as I steer us onto the highway onramp toward home. "Yeah. I'd like that," she says, real warmth in her voice. To my surprise, she reaches over to touch my hand where it rests on the gearshift, her fingertips soft, tentative. "Thank you," she adds, voice lower than before. "You were right. I needed something like this."

I rotate my hand, catch hers and squeeze gently. "Kind of suspected. You've seemed—we've both seemed more than a little in over our heads lately." Jennifer pauses. I can hear her turning that sentence over in her head, debating whether to take offense, so I hasten to add, "Not that I don't understand why. You take on so much for this family. And things are… different than they were before. Our lives are different."

I'm sure both of us are still reliving the echo of that night, a few weeks ago. It's not what we imagined. But that doesn't mean it needs to be all bad, right?

"Maybe, I don't know, a little sweat and healthy competition will get our blood pumping again."

Jennifer laughs. But she keeps her hand in mine, her mouth pursed thoughtfully, rather than in disapproval. "Yeah. Yeah, maybe this could be just what we needed."

Riding high on that thread of hope, we keep our hands clasped until I have to release her to turn off the highway and onto our back streets. We're still smiling when we park outside the house and step inside. But we're barely a foot inside the door before Mia's shout accosts us.

"Mom? Dad? What are we eating tonight? I'm starving to death here."

We trade another look, both clearly struggling to suppress our laughter, and follow our daughter's plaintive whines into the kitchen to figure out what's on the menu.

Chapter Seven

Jennifer

By our third lesson with June, I manage to beat Sebastian in a one-on-one. I crow with excitement, leaping around the court, not even pausing to think about how I must look, or whether it's in any way dignified for a woman my age to behave like that.

For his part, Sebastian only grins as he watches me be a terrible winner. "Rematch?" he shouts, and I full on stick my tongue out at him before I square off across the net once more.

"Oh, you fucking bet."

"Jennifer, watch your feet," June scolds, which brings me crashing right back down to reality. Without realizing it, I've stepped a whole foot across the baseline, too eager for Sebastian's next serve to keep myself behind the proper line.

I retreat behind the baseline and hover there, anxious for the game to start again. The win sings in my veins, makes me prickly all over with a sensation I haven't experienced in years, one that takes me far too long to recognize. It's the way I used to feel after a soccer win, when all the girls collided in messy, excited, screaming piles right there in the middle of the field, back-slapping and shrieking victory cries.

I've missed this high-on-life feeling, the sense that, just for this short moment, I really am invincible.

Sebastian serves, and I bounce on my toes, tracking the arc of the ball and then sending it right back over the net. He returns it, and we start to volley, both of us on fire, lunging for hard shots and barely squeaking sneaky dribbles over the net. He misses, and I let out a triumphant whoop—my serve again.

On the sidelines, June laughs. But it's a pleasant, involved sort of laugh—not at us, but with us. "Now you're getting it," she calls. Cheered on by her, we keep going, both of us throwing our all into this rematch.

The game winds up a very tight one, with Sebastian sneaking out the win at the very last second. "Best of three?" he asks me with a grin, a single eyebrow arched.

I'm about to say hell yes, when June interjects. "Hate to break up the party," she says, one eye on her watch. "But that's our time for today."

My shoulders slump. I'm surprised by how disappointed I am—and how quickly our hour here flew by. Before I can get too disappointed, though, June meets our gazes again, her eyes sparkling.

"What would you two say to trying an actual game next week?"

"Haven't we been?" I ask, swinging my paddle distractedly.

But Sebastian and June trade knowing looks. "A doubles' game," June clarifies. "Against actual opponents. There're some friendly matches going on at one of the courts where I teach. I could sign you up for some rounds, but we'd need to get you in quickly, because the courts fill up fast."

I glance at Sebastian again, debating. But of course, his face betrays nothing except obvious hope and excitement. Again, I feel that little twinge inside, the part of me that still thrills whenever he's happy.

"How soon do we need to let you know?" I ask. "I need to check our children's schedules, but…"

"Soon as you can." June smiles. "No pressure, of course."

I don't feel pressured, though. I feel excited, actually. Especially once Sebastian and I put our heads together and realize there's a day and time slot that would work for us. It's been fun learning how to play and getting to know one another's styles, but I have a feeling it'll be even more fun to play together, on the same team. The whole drive home, we discuss our styles, our strengths and weaknesses—Sebastian has a wicked overhead shot and a strong arm, while I'm the more dexterous, quick on my feet. The yoga classes I used to take back in my early 20s, fresh out of college and yearning for something to fill the hole that team sports left in my life, come in handy now too. I know my body pretty well; exactly how far I can push myself and in which directions.

So, when the next week rolls around and we stride onto the public court for our first game together, I'm overall in a pretty great mood. Sure, the courts are packed when we arrive, and there's already a line out the gate to sign up for any vacant slots if people miss their pre-booked times. But it's my first experience being among this many people all interested in the sport.

It's fascinating to watch from the sidelines as we line up to wait for our first game to begin. I try to figure out which teams I think work well together, versus which might be newer teams like us. But everyone seems good, frankly.

I watch a doubles' team on the nearest court volley so fluidly, the two of them seem like one being, each an extension of the other, moving perfectly in sync.

Due to the delays of some previous games, our scheduled time gets pushed back further. While we wait, Sebastian paces—he's never been good at waiting long periods for anything, especially not if he has to stand still. As he strides around the courts in circles, pausing to examine each game he passes, I can feel my own nerves starting to kick in.

I wasn't nervous when we first got here. Now, though, I've got plenty of time to stew in my own thoughts and let all the second-guesses I've been suppressing well up.

What if I'm not any good at this in a real game? What if I let Sebastian down, when he so clearly wants this to work out? What if—

I catch myself, squeeze my eyes shut, and remind myself what June always says. Our number one goal is to have fun. It doesn't matter if I suck. It doesn't matter whether we win this game, either.

It's about having fun.

I settle back in to watch the tail end of the game that caught my eye earlier. The players on both sides really are good. I'm still staring at them, more than a little awed, when Sebastian nudges me. "We're up." He points to a neighboring court.

Our opponents seem nice enough at first glance—a man around Sebastian's age and a woman maybe a few years younger than me. Her hair is up in a high pony, and her partner—husband? Boyfriend? Just a friend?—steps forward to shake Sebastian's hand.

"We've got a first-timer here," Sebastian says, jutting a thumb in my direction with a friendly smile. "So go easy on us, eh?"

"Of course," the man says, though I notice a tightening around his mouth as he says it. He flashes me a tight, forced-seeming smile, then turns around. As he does, I catch the look he directs at his partner, when he thinks neither Sebastian nor I will notice. He actually rolls his eyes.

A knot forms in the pit of my stomach. Great. So they're going to be hard-asses with the newbie. But I shake it off, try not to let them get to me. It's all about having fun. I won't let one grumpy guy ruin this for us.

We take our positions, since our opponents have the first serve. "Zero, zero, two," calls the man before he swats the ball our way. I trace its trajectory and study the angle of its bounce.

Sebastian catches my eye and gestures for me to take the hit, so I do, stepping over and returning it easily, just like I did in our coaching lessons against him.

Almost immediately, our opponents return it, with a hit

so fast and strong it reminds me of Sebastian's swing. I lunge for it, but so does Sebastian, and we collide along the center line, neither of us accustomed to considering someone else in our space.

"Shit, sorry!" I blurt, as Sebastian catches my arms to steady me. Forgotten, the ball dripples away between our feet. Sebastian doesn't go to grab it yet—he's too busy looking at me with concern.

"Are you alright?"

The collision surprised me more than it hurt, though there is a twinge in my elbow where it connected with Sebastian's paddle. I nod, forcing a smile. "Fine, fine. Sorry," I call over the net. "Still figuring this out."

"Obviously," the man says, a little louder than I think he intended to. Beside him, his partner covers her mouth with one hand, though not before a single snicker escapes.

Face flaming, I jog over to fetch the ball and toss it back to them.

"One, zero, two," calls the man, before he serves again. Our next few rounds go like that—I make stupid mistakes, give away easy points. Sebastian gets us the serve a couple of times, and even manages to eke a point past them, but before we know it, the score is narrowing down on the end of the game. They've got eight points already, and we only have one. We might as well let them walk off with the win now—it's first team to eleven to win, with a two-point lead.

My face hasn't stopped burning since they scored their

fifth point in a row. Every time they do, the man just curls his lip. He doesn't high-five his partner, or celebrate the score—that much I could understand. I might have done the same, if we were trouncing someone, although I like to think I'd be a bit of a better sport.

Instead, though, he seems irritated by every shot I miss or return I fail to make. Like my ineptitude is somehow a personal attack on him.

The next volley I fail to return, he actually scoffs.

"You should really practice at home before you come out on these public courts," he says, like he's giving me some sort of helpful tip, and not being an absolute dick.

Beside me, Sebastian bristles. "I'm sorry, do you play this professionally? Are we somehow hampering your dreams by trying to have fun here?"

The man rolls his eyes again, but he does seem a little cowed. At least he doesn't make any snarkier remarks as he accepts the ball I toss back to his partner, who readies for another serve. "Nine, one, one," she calls, and starts our game going once more.

My spirits are buoyed somewhat by Sebastian's comeback, but I still second-guess my every move. All of June's advice and training seem to fly right out of my head, driven away by my anxious nervous system. I manage to return a shot, and then another one right off the bat, a tricky nearly out-of-bounds shot I needed to race for. This should boost my confidence, but across the net, I can see that asshole smirking, and it gets under my skin, inside my skull.

I find myself thinking about how I look to everyone else, instead of where the ball is headed next or where my feet should be going.

It's no surprise to any of us when I miss yet another shot.

"Game point," the guy calls, and then, in a not much quieter voice, to his partner, "Hopefully next game will be a halfway decent challenge."

Sebastian bares his teeth now. He's been slowly getting more and more irritated all game, but now, I can sense a storm about to burst. "You were a beginner once too, you know, asshole," he says, loud enough that a couple of people on the neighboring court glance over at us, startled.

I go to catch his arm, but not before the man across from us turns bright red. "What the hell did you call me?" he shouts.

"Something I'm sure a lot of people have called you before," Sebastian replies coolly. "Based on your attitude today."

The woman glances between us all, mouth pulled flat in a grimace. She looks embarrassed, though whether by us or her partner's behavior, I can't be sure. "Come on, Mark." She grabs his arm. "Let's just call it quits."

"No fucking point finishing anyway," the guy—Mark? —mutters.

Sebastian opens his mouth, starting toward the net, but this time I'm ready. I catch his elbow, leaning in to lay a hand on his chest. I can feel his pulse beating hard beneath my palm, as I lean up on tiptoe to catch his eye. "Leave it, Bash."

The old nickname, one he acquired in college for the force of his penalty kicks, brings him back down to reality. He blinks, tearing his gaze from our opponents to lock eyes with me instead. Slowly, his fists unclench at his sides, his expression softening.

"Don't let him get to you, Jen. You were doing great today."

I arch a single, pointed brow, and he quirks a faint smile.

"Okay, so you've had better days, true. But it's no wonder you were a little off your game, with that fucker making you self-conscious."

"Thank you," I say softly. "For standing up for me."

For a moment, we both go quiet. His eyes search mine, like he's looking for something specific. What, I'm not sure. But the longer the silence stretches, the more aware I feel of the scant few inches of air between us, and of my palm still splayed on his chest, his heartbeat slowing, beat by beat, beneath my fingertips.

His lips part, his eyes dropping just an inch, before they flick back up. I can't be certain, but I get the feeling he just stole a peek at my mouth, which makes me wonder whether he's thinking the same thing I am...

"Hey." A new voice interrupts our reverie, makes me startle backward, hand dropping empty into the space between us. "If your game is over, we've got this court next," says a woman in a tight athleisure outfit, short pixie cut swept back from her face. She jerks a thumb at her doubles partner, and another pair who are already warming up across the court from us.

"Right. Of course." Sebastian grabs our paddles and starts off the court. "Sorry about that."

I hurry after him, trying my hardest to follow his advice and forget about that asshole. But try though I might, Mark's taunts follow me the whole way home.

Chapter Eight
Sebastian

Twice a week for the next two weeks, we head to public courts like the one June recommended. We didn't get a good vibe at that first place we tried, so we test out different ones anytime we have a spare hour or two. There's one, almost a forty-minute drive away, that has less of a wait for the courts, but that drive eats into our playing time, so even when we can make it that far, we're only able to squeeze in a single game before we need to head back home.

I can feel Jen's enthusiasm ebbing with each loss, with every sideways glance we garner at the courts. I want to punch that asshole who stole her confidence that very first game, because now I watch her bracing herself at the start of every new round. Even when people aren't assholes, and treat us nicely, Jennifer still plays with a wary tension in her shoulders, like she expects our opponents to pop off at any moment.

This isn't working, I think, a little desperately. I know it's just a game, but I had such high hopes about what this could do for us. I envisioned victory chants and stopping on the way home for celebratory meals the way we used to after soccer wins in college. I pictured our reignited passion on the court to carry over into other areas of life, the same way it seemed to for me and the guys at the firehouse on calls.

Instead, with each week that passes, Jen seems to get more tense, more wound up. At night, she's always tucked under the covers by the time I come upstairs, waking only to offer me a mumbled goodnight, her backside turned.

But I refuse to give up. Not yet. I've seen how much people enjoy the game—maybe it's just the specific courts we've picked.

The next day at work, I stop Ryan on his way in. "Where do you and Maria play again?" I ask him. "We're struggling with the public courts."

"Oh, god." Ryan shakes his head. "No wonder. They're the worst. Gotta wait an hour sometimes just for one round, and people can be such dicks."

"Tell me about it," I mutter.

"That's why we joined Riverbend. Here, let me see…" Ryan digs his phone from his pocket and shows me Riverbend Country Club's social media page. It's glossy, like one of those Instagram influencer pages, which makes me trepidatious at first. But I've got to admit, the pictures are enticing. There's a shot of two attractive couples in expensive-looking athleisure-wear facing off on a brand-new court, outside under the bright North Carolina sun, which glints off their matching tans.

Another shot shows the clubhouse, a stately white-columned building that looks like one of those fancy clubhouses at members'-only golf clubs, the sort my wealthier friends' parents back in college belonged to. Speaking of golf courses, there's one in the back of the clubhouse too, along with a pool where more attractive couples sip poolside cocktails, I presume after winning their games handily.

"Looks great," I say, eyes widening. "But pricey."

"It looks more expensive than it actually is," Ryan assures me. "The pickleball memberships are priced differently than the full club memberships with golf and everything included. Plus, I think you get a discount if I refer you too— let me talk to the manager and let you know." Then he grins and slaps my shoulder. "Besides, when you add up all the perks, subtract all the hassle of time and sanity you waste on the public courts, it pays for itself in no time."

I nod, even as I wonder how the hell I'm going to convince Jennifer to go along with this new idea, especially with tax season coming to a head in just a couple of weeks.

As it transpires, it's a few days before I get up the time to even ask, because Jen stays overtime at the office all the way until the weekend. Then on Saturday, we have a flurry of activities for the kids to contend with. We drop Logan at school for a tutoring session, and then Mia has a jazz band rehearsal. Afterwards, we pick up Logan again and drag him to watch Mia present in the science fair, because there's no time to take him all the way home first. We all nod and pretend to follow the descriptions of all the in-depth chemistry experiments.

Watching Mia up on stage when it's her turn to present

makes my heart swell with pride—not even dimmed by Logan slouching in his chair, texting friends while he mutters complaints under his breath.

I elbow him. "Show your sister a little support," I say. "She comes to your musical performances, after all."

Logan does straighten at that, shooting me a sideways glance before he stares front. "Yeah, well. I don't ask her to. I don't ask any of you, actually."

"You don't need to," I tell him. "We're family. Families support each other."

His cheeks turn bright red, but at least he doesn't say another word for the rest of the presentation. I study him from the corner of my eye as the presentations wrap up, and we all go to shake Mia's hand. Logan has been working hard at practice for this musical, I know—getting home late, struggling to keep up with his homework. Maybe he's nervous?

That's not like him—usually he loves the attention he gets on stage, even in bit parts. But this year, he scored a role with more speaking lines than ever before. I make a mental note to talk to him, see if he wants help. We used to run lines before rehearsals all the time, but it's been years since we did that. Now, he prefers to practice with his friends, other budding actors who "get it," as he says.

Fine by me, though I can't deny that I miss a bit of that together-time we used to share.

Jennifer is all tears when they announce Mia as the third-place winner. "We're so proud of you, sweetheart."

She wraps Mia in a giant bear hug, and even though I can see Mia rolling her eyes over Jen's shoulder, I can tell she's enjoying it, too.

I step forward and fold my arms around Jen and Mia at once, which makes Mia groan louder. But Jen looks up at me, a flash of surprise and then pleasure crossing her features. Her hand feels warm, as it snakes around my back to rest between my shoulder blades.

Too soon, however, the moment ruptures—when Logan teases Mia and she breaks out of the huddle to playfully swat his arm.

We watch our kids taunt one another, exchanging side-eyes. "Game this week?" Jen asks, surprising me yet again.

I smile. "Actually, if you've got a chance to sneak away from work for a bit, I've been wanting to talk to you about that… Ryan had an idea we might want to try out." And I don't know if I just picked the right moment to ask, or if Jen's been as frustrated as I have with the public courts we've gone to, but to my excitement, Jennifer agrees to check out the club.

We pull up outside Riverbend Country Club the next day, a sunny Sunday afternoon. We're barely out of the car before a valet appears, offering to park it. "Free of charge for all members," he adds with a bright smile.

I hesitate. "Well, we're not exactly members yet…"

Just then, a woman in a suit bustles out of the main entrance. "Mr. and Mrs. Hayward?" She extends a hand, beaming. "I'm Nicky, I'll be your club representative today."

I extend a hand, surprised. When I'd called to book our tour, I didn't realize it would come with our own guide. "Pleasure to meet you."

"Oh, the pleasure's all mine." She takes Jen's hand next, pumping it. "I hear you two are budding pickleball stars."

Jennifer laughs. "I don't know about that. But we were having fun. It's just…" She trails off and glances sideways at me, hesitant.

"Hard to actually enjoy the game at the public courts?" Nicky asks, one eyebrow quirked. "I've heard something similar from most of our members." With that, she gestures for us to follow her inside, while the valet parks our car. Nicky has a brisk, no-nonsense walk, and an equally no-nonsense way of speaking. She points as we go, mouth going a mile a minute.

"Here's the reception area—nothing fancy, you just check in and get your complimentary towels here. You can also rent a locker from us for a slight upcharge, or add on laundry service if you'd like us to wash your workout clothes once you're done for the day." Her heels click across the paved stone-style floors.

Jen and I, meanwhile, gawk at the high ceilings and the broad marble columns all around us. Through a pair of open doors, we glimpse a dining room with multiple chandeliers and a huge fireplace, reminiscent of the venue we rented when we got married, an eternity ago.

"Here's the general restaurant." Nicky nods through the doors. "There's a complimentary buffet for all our members, plus water, tea, and coffee whenever you'd like. If you want to order a la carte, you can do that too, and you're free to bring guests. But for big events, we need at least a couple weeks' notice to plan everything."

We follow her through another set of double doors to a long hallway. On our left, enormous windows look out over a pool, sauna, and hot tub complex. "The pools are for everyone as well, though only our full club members can access the additional spa services." Nicky points at a massage parlor attached to the wood-fire sauna. "And outside, I think you can see it from here." She pauses to gesture at a series of rolling green hills. "That's the 18-hole golf course, also just for full members. But anyone with a pickleball membership can buy a tee-time slot at a discount; we just need to give priority to the golf members, you know how it is."

She flashes us a smile, which we return. As we carry on to the next stop, a couple of passing employees wave to us. A few of the members look up curiously too, from side rooms where they have their laptops open, or seem to be enjoying mugs of coffee after a workout.

Nicky nods at one such room. "These casual lounges are open for use during the daytime. Some people take work meetings here or get a bit of paperwork done in between games." She pushes through more doors, this time into a hallway that smells vaguely chemical, if very clean. "And here are the locker rooms. Mr. Hayward, if you'd like to go with my colleague?" She gestures, and as if by magic, another man appears, in a suit similar to Nicky's. "Andrew will show you the men's facilities."

She leads Jen away, the two chatting eagerly about the pool's opening times and the details of the sauna.

I watch them go for a second, then shake Andrew's hand as he takes me through a doorway into what's got to be one of the fanciest locker rooms I've ever set foot inside. "How crowded does it usually get in here?" I ask, because the place is huge—I count dozens of lockers, and Andrew leads me across the tile floor to a bank of at least twenty showers.

"Not very, except on weekend mornings," Andrew says. "Nine to eleven on weekends is usually our busiest time— people work during the week, so they can't always sneak away, and on the weekends, everybody wants to get their workouts done in the morning."

I nod. That makes sense. "So is it hard to find a court then?"

"Oh, no." Andrew smiles. "We make sure that there are plenty of court spaces to go around. Members can book them anytime, and there's a few courts we leave empty for walk-ins the same day, just for when we need overflow like on the weekends." Past the showers, he points out changing areas and a steam room next to an ice plunge.

He catches me staring at the latter and grins. "Some of our members swear by that," he says. "It really helps with muscle aches and pains, and recovering faster from any injuries." As he takes me back through the bathroom, he adds, "We have a physician on site, in case of any problems. Though, in my experience, as long as people listen to their coaches, they tend to be alright."

A thought strikes me then. "We've been going to a coach we really like..."

"June Graham?" Andrew asks, and I blink at him. He laughs. "On the entry form, we asked about your current training levels and previous lessons, remember?"

Now that he mentions it, I do, though I didn't expect the whole staff to memorize our responses before we arrived. "Sure. Would we be able to keep training with her, or would we need to switch to a club coach?"

"June teaches a couple of our members, actually," Andrew says. "It's not a problem."

I relax. There's one more of my worries vanquished. As we return to the main area, I spot Jennifer, wearing a huge smile. She practically bounces back over to my side.

"Are your showers as great as ours?" she stage-whispers, which makes both Andrew and Nicky laugh. "There's even a steam room!"

"I saw," I tell her, grinning. Internally, I can't help but think it's a shame the steam room isn't in the coed section. Then again, that might be a recipe for too much temptation.

My gaze drifts to Jennifer again, while Andrew waves goodbye. She catches me looking and arches a single brow, her eyes questioning. I wonder if she's been feeling the same frustrations I have. Whether she's missed my touch even half as much as I've missed hers.

What happened to us? I wonder, not for the first time. But the answer is as obvious as it is cliché: the same thing that happens to everyone, I suppose. Life. Kids, our jobs, our packed schedules and never quite enough sleep to do half the things we want to do.

For the first time since we arrived at the clubhouse, my spirits sink a little. But before I can mellow for too long, Nicky claps her hands and leads us onward. "Now, let's get to what you came here for," she says as she strides up an adjacent corridor.

Without warning, the corridor opens into a huge interior gym. It's incredible—bigger and better than we could have imagined. Asphalt-surfaced courts shine under bright overhead lights, with nets strung up to separate each court from the next.

A couple games are going on, the players' tennis shoes squeaking on the asphalt courts as they face off: one pair of doubles at the farthest end of the court and another right nearby.

Nicky lowers her voice while she gestures to the games, so as not to disturb the players or the smattering of people watching the games, the pair of coaches next to each set of players. "We have a set of courts inside, for when there's inclement weather, as well as a series outside. The outside courts are covered, too, so if it's just raining, they're still good to use. But we've gotten a couple more winter storms than we're used to around these parts the last couple of years, so…" Her smile thins, turns wan. "Anyway, these courts come in handy. In summer, too, there's air conditioning inside."

We note that with appreciative smiles, then go back to watching the in-progress games. The players are good—intimidatingly so. Jen and I trade apprehensive looks as one woman makes an incredible lunging return hit.

"Does everyone here play at around the same level?" Jennifer asks.

Nicky smiles. "We've got members at all levels of experience, don't worry. These are some of our more advanced players." Nicky nods at the court. "That pair closest to us won the Lake League last year."

"The what?" I ask.

Nicky's smile widens further. "There's a few pickleball leagues around the area. The Lake League's games start in May and run until the end of June. Coming up pretty soon, in fact!" she adds, unnecessarily reminding me that it's already the start of April.

Where does the time go? I wonder.

"If you're interested in playing, there are sign-up forms available at reception or with any of us employees. Just ask away."

"Oh, I don't know that we're ready for something like that," Jen hedges, glancing my way.

But Nicky clicks her tongue. "Don't sell yourselves short.

League games can be a great way to practice, and beginners join all the time. They're not like some of the tournaments, which have double-elimination games. Lake League uses round robin games, so even if you lose all of your first games, you're guaranteed to get to play four rounds minimum."

"Let's see how we get on with the rest of the tour first," I interject, sensing that Jen is getting overwhelmed again. But internally, I can't help noting that the league games will start in May—after Jennifer's busy schedule finally calms down somewhat...

For the rest of the tour—through the vast outdoor complex of courts, which dwarfs even the massive indoor section by far—Jennifer's gaze keeps darting down to her wrist. I could kick myself for asking Nicky about the Lake League. Her description seems to have pulled Jen out of this fantasyland and reminded her of reality—all the responsibilities that await us both, but especially her leading up to April 15th.

On the way back to the car, I take Jen's hand, interweaving our fingers gently. "We don't have to decide anything today," I remind her. "Let's take some time and mull it over."

She nods, a little distractedly, and casts one last longing glance at the club with a sigh.

Chapter Nine
Jennifer

All day at work the next day, the only thing I can think about is that clubhouse. Going into the tour, I'd been apprehensive. But once we got there, it surprised me how much I wanted it. I envision myself playing game after game on those courts—either outside or on the interior courts, training until I'm as quick on my feet as that woman whose game we glimpsed in passing.

I picture leisurely afternoons after said games, relaxing in the hot tub or reclining in the steam room, before taking a long shower in the spacious private stalls we glimpsed.

I catch myself picturing other things, too. Sebastian and I sharing one of those showers, the steam condensing on our skin. The way he'd turned to catch my chin in one hand, pinning me against the wall with the other…

I startle back to attention to find myself drifting off in front of an open spreadsheet. Beside me on the desk are scattered notes about the client whose files I'm currently preparing. I groan and massage my eyelids, attempting to force myself back to attention. Just one more file.

I glance at the clock over my desk, and my heart sinks. It's already past five. On any normal day, I'd be headed home by now. But not this time of year. Not when it's all hands on deck, crunch time, and we all need to go above and beyond to keep our heads above water.

A couple desks over, Ellen catches my eye and gives me a weary salute. Then she pushes her chair back and stands, picking up a mug and giving me a questioning tilt of her head, one thumb jutting toward the coffee station. Alas, I must shake my head—ever since a certain noteworthy birthday last year, I find myself unable to drink caffeine after about three in the afternoon. Any later and, no matter how exhausted I am, I'll be up all night, mind racing and body unable to collapse into sleep.

Ellen shrugs and pads away, while I force myself back to the task at hand.

But as the clock ticks later and later, my mind strays farther from my work. I keep coming back to the clubhouse. Not just the pickleball courts themselves—although those were plenty appealing. But the whole vibe of the place. It was just relaxing, from start to finish. The moment you walked in the front doors, you felt at home, like you belonged.

That was the type of place I wanted to work. Not in a crummy office with no view except of a parking lot, and nothing to face except piles upon piles of the same repetitive tasks to do ad nauseum.

Not for the first time, or even the hundredth, I daydream about a little business of my own. Ever since I graduated college, I've nursed this silly idea of opening a day spa, like the kind my mom and I used to go to together when I was younger. I can't afford splurges like that these days, but I remember always being fascinated by those places when I was younger. What would life be like, for someone whose entire job was to help people relax?

I imagine they'd feel as relaxed as their customers. Not to mention, you could pop into your own spa for a treatment anytime you wanted…

With effort, I drag myself out of these ridiculous fantasies and finally manage to finish up my last client file for the day. It's not the last of the stack—I should try to do one or two more, to save myself more hassle tomorrow. But my brain is completely fried. I'll get nauseous if I have to read through one more itemized deduction list.

On the drive home, neither Ellen nor I feel much like chatting. We listen to the radio the whole way home until Ellen pulls up our driveway. "Thanks for the lift," I tell her.

She nods, stifling a yawn with one fist. "See you tomorrow?"

"Bright and early," I mumble, sounding like a prisoner on their way to execution.

"I'll be a little later," Ellen says. "Brought some work home with me, just so I can get stuff done in between my online yoga class."

I groan. "I should've thought of that."

She reaches over to pat my arm. "Just two more weeks," she reminds me. "Then we're home free."

I repeat that to myself as I trudge up the front driveway, noticing Sebastian's car is already in the garage, and the light to Mia's room glowing bright yellow against our front lawn. But on the threshold of our house, I pause, experiencing another disorienting flash, this time to the clubhouse, and the meeting rooms Nicky pointed out. Some people take work meetings here or get a bit of paperwork done in between games. Then I think of Ellen's words. Brought some work home with me…

All of a sudden, for the first time all day, hope strikes me. A smile brightens my expression as I unlock the front door and hurry inside. "Sebastian?" I call.

"In here," he replies from the kitchen. I dart through the foyer and into the kitchen, where I find my husband at the stove, apron and all, cooking a big batch of his famous spaghetti. He glances up, and his eyebrows shoot higher. "You're looking chipper," he says. "Get a lot done today?"

I wave a hand. "Not nearly enough." I stride across the room and lean in for a kiss. He gives me the usual perfunctory peck on the lips, and I feel a brief swell of disappointment. I don't know why, when this is our usual routine, but something in me had been hoping for more today…

I quell the feeling with a forced, bright smile instead. "But I've been thinking, and I have an idea."

"Oh?" He cocks one eyebrow, a move that accentuates his dimples and the crooked, mischievous smile I've always loved. "What's that?"

"Well…" As quickly as I can, I explain what I'm thinking. Sebastian brightens with each word, until we're both grinning at one another, like teenagers about to sneak off in their car together for a tryst right under their parents' noses.

"Are you sure?" he asks, just as Mia steps into the room.

"What are you two grinning about?" she asks. "You're totally weirding me out."

"Nothing," I say, at the same time that Sebastian says, "Just making some plans of our own."

Mia's nose wrinkles. "Oh, gross. Do not tell me about your hookup plans or whatever." With that, she darts back out of the room, shouting at her brother that it's almost time for dinner.

Sebastian and I crack up, though not before I notice his eyes darting to me again, an unreadable look on his face. Not for the first time, it strikes me how long it's been. But I don't want to be the first one to break that barrier between us. It feels too dangerous, like putting myself out on a limb where I might get shot down, and I don't want to let him see how badly that would hurt.

So, I turn my back and grab plates to set the table, keeping myself busy until the kids are finished eating and we're getting ready for bed.

"You sure about this?" Sebastian asks, and for a split second, I think he means about us having sex. But then I remember what I talked to him about over dinner, the club.

"I think so," I say. "Honestly, it might help me get through the work faster, if I can take a break every now and then to work out my frustrations."

He laughs. "Sounds good." He grins at me, eyes bright

with excitement I haven't seen in a long time. "I'll give June a call and see what her availability is like this week."

Which is how we wind up back at Riverbend Country Club just two days later, brand new owners of a pair of club cards and matching complimentary club towels, warming up on the outside courts while June unpacks her things.

"We're going to try something new today," June says, which I've already learned is going to mean some wild new moves.

When we first started training with June, she gave us homework—things that were easy to do at home, like practicing paddle bumps where we bounce the ball in front of ourselves over and over, flipping the paddle from forehand to backhand while the ball's in the air. At practice, we moved up to learning how to slow the ball down and take control of the pace, things like sharks versus dolphins.

But I'm confused when June starts pulling these brightly colored flat rubber disks out of her bag, and laying them on the opposing court like targets.

"We call these dot shots," she explains. "I want you to aim for these when you return my hits—try to place the ball as close to these circles as you can get." With that, she lobs the ball over the net to us and we get started.

It's harder than it looks to guide the ball into one exact spot on our opponent's court—and it looks pretty hard to start with. By the time we've gotten through a whole lesson, both Sebastian and I are sweating our faces off, and we've not even played an actual game yet.

June is grinning, though, which feels like a reward enough in itself. She's sparing with praise, never doling it out unless you really earn it, which makes it feel even better when she gives me a proud nod off the court. "You've come a long way, you know. And you're getting better every time I see you." She glances at Sebastian, laughing. "Who lit the fire under her, you?"

"Oh, no." Sebastian shakes his head, laughing. "That's all Jen. She's been like that from day one."

I flash him a bright, pleased smile, even as my cheeks flush from all the compliments. It's good to know he still sees me that way—like the competitive firecracker I used to be in college. Sometimes even I forget it, how eager for a challenge I used to be. "All thanks to our coach," I say, but June shakes her head.

"Nah girl. That kind of fire can't be taught." She waves goodbye, and Sebastian shoots me a look, like he's bracing himself for a letdown.

"Should we head home?"

I check the clock. It's after hours already, but I did take home some work from the office. I hedge, debating. "Let me knock out one file," I say. "Then maybe we can play a pickup game?"

He brightens. "I'll ask around while you're working."

I beeline to the offices Nicky showed us, understanding now why a club like Riverbend would go to all the trouble of installing them. The first one I check is occupied by a guy in a suit having some kind of yelling match over his cell phone. No thanks. I move on to the second office, empty for now, and set up at one of the desks.

To my surprise, once I pull out my laptop and get everything organized, it takes much less time than I anticipated for me to whip through the file. My mind feels clearer, my body still energized from the coaching session.

Or maybe this client file was just one of the easier ones. Whatever the reason, I knock through it in no time, and hurry back to the courts to find Sebastian chatting to a couple of familiar faces.

"Hey, Ryan!" I wave, approaching. As I do, his wife Maria turns around, and I have to resist the urge to do a double-take. I hardly recognize her. The last time I saw her, at the firehouse's annual Christmas get-together, Maria was dressed as usual in a several sizes too-large dress, something that looked like she'd nicked it out of her mother's closet. Her long hair was down, pulled half over her face like she wanted to hide behind it.

Today, she looks as sleek as any of the well-heeled ladies we've passed in the club, dressed in slim-fitting athleisurewear, her hair done up in a ponytail to reveal surprisingly pretty features. I realize I've never actually seen her whole face at once, and I definitely don't remember the big smile she's turning on me.

"Jennifer!" She darts over to hug me. I don't remember her being a big hugger, either. "Sebastian was just telling us you both joined. Isn't Riverbend the best?"

"It's definitely growing on me," I say, shooting a curious glance at Sebastian over Maria's head. But he's distracted, deep in conversation with Ryan about something. I glance back at Maria. "You look incredible."

"Oh, thanks." She flushes, tossing her ponytail back over one shoulder. "One of the other ladies forced me into a spa weekend and, well, between that and all the pickleball, I guess I do feel pretty great."

"Spa weekend?" I ask, trying to conceal my jealousy. "God, I'd give anything for one."

"You should come with us next time!" She nudges me with one elbow. "We're planning to go in another week or two."

My heart sinks. "Maybe later," I say. "After tax season ends."

"Oh, right." Maria's face softens. "Is it super hectic right now?"

"The worst." I give my paddle an experimental swing. "But hey, that's what blowing off steam is for, right?"

"That's the spirit!" Maria crows, right as Ryan and Sebastian break off their discussion. The four of us claim an open court and shake out our muscles, getting ready to play.

"Watch out for this one," Ryan calls to his wife, with a nod at Sebastian. "They don't call him Bash for nothing."

I laugh. God, I haven't heard anyone else use that old nickname in ages. "You whipping out your soccer glory days at the firehouse?" I ask him.

"Nah, just creating some new glory days," he replies with

a wink. Then raises the ball to serve.

We fall into an easy rhythm. Ryan's a bit of a banger—anytime I aim the ball his way, he fires a hard one right back at me, so fast I have no choice but to send it back at speed. June always scolds us about that, warning us that when we slow the ball down, we control it, rather than the other way around.

But it's difficult when your opponents seem to want speed over anything else. And a few of those speeding shots get past me—though a few more either me or Sebastian manage to get a handle on.

June calls hard-hitting pickleball a dumpster fire—unpredictable, hot as well, and it stinks to find yourself in. I find myself agreeing with her. Halfway through the game, our scores nearly neck and neck, Sebastian calls for a time out. He draws me in, leans down for a conference.

"I think we need a little more dolphin, a bit less shark," he says. In other words, slow the ball down, control it, like June's always telling us.

"But how?" I ask.

"Follow my lead," he says.

On our next serve, when Ryan returns one hard, Sebastian claims it. He gets to it first, hits it slow on the side, a perfect third shot drop. Sure enough, it does go over slower, aimed right at Maria. She returns it, just barely, and I lean into the kitchen to delicately dribble it over their side of the net. They don't stand a chance. It puddles onto the ground, and Ryan curses, while Maria sighs, deflating.

Our next few rounds go the same way, until Sebastian sends the winning return straight down the center line, and Maria nearly collides with Ryan chasing it. We whoop and high-five, both of us dancing a little in victory. Then I wince and glance over at Maria and Ryan, feeling bad for rubbing it in.

But they're taking it in stride, grinning at our antics, and they come up for a handshake with no hard feelings. "You guys are good," Ryan says. "Are you thinking about joining the league next month?"

My cheeks flush, even as Sebastian answers for us. "I don't know. We only just started here at the club. Let's see how this goes first."

I could kiss him for that. But I keep it to myself, because just then, my phone alarm goes off, reminding me that I have two more client files to get through before I can really relax. "Crap. Thanks for the game, guys. I'll catch you all soon?" Then I dart off, back to my makeshift office.

There's one other person in there now, a woman with her laptop open, writing something. She gives me a brief but friendly smile as I enter, then gets right back to it. More power to her.

I settle in at my computer, braced for more hard work. But to my surprise, this client file flows as easily as the last one. Either I took home a lucky batch tonight, or something about the adrenaline and sweat is good for my brain too, priming me to be in a better, more productive mood once I finally do put my ass in the chair and get down to work.

I finish both files in plenty of time to play another cheeky pickup game before Sebastian and I need to jet home to make dinner for the kids. The whole way home, a grin remains plastered on my face. Yeah. Maybe this is exactly what we needed.

Chapter Ten
Sebastian

We spent almost every night at the club over the next week. Any spare chance we can sneak away, we take it. Jen is getting fearsome with her backhand, and her overhead shot has improved loads from where she started too. We make other new friends at the club besides Ryan and Maria, meeting a few other couples, as well as some pairs who play with friends or siblings. We even meet one father-daughter pair, the father well into his seventies but spry as any of us younger bucks, his daughter thirty-something and a wicked backhand shot.

Ryan mentions the name Bash to a handful of people, and before long, it's all anyone calls me.

"Good morning, Bash," says the receptionist whenever we arrive to check in—me usually running a bit late after I got off work at the firehouse, and Jen already here, working in the office she's practically claimed for her own in the late afternoons and early evenings. Her boss doesn't mind where she gets her accounts finished, so long as they get finished, and nobody can deny she's been more productive working here at Riverbend than she ever was in her old office.

"Change of scenery, maybe?" she muses one day when I ask her about it.

Could be. But if you ask me, I think it's probably the breaks to get the blood flowing back into her brain. Sitting at a desk all day really shoots your concentration. But go back and forth between the desk and actually getting to move around on your feet? That'll liven you right back up.

We have a few more lessons with June sprinkled in among our casual games. Every time, she seems more full of praise than the last, which buoys my spirits. June's a fair coach, but she can be a tough one. She spares no punches when it comes to things we screw up.

So, it's with some excitement that I track the clock, the days ticking ever closer to the deadline to sign up for the Lake League. I haven't dared broach the subject with Jen yet, but seeing how excited she is every time she comes to the clubhouse—not to mention how she's rearranged her schedule during her busiest month of the year to make this work—I have a feeling I'm not the only one idly daydreaming about us signing up for the league.

Besides, like Nicky told us, there's no pressure around the league. It's all round robin games, above all for fun. So what if we lost out at the start of the tournament? At least we'd get the practice, learn more for next year, if we're still doing this by then.

God, I want to be. But I swallow that particular hope for now. One day at a time. For now, I'm just grateful Jen and I are here, today, warming up for another club game against some new friends we met last week. Scott and Laura, like us, picked up pickleball recently. They, too, started playing on the public courts before they found Riverbend. They've been at the club a couple months longer than us, but they seem to love it every bit as much as Ryan and every other member we've played with.

It's a busy day today, probably because we're coming up on the weekend. I've noticed the courts clear out early in the week, then slowly fill with every day closer to Saturday, when it's an absolute madhouse. We'll need to get here early next Saturday, if we want to get in a decent amount of court time outside. The inside courts aren't as popular, but we had to resort to them last weekend.

Not that that's a bad thing, in comparison to the public courts, and playing maybe one or two games if we were lucky.

With every game we play together, I can feel us improving. Not just individually, but as a team. I learn to call the shots that come our way, even the obvious ones, so that Jen and I always know who's going to take what. The constant refrain of our games becomes a steady stream of "yours," "mine," "yours," and the occasional "switch" on a high-ball, or "let it go" if one's going to go over the boundary and either of us think we might accidentally lunge for it.

So it's with the usual mix of eager anticipation that Jen and I join Scott and Laura on the court, shaking hands as per usual before our friendly match begins. Before we even get a shot off, though, shouts from the neighboring court steal our attention.

Two people I've never seen before, both long and lean and blond, face down an older man I've played a few times. "That wasn't out of bounds!" the old man is yelling. His wife looks angry too, red in the face, arms crossed.

The blond man spreads his arms and offers the kind of winning smile you see on toothpaste commercials, all polished and too straight to be natural. "Look, I'm just telling you what I saw, that's all. No need for the theatrics."

"This is the fourth time you've called something out when it's in!" the old man bellows.

"Can we get a second opinion here?" Blondie asks, turning left and right. Beside him, his wife—or maybe sister, they look pretty similar with the blue eyes and sharp, angular faces—taps her foot.

"It was out," she says, voice curt and clear, with an unfamiliar accent. Up north somewhere, but one of those fake polished accents people used to trot out in the 50s, the way nobody actually talks. Except this woman, apparently.

"Dorothy, tell them." The old man turns on his wife, but she raises her hands, face the picture of surrender.

"It's not worth it, honey. Just let it go."

The old man fires dagger glares at their opponents, who exchange looks. Blondie steps forward, ball extended. "Look, if it means that much to you, you take this next serve. On us. We don't mind."

The old man sets his jaw, scowling. "I don't want your pity shots. I want to play the game, fair and square. Same as we all do around here. Where'd you two even come from, eh? Never seen you around before."

A lot of people use this club, but I have to admit, this couple seems like they'd stand out, even in a crowd. I don't know much about clothing, but even I can tell from a hundred paces that their outfits alone are worth as much as some of the cars in the parking lot.

"We're guests of Susan Morrison," says Blondie's wife pertly, lips pursed. "You know. The owner of this establishment?"

That shuts the old man up. He shoots his wife another look, this one less irritated and more pleading. The wife—Dorothy, I guess—lays a hand on his arm. "It's all right, dear. Just play out the game, that's all."

Blondie tosses the ball, still extending it over the net. "No? Offer going once… twice…" He shrugs when neither the old man nor his wife moves a muscle and turns to go back to the baseline. "Suit yourselves. Eight, three, one," he says, and serves.

I glance over at our own game. I'm not the only one distracted by this interaction—Jen, Scott, and Laura were all gaping at the scene playing out too, along with half the other courts within earshot.

"Who are they?" Jen whispers to me.

I shake my head in mute confusion, but to my surprise, Laura interjects. "Chris and Crys Basso. They belong to Utopian Country Club—dunno if you've seen their promo ads around, super swanky, uppity place. But they're friends with the owners of Riverbend, so sometimes they come over here to guest play. Usually when it's super crowded and we could all use the courts they take up," Laura adds, with a surprisingly vehement scowl in their direction. Normally Laura seems super sweet and even-tempered.

"Steer clear of them if you can," Scott mutters, unnecessarily. "They're good players, don't get me wrong, but, well…" He glances back over at the old man currently getting his ass thrashed by Chris and Crys. "Let's just say, that was a pretty standard display for those two. They like to fudge the rules, when it comes to their own games. Push to see how much they can get away with."

"So they're cheaters." Jennifer narrows her eyes at their court. I know firsthand how strongly my wife feels about anyone who cheats to get ahead, especially in something as sacred to her as sporting competitions.

Let's just say, not all college soccer players are angels—on the women's teams, especially. It stunned me back then, how vicious some of those girls could be. Jen's friend nearly lost an eye when one of the girls snuck metal cleats onto the field. The refs had banned them at that particular match, since the schools had a fairly heated rivalry, but one of the players snuck a pair past the referees somehow. During a particularly tough scrimmage, one girl went down just as the other went for a kick—to the ball, she claims, though to my eye from the stands, it looked like she was aiming to take out somebody's knee.

Her cleat caught Jen's friend in the cheek. It broke her eye socket, and they had to stop the whole game while she was rushed to the hospital.

Those are the kind of players Jen used to run among. Dominate, in fact, one of the top players in her varsity team. Not good enough to go pro, according to her—though, if you ask me, she ought to have given it a shot at least for a year—but certainly good enough to graduate without debt, her scholarship paying for almost all of her tuition.

So when she sizes up this duo beside us, I trust her judgment. She falls back into line beside me on the court, teeth bared. "Let's play them next."

My eyebrows shoot up. I want to argue—didn't Scott just warn us not to? But then, it's been so long since I've glimpsed this side of Jen. The feral, wild side she lets out on the field and almost nowhere else. There's a fire in her eyes, one I've missed. She wants to take those assholes down a peg. And damned, if her plan doesn't make me want to join right in.

I find myself grinning, even as we square off against our friends. "Sounds good to me."

We beat Scott and Laura handily—sometimes they give us a good match, I can't lie, but today they seem off. That, or maybe Jen and I have just been practicing so frenetically that we're unstoppable today. We certainly feel like it, marching off the court and up to the blond couple smirking on the next court over, clearly pleased with beating an old couple by questionable means.

"Hey." Jen sticks out her hand. "I'm Jennifer, this is Bash."

Crys peers down her nose at us, not moving a muscle to return the handshake. "Charmed."

Jen's smile widens, forceful now. "Saw you play earlier. You two are great. Up for a match?"

Crys shoots a sideways look at Chris—who yes, Scott confirmed, is her husband, and not a long-lost Scandinavian cousin of some sort. I watch the debate play out between them, before Chris grins. His wife returns it. "Sure. Why not."

We face off opposite them, and I shoot Jen a reassuring look of my own. We've got this, I think. Her small, private smile seems to answer, I know.

But for all our confidence, we do not, in fact, have this one. That much becomes apparent within just a few minutes of the match. I'm in awe of the amount of control Chris and Crys have over the ball—it's almost like it obeys their every whim, slowing when they need it to slow, sharking past us when they need it to be a banger.

The only thing that pauses the rapid-fire game is about ten minutes in, when Crys raises a hand to force a halt. "Who is making all that racket?" she shouts to the courts in general.

To be honest, I hadn't heard anything beyond the usual sneaker squeaks and the soft tick, tock, of the ball hitting paddles or the court's hard surface. But something must have distracted her, because a moment later, Chris starts nodding, too.

"People are trying to play here," he calls out to the general hubbub of the courts. "We need to focus."

Several heads turn, a few games beside ours pausing. Now who's making the racket? I wonder, Jen and I exchanging sideways looks.

When no one says anything, Chris nods, like someone's just affirmed his insane request. "Thank you." He turns to us, readying to serve. "Five, two, one." He serves, and we brace ourselves for the incoming.

Crys protests "the noise" twice more, however—only ever when Jen and I manage to sneak one by them, I notice. Like she's blaming being on a court with other people for any minute amount of distraction. Like that's not the entire premise of joining a club to play this game, instead of just playing on your own at home with nothing but your air purifiers to distract you.

But it hardly matters anyway. They're too good for us to put a dent in their score, noisy distractions or otherwise.

When Crys sneaks a shot right past Jen's outer right edge, she straight-up laughs—an ugly, tinkling sound, like glass shattering. I expect Chris to say something, maybe even tell her off, but he just starts chuckling too. "Beginners these days," he says, pitched loud enough for us to hear on purpose, I'm certain of it. "They're always biting off more than they can chew."

"Yeah, well, at least we haven't had so much plastic

surgery that our jaws don't function anymore," Jen mutters, under her breath, startling a laugh out of me.

I hadn't noticed the telltale smoothness of their foreheads, or the disproportionate size of Crys's lips. Even the shape of their faces, Jen will inform me later, indicate fillers and work. It's why I thought they looked so much alike, at first. Turns out they planned it that way.

But hey, whatever floats their boat. It's more the personality flaws I'm concerned with. Crys keeps her next snipe about us under her breath, but from the way Chris breaks into hysterics, I'm sure it wasn't anything kind. And bad jibes aside, the Chrises really are good. We only manage to sneak in two more points before Chris and Crys whip out an eleven to four win.

Afterward, wiping our brows, Jen and I go to shake hands, but our opponents have already moved on, striding over to the next court to inquire about another match. I stare after them, wondering how their workout clothes still look so pristine. "Do they even sweat?" I mutter.

"Maybe they Botoxed all their sweat glands," Jen replies, sotto voce, and we trade undignified snorts.

"Don't let them get to you," I say. "Sore winners all around."

She wrinkles her nose. "You can say that again." But I notice she turns to watch as Chris and Crys set up for their next game, eyes shining a little too brightly. "Still, can't deny they're good. Like… really good."

I clap a hand on her shoulder, reassuring. "We'll kick

their asses someday. I promise you that."

She laughs, reaching up to wind her fingers around mine. "Here's to defeating C and C someday."

That rings a bell. "C+C. About the farthest cry from the Music Factory you can get, though."

Jennifer snorts, a mischievous grin crossing her features. "C+C Non-Music Factory, more like."

I let my arm slide down around her shoulders, grip her tight against my side, sweat and all. "Suits them. What with her bat-hearing, she probably can't stand listening to music at all."

Still giggling like a couple of resentful teens, we make our way off the court and into the locker rooms. It's strange, since we lost that last match, but somehow the competition hasn't dulled our spirits. If anything, it's given us a goal to work toward.

Chapter Eleven

Jennifer

Tax Day comes and goes. Usually it's a mad flurry of work leading up to it, followed by a hungover-feeling week afterward, where I sleep in late and generally go around acting like a crabby asshole.

Instead, this year, I get all my work turned in, and I come out of it feeling… well, still tired and overworked. But alive. Burning with excitement, because now, with my biggest work week of the year behind me, I have more time than ever for the place I really want to be.

To celebrate, we plan a whole weekend at the country club. We get there early on Saturday to take advantage of the outdoor courts, then switch to the inside ones when things get hectic. For a break, we splurge on a meal at the country club restaurant—their Italian food is to die for—and take a soak in the hot tub before we go back for another evening round.

On Sunday, the club has a tradition, a sort of round robin type game where everyone plays everyone who comes. Of course, C + C Non-Music Factory show up again, to everyone's chagrin, but especially mine. There's just something about the Chrises that rubs me the wrong way. Part of me feels a little guilty for crapping on their plastic surgery—who am I to judge what someone wants to do with their own face? But the thing is, they're just so unrelentingly petty.

They get into arguments during every match they play, sniping over technicalities, fudging the out-of-bounds line. And Crys, I swear to God, must have hearing like a superhero. A single gnat a million miles away can supposedly so disturb her concentration that it makes her miss key hits.

But Sebastian and I manage to enjoy ourselves despite those two's mood-dampening presence. We win a few friendly rounds in a row, lose a couple close games. We face off against C+C again, this time to the tune of 11-6. Still not great, but hey, two points better than our last loss. I'll take any win where I can get it.

The whole match long, I keep laser-focused on Crys's smug smile. I know her type. I went to high school with a whole gaggle of them. Pretty and wealthy, they expect the whole world to kiss their ring simply for the privilege of witnessing their existence.

Someday, I promise myself. We'll get good enough to thrash these two.

Maybe that's why, when our club rep Nicky stops us on our way out of the club to remind us that the deadline to register for the Lake League is end of day, I glance over at Sebastian and nod. "Let's do it."

He brightens considerably. Knowing him, he's been dying to sign up, but he didn't want to pressure me. I feel a rush of gratitude for him. Whatever difficulties we've had lately, however much pressure we've been under, this is a much-needed reminder: Sebastian knows me so well.

We cook together tonight, both of us moving seamlessly around the kitchen. Normally either he or I take charge of dinner, because we're in each other's way—and eventually at one another's throats—when we try to cook at the same time. The way he insists on chopping every single vegetable to the exact same size, no matter how slow the process, drives me crazy, and he hates the way I toss every which spice into the pot, no measurements, just eyeballing it.

But tonight feels different. We divvy up the chores without argument—Sebastian washes and chops, while I start the stock going, tasting and adding more things and tasting again until the balance seems just right. "Passing," Sebastian calls whenever he ducks behind me, and I take to murmuring, "On your left" anytime I sidle up to the stove to add more things to the pan, once he gets the steaks frying.

We're still working like that, in concert, when the kids get home. Mia tromps into the kitchen like a herd of elephants, as per usual—how does she make that much noise with such a little body?—while Logan immediately heads upstairs.

"You and your brother can set the table," I tell her, but Mia just pauses in the doorway, eying us. After a moment, I turn to shoot her a questioning look. "What?"

She jerks her face away, though not before I catch a hint of a smile on her mouth. "Nothing. Logan!" she screams, headed for the staircase.

Normally I'd tell her off for yelling at that volume—we have neighbors, after all. But Sebastian and I just trade looks and burst into laughter. I'm in too good a mood tonight to burst it.

Logan somewhat ruptures that mood—he refuses to come down and help his sister with the table, claiming he's behind on homework. That part, I know, is true—we've gotten another call from his teacher about his poor performance. Enough to worry me.

Leaving Sebastian to finish up, I head upstairs to Logan's bedroom. I knock on the door, first quietly, then louder to be heard over the music blaring inside. "It's me, honey."

A momentary pause, then the music cuts out. Logan strides to the door and opens it a crack. Over his shoulder, I note the room is a disaster zone—boxers everywhere, dirty laundry in piles, plates with caked food around the edges.

"What did I tell you about your room?" I say. Both kids know this—they are entitled to their private spaces as long as they keep them relatively tidy. I don't need them to be neat freaks, but we cannot afford to get a bug infestation in this house.

"Sorry, Mom." He runs a hand through his hair. There are visible bags under his eyes, which make me frown and push the door open wider.

"What's wrong? Are you sleeping okay?"

He rolls his eyes, but at least he steps back to allow me into the room. A whiff of teenage boy hits me: BO, old pizzas, and mildew. I wrinkle my nose and stride to the window, wrenching it open to let in some April evening air. We had a very late and completely unusual frost a couple nights ago, but it's started to warm up properly now. Enough that the breeze feels refreshing, not frigid.

"It's a wonder you can breathe in here," I mumble.

Logan heaves a put-upon sigh. "I'll clean it, Mom. Promise. I've just been really busy."

I turn back to face him, arms crossed. "With the musical? I don't like how much work this new director is putting on you kids. You're only in high school, for Pete's sake. This isn't Broadway."

Logan groans. "I knew you wouldn't understand."

"Honey, it's not that I don't understand; I know you want to do well in the play. But you need to learn balance. School is the most important thing. It's preparing you for figuring out work and life balance in the future—you need to have some space for work, and some space for leisure. You can't let one or the other completely take over."

Logan snorts. "That's rich, coming from you."

"Hey. Watch your tone young man." I cross my arms, staring at him. "And what's that supposed to mean, anyway?"

"It's not like you do anything but work," he replies. "Work, work, work, all the time, even when it's not tax season. And when it is, forget it." He looks away, though not before I catch a glimpse of his expression—hangdog, like he's disappointed.

My chest clenches. I had no idea he felt this way. "Honey, we need money to survive. You know, to pay for this house, and food, and—"

"You just said balance is important." Logan looks back at me, expression hardening. "But you don't remember how to balance anything at all." With that, he turns on his heel and storms out of the room.

I linger in his wake, gaping after my son. He's right, in some ways, of course. I have been far too focused on work—I'm starting to realize that, now that I've seen what introducing one actually fun activity to my life has done for me. Paradoxically, the more pickleball I play, the more invigorated I feel, which in turn makes me more capable of tackling the piles of work on my desk. Sometimes, I even manage to forget how much the tables and excel spreadsheets bore me. I can trick myself into thinking this is all accounting work I'm doing for something more fun—the supporting work for a business I actually love, something that helps people center themselves and relax.

Now it hits me, how big of a hypocrite I've been. I daydream about helping other people calm down and escape temporarily from their busy lives. But I haven't done anything like that for myself in years.

I take a deep breath, and let it out again slowly. Part of me wants to tell Logan off for his tone—I shouldn't let him get away with talking back like that. But a bigger part of me wants to just let this one slide, because in the end… he's right.

Chapter Twelve

Jennifer

Our first Lake League match is against the Mountain Creek Club. Ryan, Maria, Scott, and Laura have all signed up too, so we have some friends to linger with on the sidelines, observing the other matches until our individual rounds get called.

It's both exciting and nerve-wracking at once. I can't stop gaping at the more professional-looking players, some of them in matching uniforms with their partners, and paddles with brand names I recognize from my own search for an upgraded paddle. Some of those cost loads more than the ones Sebastian and I settled on.

With every new impressive performance, my nerves ratchet higher. I feel strung high as a kite when someone finally calls our names. "Sebastian and Jennifer Hayward?"

"Go Bash!" Ryan shouts from the sidelines, where he and Maria are drenched in sweat, having just won their first bout against a Mountain Creeker. Each opponent plays one another to best of five, and then after your games, you have the option to take a breather in the lounge area near the locker rooms before your next match, or stay to watch. Most people are staying to watch, though I notice a few couples slipping off together and exchanging mischievous looks.

The sights of them sends a pang of envy into my gut, but I suppress it.

We're playing away, at the Mountain Creek Clubhouse, which is a lot sleeker and more modern-looking than Riverside. I try not to get distracted by the view beyond the courts, a rolling hillside down to a glittering lake, with trees in the background just beginning to bud for spring. It's the kind of view you could spend all day admiring, but now we have bigger fish to fry.

The team we're playing look every bit as glamorous as the others we've watched so far. They shake our hands, seeming nice enough. Then play starts, and Jesus, are we in for it.

They pepper us both for the first half of the match, keeping us on our toes at the edge of the kitchen. I admire their moves—sleek hits and effortless-looking returns. Sebastian and I try our best to do the same. Our friends' chants from the sidelines buoy our spirits: Go Bash and Smash it, Jen!

Someone—probably Scott, knowing him—comes up with the nickname Bashifer, and they all run with it, chanting that repeatedly as we race to keep up with our opponents.

Unfortunately, all the encouragement falls flat. We miss a few hits in a row, and before we know it, the match is ending with a decisive 11 to 4 in our opponents' favor.

"That's okay." Bash touches my shoulder, grips it gently. "We've still got four more. It's not over till Bowie sings."

I snort. Our own inside-joke, because I never liked the

whole fat lady singing thing—it felt like shaming opera singers or something to me. "Be hard for him now," I say, and we both bow our heads in a quick moment of silence, the way we've done ever since the news broke of the loss of our favorite singer.

"May he bless this next match," Bash jokes. But maybe he does, because in our rematch, we squeak out a win—11 us to 9 the other team. When the winning point sails past the opposing team's paddles, we leap at one another, shouting our heads off.

Sebastian's arms snake around my waist, crushing me to him, and I get a whiff of his scent—not the cologne he usually wears, but the real him. The guy I fell for back in college. It sends a thrill along my spine, a pulse of desire that I force myself to quell, because we're in public first of all, and second of all, we have a match to win.

Our third bout gets right back on tenterhooks, though. We're sweating bullets by this point, chugging water whenever we can. We've also lost half our cheering squad, because Scott and Laura's match was called up on an adjacent court, where more of our fellow Riverbenders battle Mountain Creeks for supremacy.

We try our hardest—at one point I lunge so hard for a ball I land on all fours, scraping one knee. The other team offers to stop, but I shake my head. A courtside spectator brings me a Band-Aid, and we get right back into playing.

Unfortunately, our hardest isn't enough. The other team

fires one past Sebastian's left side, just inside of bounds, winning them 11 points to our 8.

"We're not out yet," I tell Sebastian, the moment we step off-court for our break.

"Are you sure you're good to keep playing?" He glances at my leg again, concerned, but I brush him off.

"Please. I barely even feel it. You know what my pain tolerance is like, anyway." I grin.

He eyes me playfully, eyes narrowed. "That's what I'm concerned about. Don't push yourself if it's going to hurt more in the long run."

"I'm fine." When he nudges me, I push him back lightly, then lean into his side. "Worry about your half of the court and I'll manage mine, how about that?"

He grins and leans down for a kiss, surprising me. He tastes like adrenaline and Gatorade, and both of our mingled sweat. It's… kind of hot, actually. Again, I feel that pulse, deep behind my navel. When we break apart, I inhale sharply, and notice Sebastian's eyes dilate where they fix on mine.

Is he thinking what I'm thinking?

No time to find out. The next match starts by the time we've barely recovered from this one. But it's good to see that our opponents are looking as winded as we feel. Their quick motions have slowed down, and they're getting sloppy with the ball on occasion. More and more, Bash and I find ourselves in control, and we take full advantage.

He calls out moves to me, and I execute them seamlessly,

both of us moving like one well-oiled machine. We score a point, then another, and another. Our opponents regain control for a few rounds, but we seize it back and tie them, then surpass them once more.

We're neck and neck down to the final few points. I sneak one over into the kitchen that they aren't able to reach in time, even though they both lunge for it. It dribbles between them, and Bash high-fives me. The ball comes back to us, 10-9, and it's game point now.

They aren't going down without a fight. Our next volley feels like it lasts forever. I lose track of time, space, as it goes on. All I think about is the ball, the placement of my feet, the weight of the paddle in my hand. The rest of the world melts away until there's only this moment, the sound of my breath in my lungs, the squeak of my shoes against the court.

As the volley continues, though, time seems to slow. I find myself able to anticipate where the ball will go next, figuring out the exact angle to return it with my paddle to get it where I want it—using June's dot shot technique, only without the visible target to go by.

It works.

We sneak one final point past them, and the Riverbender side of the crowd goes wild. Sebastian pulls me into his arms, both of us laughing. There's still one more game to play, the final game of five to decide the whole match, but this one already feels like victory in and of itself.

This time, I'm the one who arches up on tiptoe to press

my lips to Sebastian's, fisting one hand in his hair, dragging him down to meet me. There's a split second where he hesitates—surprise? Or does he want to pull away?—but then he's wrapping his arms around my waist, crushing me against him. I can feel every inch of his hard body pressed along my length, and it quickens my breath, speeds up my heart to an almost unbearable rate.

"Careful you two," calls someone from off-sides. We break apart and turn to see Ryan and Maria watching us with barely concealed laughter. "Don't want to set the court on fire," Laura says.

"At least, not any more than you already are," adds Ryan. They lean over for fist-bumps and high-fives, then gesture back at the court. "Go out there and finish 'em, Bashifer."

We snort. "That is not sticking," I warn him, but I can tell from the sparkle in our friends' eyes that we might be doomed. It's already caught on.

Shaking my head, we return for one last bout. We wind up losing this one, though not without giving it a good shot— eleven to seven their game, in all. But the adrenaline's still pumping from our fourth match, my whole body alight with it, so I hardly even feel let down at the loss.

We shake hands, both our teams grinning like mad. I can tell our good spirits amuse, if slightly confuse, our opponents, who give us the usual "Good game" speeches and then move on to their next match.

The loss means we're done for the day, but that's alright

by me. Because a fresh idea has sprung into my mind, stoked by the feeling of Sebastian's body against mine in the frenzy after our win.

I grab his hand. "Come on," I say.

He glances over his shoulder, and I expect him to protest, to say he wants to hang around and watch the next game. Ryan and Maria play next, and somewhere on a neighboring court, Scott and Laura must be finishing up soon. But he surprises me by staying quiet, tightening his grip on my hand, and letting me pull him away.

It takes me a few wrong turns to figure out the maze of Mountain Creek Club. The rest area is a few corridors over, and we glimpse a handful of teams lounging there, some eating or drinking sports drinks to replenish their electrolytes. I drag Sebastian right past that, into the hallway I want.

I was only here for a heartbeat earlier today, when me, Laura, and Maria came down to change clothes before the matches began. But I remember something, which I haven't been able to shake ever since.

Sure enough, just as I recalled, there's a single stall door at the end of the hall—the handicap bathroom, a one person one, with a big shower inside. I yank Sebastian into it and slam the door behind us, turning the lock.

He glances at me, a single eyebrow arched. "Someone's fired up today," he says, in a low murmur, a tone I've not heard him use on me in far too long.

"You bet your fine ass I am," I reply. Then I reach up, fist my hand in his hair again, and drag him down to kiss me once more.

We're awkward at first. We stumble backward into the sink, and I groan as it bumps my hip. Sebastian pulls back, apologizing, face flushed. But I wave him off and push him into the shower stall itself. "We've both gotten ourselves pretty dirty today, haven't we?" I say.

He grins, that crooked smile I fell head over heels for in college. "Oh, yes. I'd suggest we get clean, but I think I'd rather get filthy, first." With that, he reaches over to flick the handle on the shower.

Warm water courses over us both from a rain shower head in the ceiling. Sebastian wraps one arm around my waist and pulls me under it, clothes and all. Not that the water makes them very much wetter than they already were after the sweat I worked up in that match, but still.

He crushes me to his chest, lips finding mine once more. I part my mouth, let his tongue slide between my lips. He still tastes like the post-game Gatorade he chugged, but underneath that, there's a sweat, a salty tang that's all my husband.

I lift one leg, wrap it around the backs of his thighs. He arches his hips into mine, and I gasp as I feel the hard jut of him against the plane of my belly, through both our sweat-wicking layers. The water adds another layer of sensation, the fabric both sticky and slick now. I roll my hips against him, rewarded by a faint groan in the back of his throat.

We break apart again, and Sebastian grabs the hem of my shirt, yanking it up and over my head. My hair tumbles out of its clip as he tosses the shirt aside. His hands slide expertly beneath the hem of my sports bra, and I'm surprised to find my nipples already hard where he runs his palms against them. The callouses from his paddle add an extra spark of sensation, like match heads against a fire, and I gasp.

Sebastian grins. "God, it has been too fucking long since you've made that sound for me." He leans in, lips sliding from my jawline to the edge of my neck. His teeth graze my skin there, lightly, not hard enough to hurt, but enough to make me shiver with desire. "I've missed this," he whispers, breath adding another layer of heat on my skin where the warm water pelts down. His lips shift to my ear, next. "I've missed you."

I wrap my arms around him, for balance as much as anything, because my knees suddenly feel weak. Something about breath in my ear always makes me go liquid, and Sebastian knows it. "I've missed you, too," I admit, my voice a little strained from the desire coursing through me. "It's been too long."

I expect him to tense at that, and then I start tensing too, afraid I've just started another argument. But Sebastian only strokes his free hand down my back, one still gently teasing my nipple while his other hand dips to grab a fistful of my ass. "Then we'd better make up for lost time."

He draws back just far enough to work my bra off over my head. I feel myself flush as my breasts fall free—they don't look like they did back in college anymore. Not after two kids. But if Sebastian notices, he doesn't seem to care at all. He bends to kiss my collarbone, the divot at the base of my neck. He runs his face lower, down the lines of my cleavage, and traces his tongue over one mound, then the next. Slow, teasing. He doesn't touch the nipples, not yet, but they're both hard as rocks already. When he finally sucks one into his mouth, my head falls back and I actually cry out, a faint, strangled noise.

He chuckles, breath skimming my chest. "You know I love it when you make all that noise for me."

I bite my lip, struggle to corral my thoughts into working order. My gaze drifts to the door, double-checking the lock. "Someone might... hear." The latter, spaced out, because Sebastian gently rolled my nipple between his teeth, his tongue flicking the very tip and sending sparks all the way to my toes. I inhale again, struggling to keep relatively quiet.

"So?" Sebastian glances up at me, a single eyebrow arched. "Let them enjoy the show, if they want."

Another pulse of heat, this one directly to my core. I feel the walls of my pussy fist at the idea—strangers just outside that door, listening to everything we do to one another. There's a thrill to it. I don't want to be caught—the very idea makes my whole body flush with embarrassment. And yet... the threat of it, the possibility, makes me wetter than

I've felt in months.

Not talking about the shower water, either.

"You are so… naughty," I manage, breath hitching once more as he repeats the tongue flick.

"You ain't seen nothing yet," he replies, his legs snaking around my hips. He hooks his thumbs under the hem of my leggings and drags down.

It's difficult to peel them off in the damp, but that's alright by me. It gives me plenty of time to grab Sebastian's shirt and wrench it up and over his head—two can play at this game. He chuckles, letting me toss it aside, then helping me kick off the damned leggings.

From there, we make short work of his workout shorts and the boxers beneath. When his cock finally springs free of the boxer hem, he's hard as steel, jutting straight toward me, the tip already glistening with a hint of his want. I wrap my fist around the base of him, the shower water coursing over both our bare bodies, and drag my palm up his length slowly, slowly.

Now it's his turn to groan, deep and low in his throat, a guttural sound that drives me wild. "Fuck, Jen. You have magic goddamn hands, you know that?" As he speaks, he slides his own hands down over both my hips. One slips between my thighs, parting them gently, and he runs one thick fingertip along the length of my slit.

"You're one… to talk," I whisper, distracted, as he works his finger deeper between the folds of my pussy, running his fingertip back and forth, circling my entrance like a tease.

When I look up, I find Sebastian grinning down at me, mouth inches from mine. "Oh, you are very wet. How long have you been fantasizing about this, dirty girl?"

I inhale, my breath shuddering slightly. "Since… I saw the single stall this morning," I admit.

His eyes widen for a split second with genuine surprise, and then a wicked smile curls his mouth. "My dirty wife. I'll have to make sure this lives up to your fantasy then." As he speaks, he strokes his finger faster, practically gliding back and forth along my slit, I'm so wet. When he finally presses his fingertip inside me, all the way to the knuckle in one go, it goes in so easily that I gasp in shock.

I tighten my fist around his shaft, savoring the velvet-smooth feel of his cock in my hand. As Sebastian draws his finger out of me, then drives it straight back in, I start to stroke him in the same rhythm, both of us moving in time together.

He adds a second finger, drawing another gasp out of me. "That's it, babygirl." There's a grin in his voice that unspools me, threads of nerves unraveling behind my navel like butter.

I lose track of my hand on him, of anything but the sensations sparking inside me, when he curls his fingertip to stroke it along my front inner wall. He knows exactly where to aim, exactly how hard to press, to set off fireworks behind my eyelids.

But as quickly as the pleasure started to build, he withdraws his fingers again, tsking under his breath. "Ah, ah," he murmurs. "Not yet." He grips my hips, pushes me backward against the slick tile wall of the shower. "I want to make this last."

His mouth crushes mine once more, and I grind my hips into his, fervid now, wild with want. When we break apart, I'm panting like an animal. "Fuck me," I gasp. "Bash, please."

His eyes spark with heat—he always liked me calling him that nickname in bed, especially after a big win. He still likes it, I see, to judge by how quickly he pins me back against the wall, his thick hands so tight on my hips they might leave marks. I don't care—I'm digging my nails into his shoulders just as hard, bracing myself back on the tile so I can raise one leg to hook around his waist.

He drops one hand to position himself, the tip of his cock teasing around my entrance the same way his fingertip did a minute ago. "Tell me what you want," he says, a game he likes to play. His eyes catch mine, hold them. I sink into the twin dark pools, melt into his fire.

"I want you," I say. "Every goddamn inch of you."

His lips curl in a secretive grin, just for me. At the same time, he presses forward, gentle at first. His cock presses past my entrance, inside me. He keeps going, slowly, filling me a centimeter at a time, agonizing and incredible all at once.

"Fuck, Bash," I moan again. "I forgot how full you make me feel."

And he's not even all the way inside yet. He keeps moving, keeps pressing, and I feel myself expanding around him, contracting, expanding again, as my muscles adjust to his thickness.

"God, you feel incredible." Sebastian leans down, mouth close to my ear once more. "So warm and wet and fucking tight."

I clench my muscles around him for emphasis and he chuckles, breath ghosting across my skin. Then he bends to nip lightly at my neck, before kissing the same spot, tongue and all.

"And you taste incredible, too."

I lean in to run my tongue along the edge of his jaw, stubble and all, grinning. "Not half bad yourself," I murmur, just as he gives a tiny final thrust, entering me fully.

We pause there for a moment, fully connected, and draw back to look one another in the eye. I see him, of course, but I also see a hundred other Sebastians. The confident, headstrong guy I met in college. The one who would drag me into corners after games—behind the bleachers, in team locker rooms, pretty much anywhere we could get our hands on one another.

I also see the man who teared up at our wedding, without a damn care for who saw. The nervous, excited new father. The man who has been there, beside me, through every single moment.

"I love you," I whisper.

Sebastian's smile softens, those brown eyes intense as ever. "I love you, Jen." He bends, kisses me again, and when we finally start to move together, it's slower, sweeter than we anticipated.

At first, anyway. As he picks up the pace, driving into me, our animal sides take over. He kisses me open-mouthed, wet and sloppy, and I grab him, wild and hungry again, wanting nothing more than to mold our two bodies into one. His hands dig into my ass, propelling him deeper and harder inside me. I clutch his shoulders, nails down, leaving marks for anyone to see.

Neither of us care. We are beyond words now, beyond anything but the hot rush of each other. He pounds into me, again and again, sending waves of pleasure rippling down my legs, my knees going weak. But he holds me up, pins me against the wall, and I thrust my hips back, giving every inch as good as I get.

It doesn't take long before a familiar pressure starts behind my navel. Sebastian arches his hips, angles himself so the tip of his cock drags along my inner wall. At the same time, he drops one hand between us, his fingertips gently pressing against my clit.

I moan, louder this time—too loud—but fuck it. "Fuck, Sebastian. I'm going to..." I can't even finish the sentence.

He watches me hungrily, avidly. "That's it. Look at me.

Now, cum for me, babygirl."

He barely finishes the sentence before I cry out with abandon, my legs fully liquid now, my whole body seeming to melt into him, against the wall. He holds me up, keeps going, another thrust and another, and... With a roar, Sebastian cums right after me, hot and sticky, his juices flowing into me with a warm rush of pleasure.

Not for the first time since I got it, I thank God for the IUD I got years ago. I've always loved feeling him raw, the searing heat of his finish.

When he pulls out of me, the slick wet sound it makes sounds exactly like my own disappointment. But then his arms are around me again, and he's bending to kiss me, slow and sweet, and it keeps the rest of the world at bay for just a little while longer.

Chapter Thirteen
Sebastian

Lying in bed that night, one arm draped around Jennifer's waist, I feel decades younger. As if that shower reawakened the real me, returned us both to our true selves. Closing my eyes, I still get flashes of it—Jen after the shower, wrapped in rolls of paper towels, because neither of us wanted to put our sweat-and-shower-drenched clothes back on. Both of giggling like teenagers as we cracked the door to check the corridor, before we made a break for the locker rooms where we stashed our change of clothing.

And earlier…

I feel a tightening in my groin, and my palm flattens against Jen's stomach, tracing the smooth, soft expanse. My fingertips trail idly over the arch of her hipbone, the curve down to her thighs.

Normally, Jen would squirm away from me, or grasp my hand to stop it. I understand she feels self-conscious—neither of our bodies look the way they used to when we were younger, and after two children, she bears marks. No matter how many times I tell her that I find her beautiful, just like this, I know she doesn't hear me, because she cannot believe it herself.

But tonight, she doesn't push me away. Tonight, she sighs,

a contented sound, and relaxes back against me, deeper into my embrace. I bend to press my lips to the nape of her neck, the soft, fine hair there tickling my skin.

"Today was fun," I murmur.

"Winning that game felt great," Jen replies.

I chuckle softly. "That too. But I meant our celebration afterward…"

She laughs, too, breathy and low. "I know. Just teasing you." She weaves her fingers through mine and tightens her grip a little. "Good to know we still have it in us, huh?"

"Oh, we've definitely still got it in spades." I smirk. "I just wish we'd remember that more often, you know? We let so many other things get in the way of what's good for us."

When Jen inhales again, her breath shudders a little. Not much, but I've known her more than half my life. I catch it.

"Jen?" I tighten my grip on her hand, thumb skimming the backs of her knuckles. "What's wrong?"

Definitely wasn't imagining. She takes another deep breath, sniffling this time. "I just…" She exhales hard, half groan and half stifled sob. "I hate my job. There, fuck, I said it."

I sit up, surprised. "You what?"

She reaches out to snatch a tissue from the nightstand, then rolls over to face me, dabbing at her eyes. "I've been trying to convince myself otherwise for so long. Years, I think. And for a while, I could ignore it, but now… I don't know." She sits up too, shaking her head, her eyes overbright in the dim light filtering through the curtains from outside. "I've been so happy the last few weeks, playing with you. Whenever we're practicing, or on the court, I feel free. And it's just such a sharp contrast to how I feel the rest of the time, it's impossible to deny it anymore."

I frown. "If that's how you feel, then you should quit."

She shakes her head, tears welling again. "We can't afford that. We've got the mortgage, and all the kids' extracurriculars—plus we'll need to start paying tuition for Mia in only two years, God. I wanted to have more saved by this point. It's going to be so tight, even with my current salary—"

"So find somewhere else," I interject. "People change jobs all the time. And your skills translate to lots of other fields."

She groans and blows her nose hard. "Who wants to hire a mom with two decades of experience at the same company where she's worked her entire life? I don't even know if I'm capable of learning something new."

"Hey. Don't you dare sell yourself short." I touch her knee, squeeze lightly. "You're the smartest person I know. You can do anything you want to."

She shakes her head again, laughing this time. "That's what we tell the kids, Sebastian." She meets my eyes, her own imploring. "But we know better. It's safer to stick with the devil you know."

I can see I'm not going to win the argument the straightforward way. I heave a sigh and let my hand drop, leaning back on my elbows while I watch her from the corner of my eye. "All right. Thought experiment, then. Completely hypothetical. If you could do anything in the world, what would it be?"

"What did we just say?" she chides.

"Hypothetically," I insist.

She flops back onto the pillows dramatically and runs her hands through her hair, thinking. "Mm… I mean, in daydream, lala land, I'd love to run a day spa. Somewhere women could relax and prioritize self-care, get massages or facials or whatever they like."

I smile. "Makes sense."

She snorts. "Does it?"

"Sure. You always loved doing hair for the other girls on your team in college, and you and Mia used to do those mommy-daughter spa days all the time. Plus, your mom took you a lot when you were young, right?"

Jen sighs. "Yeah, probably where I got the hare-brained idea. Doesn't matter."

"Why not?" I stare down at her. "If it's what you really want to do, we could figure something out. Maybe get a small business loan, or—"

"Oh, we can't afford for me to quit my job, but we can afford to take out a loan on the off chance we'd be able to make enough to pay it back?" She wrinkles her nose. "I'm not bankrupting our whole family for some wild daydream, Bash."

"First of all, you're assuming you would fail, which I really don't think you would. You've got a great head on your shoulders—haven't I always told you that you should be running your own company?"

"Yes, but an accounting company. Something I actually have practical experience in, you know?"

"Day spas need accountants too," I point out. "That'll save you money hiring a bookkeeper on the backend. Besides, you've got experience with spas, too."

"Not running one!"

I lie down beside her and gaze up at the ceiling. "We could at least try to save up for it. Put a little aside each month…"

"Forget it. See, this is why I didn't want to mention it." Jen rolls onto her side, back facing me. I reach for her again, but this time, she does the usual move, shrugging away so my hand falls off her back and drops to the covers between us. After a long pause, she inhales. "I know you're trying to be supportive. Thank you for that. But we need to be practical right now, okay? We have more than just our own dreams to think about."

With that, she reaches over to deposit the wrinkled tissue in the trash can, then opens the drawer to pull out her sleep mask. I watch her pull it on and curl up under the covers, my heart a fist in my chest. I wish I could fix this for her, somehow.

Part of me knows she has a point. We do need to be practical. But surely our family's future needn't come at the expense of her happiness.

* * *

A couple more Lake League matches come and go. We win our next one three games to two, and the one after that four games to one. We're really picking up speed, getting into the swing of things.

But even as our pickleball game picks up, our communication at home breaks down once more. We don't have any more moments like the shower—we barely have time to talk at all. It's the final rush of school projects for both Mia and Logan, plus Logan's last round of dress rehearsals before the spring play, and Mia's constant taxiing to and from volleyball games.

Jen seems more dejected than ever, every morning when I drop her off at work. I start to regret asking about it, like my remarking on it has reminded her of all her worries, compounded them somehow.

But I'm determined to fix this, if I can. There has to be a solution—just one we haven't thought of yet. I'll be damned if I let my wife remain trapped in a job she hates for the rest of her life.

As she usually does in the spring, Jennifer's mother Geraldine comes for a visit. This time, her trip coincides with our fourth Lake League match of the year—Riverbend Country Club's match with Utopian Country Club. I take Geraldine aside for a talk on her first night in town, explaining that we'll be busy that Saturday.

"So? I'll just come and cheer you on," she says.

I laugh. "You might get bored."

"Never. Besides, I'd like to check out this sport that has my daughter glowing again." Geraldine's eyes sparkle as she side-eyes me. "I haven't seen that look in her eyes since she was playing in college. And I hear it's down to you for forcing her to try this."

"I don't know if force is the right word," I protest, and Geraldine titters with laughter.

"Well, either way, it's good to see her enjoying herself again. I've been so worried lately… I'm sure you must be too. She hasn't seemed like herself in a long while." Geraldine sighs. "I wish there was something I could do to help."

I hesitate, debating. Will Jen take this as a betrayal? Going behind her back? "Well, I don't think her job is helping much," I murmur.

"God, no. I've been trying to talk her into quitting for a year." Geraldine shakes her head.

I blink. That's news to me, though I guess it shouldn't be. "Did she ever tell you what she wants to do instead?" I ask, before I can think better of it.

Geraldine glances my way, eyebrows rising. "Pray tell."

I pause, listening. Jen is downstairs with the kids right now, looking over their homework. I offered to carry her mother's bags up to the guest room, which means we're alone together now, a rare occurrence. Something about it seems like fate. "Well, if you really want to know…"

Geraldine takes one look at me, then strides over to shut the guest room door. Jen gets her no-nonsense, straight to business sense from her mother. "I'm all ears," she says.

So I lay it all out there. Jennifer's secret dream. Her anxieties about pursuing it. My belief that she could be great at it. Unsurprisingly, Geraldine agrees. "Leave it with me," she says, a new twinkle in her eye. "I have a plan."

What that plan is, I don't know, however. We don't talk about it before the match—which is probably a blessing in disguise. Don't want Jen to get into her head before this one—neither of us can forget that Utopian is C+C's home club. The most pretentious, expensive, snooty club in the rotation, one which all of our friends at Riverbend have warned us about. Scott, in particular, seems to be dreading this match.

Before either of us know it, Saturday rolls around. Logan's got a daytime rehearsal, and Mia's shopping with some friends, so we drive with Geraldine out to the Utopian club for the match. The moment we step out of the car, Geraldine is oohing and awwing at everything.

"The wheels these people drive." She gawks at a lot full of Mercedes, Jags, and Aston Martins. "And holy cow, that castle."

It does seem more like a castle than a clubhouse, an ancient-looking structure that would look more at home in the English countryside somewhere, probably the seat of a duke or minor prince. Except, this one was only built twenty years ago, so all the homey, historical-esque touches come across as weirdly fake.

We head to the courts, which overlook an even more

elaborate golf course than the one we glimpsed at Mountain Creek. I've got to admit, snobs or not, Utopians have a sweet setup. We introduce Geraldine to Scott and Laura, then get her settled into the stands with the other spectators. Scott and Laura's daughter came this time—she's a few years younger than Mia, not really staying home solo on weekends yet—so Geraldine settles in with her, bags of popcorn in hand.

And then we get the match assignments.

I have a sinking feeling in my gut the moment Chris and Crys stride onto the courts, a bevy of other bleached and sculpted players on their tails. Sure enough, when the referee reads out who each of us will be playing, our names are right there on the list across from C+C Non-Music Factory.

Jennifer sets her jaw, a determined look coming over her. "Right. Time to get payback."

I grin, buoyed by her optimism. "Let's show them who they've been messing with."

But our first match ends in a frankly embarrassing defeat. We put in what feels like a good show, but C+C are just too well-oiled. Well, that, and their home referees seem determined not to call anything against them. After the fourth obviously out-of-bounds ball gets called as in, another point to them, I stop even bothering to argue.

"Go for everything," I tell Jen, under my breath. "Even the stuff that looks like it'll go out."

This improves our game somewhat, but we still lose a

whopping two to eleven. Chris and Crys smirk over their matching water bottles, making comments just loud enough for us to catch snatches. Amateurs, is one word we notice, along with out of their league.

Jennifer grits her teeth as we head to the sidelines before our second game. Geraldine meets us there, Scott and Laura's daughter Andrea in tow. "Those bastards," Geraldine says, before we even get a word out. "Oh." She bends to cover Andy's ears. "You didn't hear that, got it?"

Andy giggles, while Geraldine passes us Gatorade and snack bars. "Are they always like this?"

"Pretty much," I say, jaw set, as I glance back across the court at Chris and Crys. A few of their fellow club members mill around them, but they don't seem like spectators so much as adoring fans. One woman asks Crys for a photo. Crys wrinkles her nose and covers her face when the woman snaps one anyway.

I bite the inside of my cheek to keep from laughing. God. They really do think they're celebrities or something.

"We'll get them this time," Jen insists.

Geraldine claps her shoulder. "Hell yes you will. Oh, gosh, sorry again," she quickly covers Andy's ears once more. "Who let me go unsupervised around children?"

We snort. Then it's time to head back onto the court. Jen and I trade a long glance, a sharp nod, before she serves first—our turn, since they won the last match.

This time, we're warmed up—primed and ready to go. The

adrenaline flows through us both, and our communication feels seamless. We both, by agreement, lunge for the balls we'd normally let go as out-of-bounds, having learned our lessons about the bias in this clubhouse. Jen's on fire, light on her feet, quick as a whip.

The Chrises give it their all, but we manage to sneak up on them, point by point. Before long, it feels like the attention of the entire clubhouse has focused on us. Someone—probably Scott—chants our name in the distance. Bashifer, Bashifer.

I even catch a few of the Utopian people chanting it out of the corner of my eye, which makes me think Chris and Crys might be as unpopular at home as they are at the other clubs they visit. When we sneak a tenth point past them, it feels like the entire clubhouse erupts in cheers.

As the eleventh sails by them too, Jen and I whoop, my wife's grin feral and so fucking sexy I envision grabbing her right here and now.

But C+C Non-Music Factory aren't about to go down that easily. They seem energized by defeat, fired up by the cheering for their opponents. When Chris starts off the next game, there's fresh speed in his arm, flames in both their eyes. We struggle to get the ball down low, all of our return shots going waist high or even higher when we send them back over the net.

That makes it far too easy for C+C to fire them back in unattainable long shots, whipping between and around us no matter how hard we run for them. We lose our third match four to eleven, and our fourth one three to eleven.

There's no point in even playing the fifth game—they've already won best of three—but in friendlies like this, you always play out the full matches.

I try to channel June's mantra, and to remind myself that it's all about having fun at the end of the day, not winning. But that's hard to remember when Chris is mocking your every move, pausing between shots to mimic the way I hold my racket. Crys, for her part, keeps making loud comments like, "you can do it, sweetheart! Better luck next time!" Anytime someone misses the ball, she gives an exaggerated pout, then turns to whisper to Chris, both of them snickering like children.

Pretty much any way she can insult us, she does, all while maintaining the sickly-sweet smile on her face, as if she's Miss Angelic.

We keep our mouths shut, having learned in game one that the refs here won't step in for anyone but their home club's darling duo. Still, it stings to lose the fifth game just as badly. Three to eleven, their win.

We don't even bother to approach the net to tap paddles. C+C have made it obvious before how they feel about that. Chris smirks at us, raising one of his hands for a finger-wiggling goodbye wave as we turn to go. "You've been measured, little newbies, and you've been found wanting."

I open my mouth to retort, but Jen grips my arm, her fingers tight. "Don't," she murmurs. "We showed more class. We're going to be respectful losers, and we'll walk off this court the real winners."

She's right, though it rankles to swallow my anger. I wrap an arm around her shoulders and we walk off together, both of our nerves on edge.

Geraldine meets us in the stands with a fresh refill. This time, she's procured something a little stronger than Gatorade for us. Jen and I toast her before we sip, and Geraldine pats Jennifer's knee. "You did very well out there, darling. I know you hate to lose, but frankly, those…" She pauses to glance around, making sure Andy's back with her parents before she adds, in a lower voice, "Those assholes don't deserve a second of your headspace."

Jennifer sniffs airily. "Oh, I know." She shoots her mother a smile, then gives me a longer one, her expression softening. "You were great out there today."

"You too." I hold her gaze, hoping she can see what I'm thinking. Flashing back to our last big win, to how much it meant to me to celebrate it with her.

Geraldine clears her throat. "Not to interrupt, but…" She glances my way. "Is now a good time?"

"A good time for what?" Jen asks, confused.

Her mother smiles. "Well, Sebastian and I have been talking."

"Uh oh." Jen eyes me, one brow lifted.

"Nothing bad," I promise her.

"Not at all." Geraldine grins. She's got Jen's same smile, the kind of smile that lights up a person's whole face, and makes them seem years younger. "In fact, it's great news. He told me that you've been having a tough time with work lately…"

Jennifer flushes. "Bash, I told you that in confidence."

"I'm sorry," I say. I really am. "It just came out. She knew you've been upset lately, and, well, she agrees with me. We don't want you to suffer at that job if you don't need to."

"But I do need to," she argues.

That's when Geraldine clears her throat. "You know how I've been retired a few years now?"

"Sure," Jen says slowly, eyes darting between me and her mother, not following yet.

Meanwhile, a rush of surprise floods my system, as I realize what Geraldine's plan must entail. I'd suspected, on some level, but I wasn't sure until now.

"Well, I've been speaking to my accountant. I have quite a lot saved up, you see. And what with your father's pension money, and my 401K, I've got more than enough to sustain my own lifestyle at the moment."

A line appears between Jennifer's brows. "I know, Mom. You've always been really careful with money."

"Maybe too careful. You've never asked me for help—"

"It's your money," Jen interjects quickly. "I couldn't burden you. You paid for my college tuition—that was more than enough. You gave me a huge leg up in the world."

"And I was happy to do it." Geraldine pats her leg firmly. "Just like I'm happy to do this." She shoots me another look again, eyes sparkling. "Sebastian told me about your spa idea. Frankly, I love it. I don't know why I didn't think to do something like that myself. But I want to help you get it off the ground."

Jen's mouth falls open. "But, Mom—"

"Don't but me, young lady." Geraldine still knows how to turn on that stern voice when she needs to. "I've got a nice little egg saved up for a rainy day, and it seems to me this would be the perfect way to incubate it." She lifts her hand from Jen's knee to cup her daughter's cheek. "I've seen how stressed you've been lately. Sebastian didn't need to tell me that part. If your job is the cause of it, then I want to help you establish a new career, something you really love."

Bright red spots form on both of Jen's cheeks. She glances from her mother to me and back again.

I brace myself for a scolding. Neither of us have ever gone to our parents for money—we both feel the same way. Our parents helped raised us, gave us everything when we were younger. Now it's our turn to support them. But this happened so organically. I didn't even know that was Geraldine's plan—not really. And if she wants to help...

Jen's expression crumples. Tears rush to her eyes, and my heart sinks at the sight. "What if I let you both down?" she whispers, the tone heartbreakingly sincere.

I step around her mother, wrap both arms around Jen. She turns to bury her face in my chest, and I hold her there, tight against me, as her tears soak the fabric of my shirt. "You could never let us down," I whisper into her hair. "Never."

Over the top of her head, I catch Geraldine's eye. She's smiling at us both, teary herself now. Holding her gaze, I mouth, Thank you.

Chapter Fourteen
Sebastian

The rest of the Lake League games finish without much fanfare. To everyone's annoyance, C+C Non-Music Factory win the whole league at the championships. Our rematch with them during the finals was even more brutal than our match at Utopian—Crys hit Jen with six balls in a single game, one of which left a face welt. I went ballistic at that, and the refs wound up giving me a hard time about controlling my anger?

But we wound up placing fourth overall—not too shabby for our first league championship.

At the afterparty back at Riverbend, Scott and Laura share a table with us. While we sip rounds of specialty cocktails, Scott and Laura tell us about another series. "It's not like the Lake League," Laura says. "It's much bigger, and there's a bit of travel involved."

"How much travel?" I ask, thinking about the kids. It's June now, with the end of the school year a handful of weeks away. I'm looking forward to actually seeing them more, but we will have to figure out a schedule, maybe cut back on the number of days we've been playing.

I glance at Jen, who shrugs. She's still hedging about the day spa, though between me, Geraldine, and now Mia and

Logan both egging her on as well, I have a feeling she's going to cave and accept her mother's offer soon. But still. The spa itself will need a lot of work to get off the ground.

"It's called the Southern Pickleball Championships," Scott says. "There are ten tournaments in all—round robin events instead of just double elimination. They're really fun—Paul and Mark are the organizers, they're great guys."

"But it's all summer and fall," Laura adds. "A weekend day here and there. Easier to make it to than all the league games in a row. The first one's in Myrtle Beach in a couple weeks."

Myrtle Beach isn't too far—just under a four-hour drive, give or take. "That might be doable," I say. "But where are the other tournaments?"

"Raleigh, Asheville, Greenville... The farthest one is in Orlando," Scott says. "But the real key is the Atlanta one. If you play in at least six of the other tournaments, and win gold in one of them, then you qualify for the Southern Pickleball Championship in Atlanta. That's on Veteran's Day weekend, so not until November."

"Huh." I glance at Jen again. "So we'd only have to play six tournaments before November?"

"Yeah." Laura grins. "And you can pick the ones that work best for you, depending where they are and what time of year and all."

"Sounds doable," Jen says, starting to smile now. "What's the prize for the championship?"

Laura's grin widens. "That's the best part." She leans

forward for emphasis. "If you win your bracket, getting gold at Atlanta, you qualify for a golden ticket to the nationals. Those are in Palm Springs every March. It's a massive party—everyone I know who's been says it's to die for."

I feel a spike of excitement. It's been a long time since Jen and I have traveled much outside of North Carolina, save a few beach trips to neighboring states. It would be fun to get away together. Especially somewhere like Palm Springs, which I've always wanted to visit.

Jen's eyes are sparkling with a telltale eagerness. I know she wants this too. Still, it catches me off-guard when she leans in to murmur, "Once the spa is up and running, maybe we could bring the kids along for some of those tournaments. The Orlando one sounds perfect."

My eyebrows shoot up, a smile that has nothing to do with pickleball spreading across my face. "You mean you're going to do it?"

"Well, if my mom's offer still stands..."

Scott and Laura glance between us, expressions of polite confusion fixed on their faces. Meanwhile, I whoop and lift a hand to wave at the clubhouse waiter. "We're gonna need another round," I call to him, beaming. "My wife and I are celebrating."

"What's the occasion?" Laura asks, tilting her head.

I glance at Jennifer, pride practically oozing from my pores. "My wife just decided to open her own business."

Our friends expressions brighten. "That's so exciting!"

Laura cries. "What kind?"

The waiter returns with our next round of cocktails while Jen explains her plans. She's given this a lot more thought than she had the last time we talked about it—now she's got names picked out, color palettes for the spa, treatment ideas.

"I've been researching the offerings at other spas in town," she says. "And I haven't been able to find anywhere that's offering hot stone massages or aromatherapy. I thought those might be a good place to start, and maybe work up to infrared saunas and LED facials once I can invest in some more technology."

"What about a sound bath?" Laura asks. "I used to go to one all the time when we lived in Atlanta, but I haven't been since we moved. I've been dying without my weekly relaxation ritual—I can't tell you how relaxing it was."

Jen brightens. "That's an interesting idea. I wonder if pairing that with aromatherapy would work, too, almost like a full sensory experience…"

The women shuffle closer together, talking shop. In the meantime, Scott leans my direction. "Listen, if y'all can make it work, I really think you ought to go out for the tournament series. I've never seen someone so new to the game place as high as you two did in the Lake League before. Even the Chrises came in twelfth or something their first year."

We both trade grimaces. "Let me guess. They play in the Southern Pickleball Tournaments too?"

"Of course." Scott rolls his eyes. "But don't let those

assholes stop you. Besides, they only play six tournaments out of the ten, like most people, so you probably won't run into them at every stop."

"How have they not been kicked out yet?" I can't help muttering. "You saw Crys targeting Jen today. She purposefully aimed for Jen's head with every power shot she got."

Scott glances over his shoulder, then lifts a hand, rubbing his forefingers and thumb together.

I roll my eyes. "Seriously? They're both bribing people over a game?"

"Losing ain't a game to people like that. At least, not in my experience." Scott shakes his head, then picks up his drink again, taking a long sip. "But like I said, ignore them. Most everyone else is great, and you'll have fun."

"Hell yeah we will." I toast to that.

But as it transpires, we stumble onto a shitshow to clean up before said fun can begin. The next week is supposed to be Logan's big performance—the musical he's been working so hard to practice for all semester.

Exccpt, when we show up at the theater, all dressed to the nines, and accept our programs… Logan's name isn't in the program. We read and reread it, both confused as hell. Beside us, Mia shifts uncomfortably in her seat, frowning at the packet.

"I thought he was playing this character." Jen points at a name near the top. "But he's not even listed as the understudy."

"It must be a mistake," I say, standing. "I'll go speak to someone about it."

But Mia catches my arm. One look at her face turns my blood to ice. "Dad. I don't think it's a mistake."

"What are you talking about?" I demand.

She won't meet my gaze. She stares anywhere else—at the ground, the stage, the seats around us. "I… don't think Logan's actually been going to rehearsals."

"Honey." Jen touches my arm. Slowly, I sink back into my chair. "What do you mean?"

Inch by inch, we drag the story out of Mia. She's not sure, she says, and she keeps hedging—probably not wanting to be the one to rat out her younger brother. But it's not like we aren't going to find out—the truth is staring us all in the face. "I heard rumors that he quit back at the start of the semester, but I didn't want to believe it."

"Why didn't you say something?" Jennifer whispers.

But I understand. I catch her eye, shake my head a little. "It's not your fault, honey. Do you know where he is right now?" Because that's what's really thundering through my mind, turning my veins to ice. He's been staying late at rehearsals for months now, the whole semester, every night another late rehearsal, another reason he's behind on his classwork. If all of that was a lie, then…

What the hell has my son gotten himself into?

"I don't know," Mia mumbles, miserable now. We both give her The Look, and she bristles. "I really don't! He's been hanging out with some new guys; I don't know them."

I do not like the sound of that. I whip out my phone and

excuse me my way back up the aisle of the theater, outside to the lobby. There, I dial Logan's number. It goes straight to voicemail. Small wonder—he must have known tonight would be the night his house of cards collapsed. He could lie to us until tonight, but we were destined to find out the truth now.

I type out a text. Call me. Now. It sends, but remains unread, which means his phone is on, but possibly in Do Not Disturb mode. Or he's screening my messages. Cursing, I pocket it and storm back into the theater to collect my family. Mia's hovering next to our row of seats, but Jen has vanished.

"She went to talk to the director," Mia says. She squints up at me in the dim theater lights. "I'm sorry I didn't say anything sooner."

"Your brother is responsible for his own decisions," I say. Then I set my jaw and exhale hard. "But he could be getting into trouble, Mia. Worse trouble than ditching theater practice, I mean. I know you don't want to betray his trust, but as his parents, we need to know about that sort of thing. Understand?"

She squirms, clearly uncomfortable. But after a minute, she nods.

Jennifer finds us outside the theater fifteen minutes later, arms folded, jaw set in a look I instantly recognize as her I mean business face. "The director says he quit four weeks into rehearsals."

I quickly do the mental math I'm sure Jen has already done. "So he's been lying to our faces for four months."

"That boy is so grounded." Jen storms past me toward

the car. "The minute we find him, I swear to God..."

I jog after her, Mia in tow. "Honey, where do the kids go to hang out these days, still the mall?"

She wrinkles her nose. "God, no. We're not eighty-year-olds. Mostly we just go to each other's houses. Or—well..." She trails off, eyes widening.

"Or where?" I stop in my tracks, facing her. When she doesn't respond, I add, "Mia, this is serious."

Mia takes a deep breath. "Um, well. There is a place, out NC-80... This abandoned old hospital. Some of the older kids go out there to, uh, smoke..."

My pulse ratchets up at least a dozen notches.

"But I'm sure he wouldn't do that," she quickly adds. "He's probably just at TJ's or Andy's playing video games."

"Text him," I tell her. "See if you have better luck than I do."

Obediently, Mia pulls out her phone. She types something out.

Less than a minute later, my cell rings. Figured. I grit my teeth as I pick up. "Where are you?"

"Dad." Logan's voice sounds all tight and watery, on the edge of tears. For a moment, guilt washes through me—I haven't heard him cry in I don't know how long. At least since he was much younger. "I'm sorry, I panicked, I didn't know how to tell you..."

I remind myself what he's done. Why he's crying. And the steel hardens in my tone. "I won't repeat myself, Logan. Where. Are you."

Beside me, Jennifer's face is a mask of panic, mirroring exactly how I feel.

"I'm just at my friend's house. I'm fine it was only—"

"Text me the address. We're on the way," I interrupt. He can save the explanations for once he's safely locked in our home again, presumably for the rest of the summer.

Christ. Was I this much of a handful at 15? I make a mental note to ask my mother the next time we see her.

The whole drive over to the address Logan texted, Jen chews her nails to the quick. In the backseat, Mia scrolls her phone moodily. I don't recognize the address, which rules out TJ and Andy. Who the hell is this, to help Logan lie to his entire family for months? Do the kid's family know what he did?

When we pull up out front, I'm relieved to see a relatively normal house. In my anxious state, I'd been picturing some illicit den of evils, like the abandoned hospital Mia mentioned. But it's just your average cookie-cutter home, two cars parked out front, a cheerful spring wreath on the front door.

Jen goes to get him, saying I'll give him a heart attack before we even make it to the car. The suggestion irritates me, but deep down, I know she's right.

I watch from behind the wheel as Jennifer speaks to the woman who answers the door—a woman who looks around our age. Her expression darkens the longer Jennifer talks, answering at least one of my questions. No, it does not seem that this new friend's family was aware of Logan's lying streak.

I don't fully breathe again until my son appears in the

doorway, hoodie pulled up to conceal his reddened eyes, arms tight around a backpack.

Jen points him toward the car, mouth pressed tight and thin. I might be the family hard-ass, but when you piss her off, that's when you know you've really screwed up.

Logan knows it, to judge by his slumped shoulders, his head dropping almost to his chest. He flings himself into the backseat with a sideways scowl at his sister, who mouths I'm sorry.

I catch that in the rearview and scowl. "Don't go blaming your sister for your choices. Least you can do is own up to your actions."

Logan flushes and turns to face the window instead. We drive the whole way home like that, in stony silence. Once we arrive, Mia bolts for her bedroom like a frightened rabbit seeking its den.

I don't blame her. I'd do the same in her shoes.

Jen and I sit down at the kitchen counter opposite Logan, the overhead lights all on, beating down on him. It's been a while, I realize, since I properly took stock of my son. He's grown somehow, since the last time I remember truly looking. His shoulders have broadened out from their earlier scrawniness, and his limbs, always long and gangly, look fuller, more defined.

His face, too, seems more mature, even now, flushed with a mixture of guilt and defiance. "I should've told you sooner," he says, before either of us can say a word. "I was being a coward, I know. But... I just didn't want to disappoint you.

And the longer it went on the worse I knew it'd be when I told you so I just wanted to keep ignoring it and hoping..."

I arch an eyebrow. "Hoping that what, we wouldn't notice when you failed to appear onstage for your big show?"

Logan's shoulders hunch miserably. But there's a tiny hint of defiance in his eyes. "I didn't know if you'd even come."

Jennifer frowns. "We always come to your shows, honey."

"You didn't come last fall. To the play."

We trade sideways looks. I'd been scheduled overtime the week the play was on, and Jen had been busy onboarding several new clients at once. "So you quit your favorite activity just to get back at us for not supporting you?" I reply.

"It's not my favorite," Logan mutters. "Not anymore."

Jen reaches across the table to touch his hand, concern radiating from her features. "Since when? I thought you loved acting."

"I'm no good at it. I can't remember the lines. I don't even know why they gave me this part; I was happier in the background."

I frown, thrown temporarily off-course from my anger. "I thought you were excited. You seemed thrilled when you first got the casting news."

"Yeah, well." His shoulders hunch higher. "That was before we started rehearsing, and everyone kept getting pissed at me for forgetting every other line."

Jennifer exhales slowly, casting me a sideways look. A few weeks ago, I might've had difficulty interpreting the glance.

Now, however, after all the silent looks we've traded on court, I recognize this one. My ball, she's thinking. Let me take this one. Jennifer reaches across the table to take Logan's hand gently. "Honey. Look at me." She waits until he raises his head, expression miserable. Then she smiles, sweet and gentle. "If you don't want to keep performing, you don't have to. Nobody's going to force you into it, especially not us. It made you happy before, but if it doesn't anymore, there's no shame in moving on to something new." Her smile curls gently into something more serious. "But. You need to tell us the truth about things like this, Logan. Where have you been spending all the afternoons you were meant to be at rehearsal anyway?"

He winces. "With friends mostly."

"Like that boy Jonathan whose house we picked you up from tonight?"

"Yeah. Or TJ, since he wasn't cast in the musical."

Jen heaves a sigh. My expression darkens, but before I say a word, Logan quickly interjects, eyes darting to mine.

"They didn't know I was lying, ok? So don't go after them."

"I won't," I say, meaning it. "But I will need to have a talk with both of their parents."

Logan's shoulders tighten. A flash of defiance crosses his features, but he quells it. Good idea.

"You understand how serious this is, don't you?" I say, my tone softer, but still with a measure of steel underneath.

He nods, head bowed.

I exhale, glancing at Jen. "Trust is earned, Logan. I'm

afraid that after this, it's going to take you some serious time and effort to earn ours back."

"You're grounded, obviously," Jen adds.

He glances up again. "For how long?"

"Let's just say for the foreseeable future," I reply, eyes on my wife.

Later that night, alone in our bed, she curls into my side. "What happened to the little boy who used to cry every time I dropped him off at daycare?" she whispers.

I wrap an arm around her shoulders, tuck her head under my chin. "Teenagers act out. We knew this."

"But to lie to us for that long." I can hear the hurt in Jen's voice, even without seeing her face. "What else might he be lying about?"

I flinch. I don't want to think about that. But it must be considered.

She shuffled backward a little, lifts her face to mine. "Are we complete fuck-ups? Maybe if we weren't so busy with our own shit, we would've noticed this sooner."

I grimace. The same thought had occurred to me. But... "Or maybe we need more things to do together. All of us. As a family. Look how spending more time together worked for us," I point out, rubbing her arm.

But Jennifer's gaze shifts over my shoulder, to the distant bedroom door, her expression pensive, brow scrunched with anxiety. "Maybe..." she murmurs. But she doesn't sound convinced.

Chapter Fifteen

Jennifer

It takes me another four days to wheedle the full story out of Mia, who in turn badgered it out of some kids she knows in Logan's grade—because my son, God love the stubborn streak he inherited from me, would rather die than admit any of this.

Apparently, other kids laughing at his line delivery was an understatement. Another kid who'd gotten passed over for the part started a whole petition to get Logan recast, which he convinced a decent amount of the cast to sign. It breaks my heart, both that any kid would treat another that badly, and that Logan didn't feel comfortable talking to either of us about this.

On the bright side, being grounded, he's home a lot more often now. There's only a couple weeks left of school, after which we'll need to figure out what to do with a grounded kid over summer break. But in the meantime, I come home every day after work to apology dinners in the process of being cooked, or a kitchen halfway through being cleaned.

I've handed in my notice, so on the bright side, I'll finish up work right around the same time that Logan finishes school. "Maybe you can help me get started with the spa," I suggest one day as we putter around the kitchen, him chopping onions and me preparing a lasagna.

Logan's nose wrinkles. "I don't know anything about that kind of stuff."

I laugh. "Not with the treatments. But we're going to have to pick out a space to rent, then get it fixed up with all the furniture and supplies we'll need. I'll be hiring contractors, of course, for the heavy lifting, but the smaller stuff like furniture…" I hesitate, trailing off. Not for the first time since I, in an uncharacteristic rush of confidence, agreed to accept my mother's offer, I find myself questioning what the hell I was thinking. Am I really ready for an undertaking like this?

I'm used to being an employee, not an employer. I'm good at following orders, but I've never been the one calling the shots. Going forward, my decisions will determine how my company performs. Whether my business lives or dies.

It's a stressful as hell position to be in.

But even as I focus on the anxieties, I feel a familiar rush of adrenaline. It reminds me of when I was first getting started on the pickleball court—the rush of nerves-plus-eagerness that I got every time I stepped onto that court. Like I was afraid of what was about to happen, but in equal parts could not wait to find out, because there was a chance—however slim—that I would walk away from that game a victor.

"Sure," Logan's saying. I notice him watching me with a strange expression, and realize I trailed off mid-sentence. "I could help with furniture, I guess. If you pick it out. Just like, moving it and stuff."

I smile and nudge his arm. "Who knows? Maybe it'll be fun. We can make the whole project a family affair, huh?"

He sighs, drawn out and exaggerated. "Oh sure, just what every dude dreams of. His name on a spa."

I snort. "Who said anything about your name?"

"What are you going to call it then, Jennifer's Spa of Dreams?"

"Actually…" I tap my chin, faux-serious. "That has a nice ring to it."

"Oh, my God, I was joking, Mom. You can't call it that; it sounds dirty."

I arch a brow. "You're the one who suggested it. Should I be concerned about the sorts of spa treatments my son is seeking?"

He turns bright red. "Jesus, no. Eww. Mom!"

I shrug and turn back to stirring the sauce for the lasagna. "Don't dish the dirty jokes if you can't take them," I reply. But truth be told, it feels good to joke around. To act like a normal family. I know that Logan's of an age when testing our limits is normal, and I understand now why he wanted to quit the musical. I even understand, kind of, why he was scared to tell us—especially Sebastian. Bash has always been a stickler for responsibility, for sticking with any project you start, not quitting when the going gets hard.

But I can't help but wonder if some of this is on our heads, too. After all, when was the last time Logan and I spent time like this together? Or me and Mia? I especially can't recall the last time the four of us all hung out. Between all their school activities, and now my and Sebastian's busy schedules…

Before I can second guess myself, I find myself opening my mouth. "Logan. How would you feel about a weekend trip to Myrtle Beach?"

He squints sideways at me, probably trying to work out whether this question is some sort of trap in disguise. "Would that be allowed, me being grounded still and all?"

"Well, it would be a family trip, so we could extend the leash a bit."

He blinks, confused now. "Why are you going to Myrtle Beach?"

"Your father and I are both going," I say. "To play in a tournament there. It's not for a couple more weekends, so you've got some time to decide. We could invite Mia too, make a whole weekend of it."

"What kind of tournament?" he asks, still eying me strangely.

"Well, you remember how I told you your father and I have started playing that new sport—"

"Pickles or something?" he interjects.

I laugh. "Pickleball. It's kind of similar to tennis, but different paddles, different balls, a different court, different rules…"

"So, not similar at all?" he replies, snorting.

"I guess not in practice. But from afar it looks that way." I nudge his side again. "Who knows? Maybe you and Mia will wind up liking it. We could play some games together, the four of us."

Logan glances away, sighing. "I don't know. Maybe."

I'm tempted to ask what else he has on his busy grounded schedule, but I bite my tongue. Even I know that there's only so far you ought to push your son when he's actively trying to show that he's sorry for something.

So, I decide not to bring it up again until closer to the tournament. In the meantime, I've got plenty to concentrate on, wrapping up all my existing files at work and getting them ready to pass on to the colleagues who will be taking over my tasks once I leave. It feels exhilarating and intimidating at once, to be closing this chapter of my life once and for all.

My last day of work coincides with the day before the Myrtle Beach tournament. My coworkers surprise me with a going-away party, spear headed by Ellen, of course. They let Sebastian know, so he was able to shift his schedule around to get off work at the firehouse early to join us.

We eat cake, sip bubbles, and I can't lie—I get a little teary. "I can't believe I'm really leaving," I admit to Ellen, her arm draped around my shoulder as we sneak out onto the seldom-used office balcony for some fresh air.

"Don't think of it as an ending," she advises, squeezing my waist. "More like a new beginning."

I grin. "Sage advice."

"Duh," she says. "I'm known for that." She gives me another sideways hug and then lifts her glass to tap mine.

"Onwards and upwards to greater things, my girl."

"Amen to that," I reply, clinking glasses and taking another fizzing sip of bubbles—the right on the edge of too-sweet kind that I love. One too many glasses of that will give me a headache, though, so I stop after two, conscious of the fact that we'll be waking up at the ass-crack of dawn tomorrow morning to drive out to Myrtle Beach.

As if reading my mind, Sebastian steps out onto the balcony to join us, smiling. "How you feeling?"

I give Ellen one last squeeze and break apart, straightening. "Like it's probably time," I say. So, with one last fanfare and farewell, I exit the office where I've spent almost my entire adult life, save for a handful of crappy straight out of college starter jobs.

I'm surprised how much it affects me, leaving the office. Maybe it's the two drinks, or all the farewell hugs, but by the time we get to the car, my eyes are teary. Sebastian notices, because of course he does, and he draws me into a tight hug, his chin resting on top of my head.

"I'm proud of you," he says, in his deep, reassuring baritone, his ribcage vibrating against mine when he speaks. I rest my cheek against his chest and smile, eyes half-shut. "It's not easy to walk away from the comfortable option, even when you've outgrown it."

"Trust me, I know." I wrap my arms around his waist and close my eyes, savoring this. Him. The feeling of stepping forward into the unknown future isn't quite so intimidating with Sebastian's arms around me.

Maybe we really can do this after all.

* * *

The kids wind up deciding not to come to Myrtle. We leave Logan and Mia at home with a list of chores to finish while they wait for Mom's flight to arrive, and then we drive out to the sunny, breezy shore. The club where we're playing is beachside, which provides some absolutely killer views out over the calm waves and white sand, dotted with umbrellas and sunbathing people of every age.

Scott and Laura brief us on the structure as we warm up with Ryan and Maria, along with a few other friends from Riverbend. There will be a few separate brackets of eight teams, and we'll all play against each other, round robin style. Whoever has the most points will advance from the round robins to the more direct competition rounds.

We watch Scott and Laura first. They win their first bout. Then Ryan and Maria lose theirs narrowly. Finally, it's Bash's and my turn. My stomach has been churning all morning, ever since I woke up. I can't tell whether it's anxiety about leaving Logan home for a two-day weekend after all the lies—will he really stick to his word and our grounding?—or if it's about leaving my job, or just plain old tournament nerves getting to me.

I thought, after the Lake League, that I'd be a little less

nervous about this tournament, since I know now that I can hold my own among good players. But I didn't anticipate how it would feel to come here with a million other threads in my life all coming apart at once.

However, the moment we step onto the court, paddles in hand, the rest of that melts away. I feel a flare in my veins, a familiar tension flooding my muscles. You know how to do this. We've been on this court before, faced a team like this before, even if not this exact one.

The moment the serve comes flying my way, my muscles react. My body knows what to do, even when I'm not entirely sure myself.

It's a relief, in fact, to step out of my head and into this game. It feels easy, like breathing. Sebastian and I play off one another, each understanding the other's strengths now, knowing which balls to let go and which ones to chase. We understand who belongs where on the court, and whose tactics will serve us better in the moment against our opponents.

We win our first match, 11-7, and it buoys our spirits, raises my confidence going into the subsequent games.

Our second match is harder. Our opponents move like a machine. Anytime we send it over, they seem to know what we're planning even before we do. The ball fires back at us every time, faster and sharper than we can catch it. We put in a decent showing, but before long, we're dripping sweat and down 8 to 5. We hang on by our fingernails for a few more rounds, but in the end, they cinch a win.

We take a breather, catching up with Scott and Laura before our next game in the round. "You guys are on fire out there!" Laura cries as we join them.

I shake my head, flushed, but Sebastian just grins. "All this one." He claps a hand on my shoulder, and I can't help it. He looks so handsome in that moment, backlit by the sunlight and the glittering waves in the distance, his eyes on fire, searing into mine.

I lean in, catching his collar, and drag him down for a searing kiss.

Beside me, Laura chuckles. "Damn, tell us how you really feel. Or, show us, I guess."

We break apart, my cheeks flushed, not quite sure what came over me. Except that, I already know I want more. I face our friends again, forcing a laugh, pretending I wasn't just having an out-of-body experience. "What can I say? All this action is getting me a little hot under the collar."

Scott barks out a laugh and snakes an arm around Laura's hips. "Oh, believe me, we know the feeling."

My eyebrows shoot up. "Really? Do tell."

Laura shoots a sideways grin at Scott and leans in. "Let's just say, these tournaments have a tendency to get a little… wild, sometimes."

Now I find myself glancing over at Sebastian, who's staring right back at me, a sly grin on his face. "How wild are we talking, exactly?"

"Well…" Laura glances at Scott again.

He bends in, seamlessly taking over, in a move I recognize from the way they communicate out on the court. "Let's just say, you don't want to go poking around the clubhouse spa rooms without knocking first," he murmurs.

We both snort. My face flames with heat, and I hope they think it's just because of the joke, and not because I'm remembering us at the Lake League game a few weeks ago, doing exactly that. Christ, did anyone hear us?

From the sounds of it, though, we weren't the only ones getting fired up by all this competition. Or the only ones to have the shower idea.

As Scott heads off to buy more drinks and Laura leaves to find the ladies room, Sebastian bends down, so close to my ear that his breath tickles the fine hairs along my skin. "Are you thinking what I'm thinking?"

"That depends." I cut him a pointed look. "How naughty is your mind getting right now?"

"Well..." His arm dips down from my waist—a perfectly respectable height—to a less appropriate for public position, his hand hovering dangerously close to the curve of my ass. He doesn't grip it, not quite. But I can feel the tension in his fingertips digging into my skin, and I long to lean back into him, surrender to that sensation. "Let's just say, those two have given me a few ideas..."

"Oh really?" I twist in his arms, letting my thigh slip between his legs as I do. From this angle, my body against his, it just looks like we're standing face-to-face in the middle of this clubhouse cocktail room. Nobody will be able to see my thigh between his, my leg grazing precariously close to his crotch, where I can already feel a hard bulge beginning to form. "And what, precisely, might those be?"

"Well..." Sebastian's hand slips around my front, his fingertips toying with the hem of my athletic pants. One fingertip slips past the band to graze the fine peach fuzz just below my navel. "Let's just say, all of them involve you and significantly less clothing. Preferably spread-eagled on one of these fine dining tables, with everything I'd like access to at the perfect height for my—"

"There you two are!" Ryan waves at us, jogging over with Maria in tow. They look almost as sweaty as we feel, but they're both beaming from ear-to-ear, which tells me their second match must have gone better than the first. "You know you're up in five, right?"

"Oh shit." I straighten, drawing away from Sebastian, my face still bright red, breath coming hard. "We should get back there, then."

Together, we head back to the courts for our next game. This one goes a lot better than the second—even better than the first. We win 11-3, which means, if we can cinch our fourth game in the round robin, we'll advance with a good ranking to the elimination round.

Our fourth game turns out to be the hardest of all. We're running out of steam by then, and the other team starts out with several lucky hits in a row. Before we know it, we're down seven to two, both of us panicking. Sebastian pulls me aside for a brief chat while the other team stops for a water break.

"Look at me." He cups my chin in one palm, tilts it until I raise my face to his. "We've got this. Understand?"

"But—" I start, and he cuts across me.

"No buts. We've got this, Jen. Say it back to me."

A small smile forms at the corner of my lips. I hold his gaze, let myself sink into those familiar dark eyes. "We've got this, Bash."

A smile splits his face open at the sound of what's become his pickleball nickname. "Let's show them what we're made of."

Together, we turn back to the court, both our veins singing with energy now. I don't know what comes over me—over us. But every swing feels easier somehow, every return preordained, like we know what will happen before it actually does.

Before we know it, we're back in the running, with them only up by one, 7-6. Then we tie it. They score a sly one, but we turn it right back around for 8-8. They score again, we tie again. The stands around us fill up with bystanders, as a few other tournament games finish. We can hear Ryan chanting our names.

When we take the lead, 10-9, the high could propel me all the way up to the rafters. All our Riverbenders erupt when we finish off the other team, 11-9, the final shot one of

Bash's infamous hard and fast overheads that they had no chance of returning.

We step forward to tap paddles, the other team all smiles despite their loss. Everyone at the tournament has been friendly so far, and I don't think it's just the salt breeze coming off the ocean or the warm sunshine brightening our spirits.

We end up taking bronze overall, which stuns me. Sebastian doesn't seem surprised, though. "I told you," he murmurs, one arm wrapped around my waist at the medal ceremony. "You and me, we've got something special. Once we get through with it, this tournament won't know who hit it."

Laughing, I let him pull me into a deep, searing kiss. A few onlookers whoop, but for once, the overt PDA doesn't even bother me. Who cares if anyone wants to judge us?

Right now, we're on top of the world.

Chapter Sixteen

Jennifer

The post-tournament high carries us all the way back home and straight into renovations for the spa. My mom decided to extend her visit for a few more weeks to help out. Ellen, too, has taken to driving over from the office on her lunch breaks to pitch in.

Logan, as promised, helps me with a lot of the hauling and organizing—what tasks we don't leave to the professionals, anyway. The contractors we hired are friends of Sebastian's friends from the firehouse, so they gave us a sweet deal—supplies all wholesale, the work on the friends-and-family discount.

Still, my heart rises into my throat with each new check of my mother's money I need to write.

"Are you sure about this?" I keep asking her. Finally, on a Friday morning when it's me, Mia, Logan, half a dozen contractors and my mother in the store, Mom asks Mia and Logan for some privacy. Then she drags me over to the window of the little downtown shopfront we signed a joint lease for once I finally decided to chase this dream.

"Look at me, Jennifer."

I do. There are new, fine lines bracketing my mother's smile—the same smile I inherited—and deeper crow's feet around her eyes than I remember. Her hair went silver years ago, but now it's bordering on white. Though, recently she went and added a few blue streaks to it ("going white is like free bleach—can't let that go to waste!" she joked).

"I know you feel bad about accepting anything from me," Mom says. "And you feel like this is an imposition. But really, me giving you this money is selfish on my part." She takes my hands, squeezing tightly. "Because it makes me so happy to watch you be happy."

I let out a breathy, uncertain laugh. "Do I seem happy?" Lately, I feel like I've just been running around like a chicken with my head cut off—making to-do lists and double-checking supplies and researching this new industry I'm throwing myself headfirst into.

"Honey." Mom lets go of my hand, only to rest a palm against my cheek. It feels rougher than usual, dry. "I can't remember the last time I saw you smile this much, busy as hell or no."

In answer, another smile stretches across my face. I hadn't noticed it, but she's right. Even with all the running around and frantic tasks to complete—and even with all the fresh worries about Logan—lately I feel... lighter. Like a weight I didn't even know existed has been hauled off my shoulders.

"I don't know if it's happiness," I say. "But I feel content. Like I'm doing what I should be doing, finally."

Mom grins. "And it shows." She gives my cheek one last fond pat. "Now, I don't want to hear another word about my investment. Far as I'm concerned, it's already paid off in spades, whatever happens now."

I laugh again. Then I'm the one catching her hand, turning it over to examine her skin. "Speaking of repaying your investment. We've got a few of the new products in. I need to start testing them." I run a hand over her knuckles. "What would you say to letting me try out a hand treatment?"

Mom arches a brow, looking severe. "Are you implying something?"

"Only that a partial owner in a day spa deserves the best." I pat her hand again. "And, your hands do remind me of the Sahara right now…"

Mom huffs, mock offended. "This is the thanks I get! I see how it is." But she waves a hand at me, gesturing to the back office. The main area of the spa is a mess, all tangled wires the electricians are sorting out in the ceiling and walls, plus heaps of furniture covered in drop cloths, waiting until the new walls and ceiling are in place and painted before they can be set up the way I envision. But the office was in decent shape—didn't need much besides a new paint job, which Mom, Logan, and I knocked out first thing.

Logan helped me haul a cute vintage desk we found at a sale inside after that, and Ellen brought one of her old laptops that I'm using until we can get a separate work computer for the store, and the room practically feels ready to go.

"Go on," Mom's saying. "Show me what this cream you've been bragging about can do."

Out in the main spa area, the contractors drill and hammer and curse away. Logan hovers around them, watching the whole process with interest.

"Mia?" I call. "Want to test some products with Grams?"

She brightens, looking up from her cell phone for the first time all morning. "Sure."

Back in the office, I give Mom and Mia our first official treatment. I start with the honey exfoliator, then lather on a hydrating rosewater and aloe mask, before wrapping both of their hands up in these bags that make Mom dissolve into laughter, because they remind her of Mickey Mouse cartoon hands.

Mia snorts. "More like alien hands," she says, lifting her clear plastic bags to wave around her face.

"Stop, it'll leak out," I admonish, catching her wrists and lowering them to her sides.

"How long do we leave the bags on?" Mia asks, clearly already itching for her phone once more.

"Twenty minutes," I say.

"What if my nose itches?" she cries out.

Mom and I laugh.

While we wait for the mask to work its magic, Mom settles back in her chair, eyelids drooping. She's clearly struggling to stay awake, starting upright every few seconds. Mia and I trade sideways glances, stifling laughter. Finally, I stand up, pretending I need to run a quick errand.

"I'll come with," Mia volunteers, and we slip out of the

office, turning off the lights as we go. "Is it just me?" Mia whispers. "Or does Grams seem a little… I don't know. Older, this visit?"

My heart fists in my chest at the thought. Of course, she is older, but not so old as all that. She had me young, at only twenty-five. "She's fine, honey," I say. "Age just makes us all a little more nap-prone, that's all."

I lead Mia to the sink, which is covered in construction dust. Someone up front shouts something about a drywall, as I gently peel off the gloves and help Mia rinse off the remainder of the mask, before I finish it up with a soothing coconut and lavender moisturizer.

"Okay," Mia admits, begrudgingly, as she runs her hands over one another. "They do feel really smooth."

I grin. "Told you so." But she's already reaching for her back pocket, yanking her phone free. "Who are you talking to, anyway?" I ask. "You've barely set that thing down for a minute all day."

Mia, like any girl her age, is borderline addicted to her cell phone. But she's normally pretty good about spending some time in the here-and-now, before she slips off to text her friends about TV shows and boys. Not today, though. Not all week, come to think of it—when I've seen her, that is.

I squint sideways at her, just as Mia's face lights up neon red. Oh. I arch an eyebrow, suddenly doing the math on the past few weeks. "Is it a boy?" I ask.

She purses her lips. But she doesn't need to reply—the

deep blush of her skin is doing all the talking for her.

"Who is he? Where did you meet? How long has this been going on?"

"God, Mom!" She flings up her freshly masked hands. "See, this is why I didn't mention him. I knew you'd make a huge deal out of it—"

"I'm just curious, honey. You haven't mentioned any boys since the whole Caden incident—"

"Oh, my God." She groans. "Do you have to bring up my ex now?"

I grimace and clap a hand over my mouth. I should've known better. Caden was her first—well, only, until now—real boyfriend in high school. They only went out for a couple of months. Then he dumped her without a word. Not even a text message. She found out in school one day when she went to swing by his locker and found him making out with a new girl instead. "Sorry, honey. I'm sorry. That wasn't appropriate."

First I don't even notice my daughter has a crush, and now I stick my foot into my mouth the instant she gets up the courage to tell me about it. Get it together, Jennifer.

Mia groans again, louder this time, and rolls her eyes. But after a moment, she relents, stuffing her phone back into her pocket. "His name's Kent. He's in jazz band with me; he plays the saxophone. We've been friends for a while, but I didn't think he liked me that way or anything. Last day of school, though, he gave me a note, and well…" Her cheeks flame again.

My smile widens. "That's really sweet. I'm happy for you."

She rolls her eyes. "We're not dating. I mean, I don't think we are? He just told me he liked me, that's all."

"Have you told him you'd like to date?"

That earns me another glare. "You can't just ask a guy that. It's weird."

"But maybe he's wondering the same thing. Did you ever think about that?" I glance over at her, watching her expression shift to one of confusion. Smiling, I pat her shoulder. "Never hurts to try a little communication." Even as I say it, my mind drifts to Sebastian. He's still at the firehouse now, though he has plans to stop by and check out today's progress after work.

I catch myself smiling, looking forward to his reaction. Mia tilts her head, squinting at me. "What? You look all daydreamy all of a sudden."

I wrap one arm around her shoulders and pull her into a reluctant hug. "I'm just glad I got a chance to talk to you today. We need to catch up more often. Promise?"

Mia makes a show of resisting. But in the end, she sinks into my hug, voice muffled by my shoulder. "Okay, okay. Promise."

Chapter Seventeen
Sebastian

Geraldine is in town again, for more spa planning and supervision. The minute I finish up at the firehouse, I'm raring to head over and see what all the girls—plus Logan—have accomplished so far. Luckily, it's not a far drive, which is one of the reasons Jen decided on this location for the spa.

That, and its general surroundings. It's in a walkable part of town, but not right in the middle—far enough out that from the storefront, you still have a view out over the long green hillside that leads down to Lake Heather. As I pull up out front, I notice Logan slouched on the curb outside, phone in hand. No sign of the girls.

"Hey, bud," I call once I've parked in an empty space across the street.

Logan startles, nearly dropping his phone. He catches it at the last second and shoves it back into his pocket. Hmm. "Hey, Dad." He surges to his feet, dusting himself off. "What's up?"

"Is your mother still here?" I glance from him to the storefront. This late in June, we've still got another couple hours to go until sunset, so there are no lights on in the front of the store. Judging by the lack of bustle, the construction workers themselves have cleared out, too.

"She's in the back with Mia and Grams."

I'm about to start past him, but something about Logan's expression draws my eye again. "Everything alright?" I ask. Jennifer told me, by way of Mia, about the bullying Logan endured on set before he quit the musical. It doesn't excuse him lying, but, it certainly clarified a few things about the whole situation.

Still, I can't help but feel like we're still missing something.

"Yeah. Fine." Logan shrugs. When I lift an eyebrow, he straightens and meets my gaze. "I mean, I'm spending my summer break working on my mom's spa, so, it's not great, but..."

I snort. "Better get used to it. This is only the warm-up." I glance past him at the interior of the store. The workers made a lot of progress on the electrical wiring, it seems, and they've got some of the floor laid already. Still needs walls and a ceiling, though, before we can get into the nitty-gritty. "Your mom's going to need our help even more once the construction work finishes."

He groans. "If you're trying to make me feel better, it's not working."

I laugh. "Hey, we all have our own crosses to bear." With that, I step into the store, leaving him to crouch back on the curb and pull out his phone again. "Jen?" I call.

"Back here!"

I follow the sound of her voice into the rear of the spa.

There's a few rooms back there: some future massage and aromatherapy areas, as well as her office, and a bathroom. I find the three of them in the office, Jennifer and Mia helping Geraldine out of a chair. The latter looks ruffled, her hair askew, eyes red and puffy. "You okay?" I step forward to help, but Geraldine's already on her feet, waving her daughter and granddaughter away.

"I'm fine. These two are just fussing." She rubs at her eyes, yawning. "Dozed off during a treatment." She rubs her hands together, then gives Jennifer an appreciative look. "It did soften them a lot, you're right."

A tiny wrinkle appears between Jen's brows—the look she gets when she's worried, but trying not to let it show. "Mom, you slept for two hours. And you seemed really out of it just now…"

"Well, wouldn't you, after an unscheduled two-hour nap?" Geraldine responds, sniffing. "That, and I'm starving. What's for dinner?"

Jen glances at Mia, who shrugs. "We could order some pizza back at the house," Jen suggests.

"Perfect." Geraldine steps forward to loop her arm through mine. "Sebastian and I will meet you there." In characteristically bossy fashion, she steers me toward the door, calling over her shoulder. "What do you want? We'll order on the way."

Mia and Jen call out orders as we go. Outside, Logan stands to follow us, but Geraldine waves him back down.

"Stay and see if your mother needs any more help before she leaves."

My suspicions, already on medium alert, shift to high now. Still, I keep my mouth shut until Geraldine and I are alone in the car. "What's going on?" I ask as I start the engine.

Geraldine squints through the window, watching the store lights in the rearview mirror as we pull away.

When she doesn't say anything, my brow furrows. "Geraldine? You clearly wanted to talk to me alone, so…"

She inhales, shaking herself a little, as though she's just been startled from a reverie. "Yes. I do." She quiets again, but this time, I can tell it's because she's trying to get her thoughts in order.

I'd been hoping this was nothing. A casual catch-up sort of chat. Or, I thought, maybe she wanted my help with some sort of surprise for Jen. Now, though, the longer she lets the silence stretch, the more worried I become. Finally, she scrubs a hand over her face and tears her gaze from the window, facing me.

"I don't want to worry Jennifer yet," she says. "It could still be nothing. But, I thought I ought to let someone know, in case…"

My nerves spike, like I'm on the court and someone just sent a fast ball right past me, one I know I've got no chance in hell of returning. "Let someone know what?" I reply, grateful that my voice, at least, sounds steadier than I feel.

"My doctor thinks I have cancer."

It takes effort not to slam on the brake. I strangle the

wheel in both hands, let the C word lie heavy between us for a minute. "Thinks?" I finally say, once I have a handle on my racing thoughts. All I can think about is Jennifer's face, once she finds out. The way she'll crumple under the weight of this.

And Geraldine... God. She only just retired. She has all these plans—trips she wants to take, places to see, now that she's got all the time in the world.

Or none of it. I suppress that thought angrily.

"Well. He says he's sure. Ninety percent, anyway. We're waiting on one last test, though, so I've decided to take the more measured approach." She sniffs, all faux-offended, and I can't help but laugh a little.

Trust Geraldine to decide to no thank you her way through a cancer diagnosis. "What kind? Did he say if it's... well..." Some forms of cancer, I know, are far more treatable than others.

"It's in my lymph nodes," Geraldine says softly. "We're waiting to find out what type. I guess there's a few, and it depends what stage it's in. But... doc didn't sound thrilled, let's say that. Still, there's an off-chance that the scans could be misleading, too. The tests we did a few days ago should confirm one way or another."

I scrub a hand over my face at the next traffic light. "But you said your doc sounded pretty sure."

Geraldine purses her lips. "What does he know?"

I stifle an inappropriate laugh. "Geraldine..."

She turns that infamously sharp gaze on me, now. Even

with my eyes on the road, I can feel her stare burning holes in the side of my face. "Don't you start in on me too, now. I know myself, and my body. This gal's got years left in her yet." Geraldine slaps her knee.

I smile. "Don't we all know it." But… "You can't keep something like this from Jen. Not forever."

"I won't," she agrees. "Not forever, anyway." Then she waves a hand over her shoulder, back in the direction of the store. "But she's got so much on her mind right now, and she finally seems like she's in a good headspace. I don't want to derail her right now. She needs to focus on the spa for the time being."

I frown, a sudden thought occurring to me. "Is this why you invested?"

Geraldine hedges, her expression suddenly cagey. "I'd support anything Jen set her mind to. I always do, you know that."

"Sure, but, if this really is something bad, won't you need money? To treat it?" She's old enough for Medicare, thank God, but cancer can be expensive, especially these days.

"Don't you worry about me." Geraldine clicks her tongue. "I've got a supplemental policy I took out when Jen's father passed. Should cover just about anything those docs want to do to me, that I'm on board with."

That relaxes me somewhat. Until I process the whole sentence. "What do you mean, that you're on board with?"

Geraldine exhales through her nose. "You remember what it was like with Ron. All those procedures, and tests.

He spent his whole last year on this earth in the hospital."

I grimace. Of course I remember how hard it was when Jen's father passed away. He had an aggressive form of pancreatic cancer, and the doctors threw everything they could at it. "The doctors tried their best," I say.

"I'm not saying they didn't," Geraldine replies, gaze shifting back to the window. Outside, the sun is setting, casting the streets in a golden hour glow. "But at the end, you know what he told me? He said he wished he'd just let it go. Enjoyed what time he had left with us, instead of chasing the faint possibility of a few more weeks."

My mouth flattens. "That was a very different situation."

"I know that." Geraldine smooths her hair back from her forehead. "But I don't want to make the same mistakes. Not if it's as bad as his."

My heart, already clenched, becomes a solid fist. Jennifer will hate this. She pushed the hardest for her father to fight; she was the one who believed, right up until the very end, that he could still turn things around. She never gave up. Not on her father, and she certainly won't give up on her mother either. I reach for the water I always keep in the cupholder, take a swig to help me swallow past the sudden lump. "Whatever you decide," I finally say, "You'll have to tell Jen. Sooner than later."

We're nearing our house now. I stare down our familiar street, the trees along it swaying in the gentle start of summer breeze.

"When the time is right, I will," Geraldine says.

I pull into our driveway, set the car in park. Then I turn to face her, expression dead serious. "I want your word on that," I say. "I don't like keeping secrets from my wife."

In response, Geraldine sticks out a hand, a half-smile on her face. "Deal's a deal." When I take her hand, she pumps mine, her grip firm like she's got something to prove. "Anyway, don't feel too bad about it," she adds, once she releases me. She grabs the door handle and pops it open, hauling herself down from the truck without waiting for me to come around and help her. Stubborn as ever. "It's not your secret to worry about."

I wish I could believe that. But I know my wife, and this is something we'll all need to carry from here on out.

Chapter Eighteen

Jennifer

By the time our next tournament comes around, in Raleigh a few weeks after my mother's visit, we are on a certified roll. We've been winning friendly match after friendly match at the clubhouse, but our day trip to compete in Raleigh confirms it: this isn't just a lucky streak. We're good.

This time we take silver, going six and one in the seven games we play. The matches are all close, but we're learning how to roll with it now. The lows don't throw us off our game as much anymore, and the highs, while incredible, don't inflate our egos too much.

Not beyond the point that they could use inflating to, anyway.

We spend the whole drive back from Raleigh talking, in a way we haven't done in far too long. For the first time in ages, I'm excited to tell Sebastian everything about my week: the progress we're making at the spa, all the disasters Mom encountered on her departure flight, everything we've got to look forward to in the coming weeks.

We talk about Mia's new boyfriend, too—Sebastian didn't know about him either, which makes me feel either somewhat better or a whole lot worse about our parenting skills, I can't decide.

We discuss how Logan seems during this enforced grounding. He's been helpful around the shop, I must admit. But Sebastian's worried that there's more going on than we realize yet. He spends all his spare time buried in his phone, but it doesn't seem like he's texting or talking to anybody. He just scrolls and scrolls, on some endless loop.

"Maybe he just needs to burn off steam," I suggest. "It can't be easy for a fifteen-year-old to be trapped at home with his parents all summer."

We agree that must be it, though there's still a niggling sense of doubt that lingers after our conversation. It leads me to watch Logan more closely at the spa over the next few days. I try to look out for whatever it was that worried Sebastian—is Logan frowning more than usual, or moping whenever he looks at his phone? But my son has a killer poker face. I can't read anything from him most days except a slight air of boredom, perhaps.

Maybe that's all it is. After all, to his credit, Logan has been taking his punishment with stoic acceptance. He and Mia might roll their eyes or trade gripes from time to time, but every day, he rides into the spa with me, and he doesn't even ask to leave until we finish up working.

Sometimes, I offer to leave him home with Mia or Sebastian, feeling guilty for working him in what little free time from school he gets. But Logan always asks to come along anyway. I think he does genuinely enjoy talking to the workers—I catch him asking them how various things work, like the sanders they use on the walls or the techniques they use to lay out the floorboards evenly.

Before I know it, we're moving on to finishing touches: paint colors and massage tables and a shopping run with Mia to a huge garden center to pick out soothing but easy to cultivate plants. None of us have much in the way of green thumbs.

Finally, halfway through July, opening day dawns.

I'm a nervous wreck that morning, but Sebastian takes it upon himself to cook everybody breakfast. The whole drive over to the spa, I recite aloud my worries: that nobody will come to the opening, that the spa will get terrible reviews right off the bat, that we'll crash and burn before we even get out the gate.

But when we pull around the last corner before the store, my jaw drops.

As I stare, uncomprehending, the whole backseat erupts in cheers. Mia leans forward to clap my shoulder, and Logan chants the name we chose for the spa, "Heather River, Heather River," a mix of the lake Sebastian and I loved so much we simply had to move here, and the Riverbend Club to which we owe so much of our recent joy.

I can't stop staring. Not only are there actual real-life people here, but there are a lot of them. My eyes run down the line outside our door, which stretches all the way down the block.

Of course, Mom is at the head of it, having flown in again

late last night for the launch. She must have come here straight from her hotel. And beside her…

We park and I hop out of the car, grinning at my best friend. "Are you responsible for this?" I demand, as Ellen pulls me into a hug.

"Don't be silly! This was all you." She steps back to grin over my shoulder at the crowd. "Pretty great turn-out, huh?"

Among the crowd, I spot a few familiar faces. Other shopkeepers from this part of town, along with friends from work and the kids' school. But I also spot some surprises: Scott and Laura, for example, who don't live anywhere near here. Ryan and Maria came too, along with a large contingent from Sebastian's firehouse crew.

My face flushes. We'd planned on a simple launch day party: cupcakes, bubbles, and complimentary hand massages for everyone who came. We only hired two staff members so far—I was planning to help do some of the treatments myself. But this… "Thank y'all for coming," I call out, raising my voice loud enough to be heard by those in the back. "And apologies in advance if we run out of supplies."

A few people laugh. "Just here to support!" shouts back one of Sebastian's firehouse buddies.

My eyes tear up. I glance over at my husband, only to find him watching me with an expression of shining, obvious pride. He takes Ellen's place at my side, bending to whisper in my ear. "Told you so."

Laughing, I elbow his side. "This proves nothing yet,"

I murmur. But I take the key to the store from him and insert it into the lock. "Welcome to Heather River Day Spa," I announce, to another round of cheers. And then I turn the key.

* * *

The rest of opening week passes in a blur of happy memories: Ryan getting addicted to the facial treatment he tried, much to Maria's amusement; our first Wednesday sound bath event selling out within minutes; every slot for massages with both of our employees and me booking up every day this week.

In some ways, I'm even busier than at my old job—at least in terms of how many hats I'm wearing now, and how many different moving pieces I need to juggle. But somehow, I feel so much more relaxed about it all.

Work no longer feels like a horrible chore to suffer through. Instead, it's a place I look forward to being every morning. I never know who will stop by today, or what new challenge I'll have ahead of me.

Things with Sebastian have been easier, too. There's a new ease to our bodies at home—our hands brush hips as we pass each other in the kitchen, our fingers grazing one another's shoulders in the bathroom as we ready for bed. Things aren't magically fixed in an instant—we've still been tired out from life, kids, even pickleball practice somedays.

We've had sex a few times lately, but nothing like the

shower stall after that Lake League game again. My body still catches fire every time I think about it. I'm not sure what made it so hot—the situation, the potential for being caught? Or just the thrill of the game we won, the high of adrenaline we were both riding?

I catch Sebastian watching me from the corner of his eye, too, and I wonder if he's thinking the same thoughts. If that memory snags him as often as it does me.

Maybe not, whisper my anxieties, whenever we turn out the lights and they're free to roam. Or else why haven't we done it again? I try to suppress that voice, to tell myself it's just timing, habit, life getting in the way.

By the time the third Southern Pickleball Tournament rolls around, a long weekend in Asheville, North Carolina, my whole body feels like it's about to explode from pent-up tension. I want that kind of frantic, intoxicating sex again. I want him to tear my clothes off; to come at me like a hungry animal who can't get enough.

But I don't know how to open my mouth and admit that.

The spa is technically open Saturdays too, but Ellen has been coming in often, helping cover for me whenever I take lunch breaks or need to treat a client myself. She volunteers to take over all by herself this Saturday, to give us time for the tournament, while Mom returns for another long weekend with the grandkids.

I feel a little pang of worry—will the ship be okay without its captain for the first time ever? But I trust Ellen, and I trust my mother to help out with any emergencies. So in the end, I leave them both to it, and Sebastian and I pile into the car with all of our gear to drive to Asheville. It's sweltering, but that's mid-July in the South for you.

We drive with the air blasting and our favorite station on. Sebastian rests his hand on the gear shift, and I try to work up the nerve to reach over and take it. But I deliberate for too long—he catches me looking and arches an eyebrow. "Need something?"

You. Way, way more of you. I bite my lip to swallow the words. I should be focusing on the tournament ahead instead. "Just thinking about Atlanta."

A smile curves the edge of his mouth. "We did well last time. Silver! We only need one gold medal to cinch our spot in Atlanta." He reaches over to pat my knee, and his touch sends a rush of heat through my veins. Before I can reach out to take his hand, though, it's gone, retreating back to the steering wheel. "This will be our weekend, just you wait and see."

The tournament is all-day Saturday, but we decided to drive down early—right after I closed up on Friday afternoon. We'll stay an extra day afterward, too, since the spa doesn't open at all on Sundays, and Sebastian has a rare whole weekend off.

Maybe some fresh air and mountain scenery will clear our heads, provide the stimulation we need. If nothing else, it might burn off some of my stress.

The spa has been exciting, but it's a lot of work. Turns out fun work can stress you out too—albeit a lot more pleasantly than work you hate. I'm looking forward to the breather. Maybe I can be the one who gets pampered for a change, rather than the other way around.

We're staying at a hotel right on the grounds where the tournament will be held tomorrow. Once we get checked into our room—a high-ceilinged, airy room with an enormous bathroom and one of those balconies that walks right out over the courts with a view to the mountains beyond—we go for a wander around the place. A few other couples are already lounging by the pool, and we wave to a few faces we recognize from other tournaments.

We don't see anyone we know by name yet, though, so we keep wandering through the clubhouse. Halfway through the interior tour, however, a familiar bark like laugh stops us both in our tracks. We trade matching looks of despair just as Chris and Crys round the corner, dressed to the nines in their usual designer gear.

"You should've seen her swing, my God," Crys is saying. "A monkey could've done better. Oh." She draws up short, squinting in our direction.

Beside her, Chris pauses, too. "Bash, right?" He glances at Sebastian.

I don't know whether we should take it as a good sign or a dangerous one, that we're finally on C+C Non-Music Factory's radar. It must mean we've improved enough that they view us as a threat—they only ever seem to remember the good players, laughing at or dismissing the rest without bothering to learn anybody's names.

On the other hand, this means they'll be gunning for us, now. "Chris," Sebastian says, his voice a lot more even than mine would've been, given the circumstances. "And Crys."

Crys sniffs, her gaze flitting to me. "I see you two are still paired up. How sweet."

My eyes narrow. I can practically hear the insinuations brewing. They've made no bones about the fact that they think Bash is a more talented player than me in the past. "You know how it is," I say, making my voice as sugary sweet as hers. "Playing with your husband can be such a… thrill." As I speak, I let my hand wander to Sebastian's back, brushing from his shoulder blade down his back in a slow sweep.

He half-turns to me, eyebrows lifted slightly, a smirk curving the edges of his mouth. "This one keeps me on my toes off-court and on," he says, eyes finding mine, a familiar spark catching behind them.

"Adorable," Crys replies, in a flat tone that says she finds it anything but. Nose wrinkled, she moves past us, Chris trailing in her wake. "Well. See you tomorrow, I suppose."

"That'd be just our luck," I mutter under my breath, pitched low so they won't hear as they walk away.

Sebastian snickers, though he keeps it quiet, too. "Let's pray we're not in their bracket."

Soured on the idea of the clubhouse now, I lead the way

outside into the sunshine. We got here early enough that there's still a couple hours until dusk, and a sign nearby proclaims the Prettiest Hiking Trail in the South will only take an hour and a half to complete. "How about it?" I ask, nerves still jittery after that encounter.

Sebastian seems to be on the same page. "Seems as good a palette cleanser as any."

Together, we start up the trail, leaving the clubhouse and all the interpersonal dramas of the tournament behind. This late in the day, we seem to be the only people out on the trail. We pass wildlife galore—squirrels chittering in the trees, birds singing and flitting overhead—but no other signs of human life. The only sounds close at hand are our breathing and the snap of twigs and leaves underfoot.

About forty minutes in, the trail opens up ahead. We stop, breaths stolen not just from the steep incline, but also from the view spread at our feet. A glittering mountain lake lies nestled in a small valley, ringed by trees in full summer bloom. There's a viewpoint, a little ways off the trail, where someone has dragged logs into makeshift seats.

We stop, faces red from the climb, sweat glistening on our foreheads, and look from the lake to one another and back.

"It's beautiful," I murmur.

"Just what the doctor ordered?" Sebastian takes a step closer to me, reaching over to offer some of the water from his canteen. He's always better at preparing for things like this than I am.

I take a long swig, then pass it back. As I do, I catch him watching me, eyes dipping to my lips before they return to my face, still with that mischievous sparkle in them from earlier. "What?" I demand.

His lip curls again, a deeper smile this time. "Just admiring the view," he says, gaze still firmly fixed on me, not the landscape behind us.

My body ignites again. I feel the same way I did after that league game, even though we haven't played yet. Adrenaline surges through my body, and when I catch Sebastian's eye again, I see the same feeling mirrored there. "You know, I keep thinking about… that time at Mountain Creek."

His smirk widens. "Oh?" He arches a brow. "What about it, exactly?"

I know he knows exactly what I mean. But clearly, he wants me to spell it out. "Well…" I take a step closer to him, leaves rustling. There's a few crickets mixed in with the birdsong. Earlier, it was scorching hot, but this time of day, with sunset close upon us, it's cooled down to a pleasant degree. The gentle breeze skirting off the lake down below helps, too. "Specifically, I think about that shower stall."

"Hmm." His smile turns sly. "You mean the one I fucked you senseless in?"

A throb goes through me, a knot tightening in my core. "Yes. That one."

He takes another step. We're barely inches apart now, the air between us thrumming with promise. "And when you think about it, how do you feel?"

I suck my lower lip between my teeth, gratified to notice his gaze drop, following the motion. "I wish we would do it again," I admit softly.

One of his eyebrows ticks higher. He reaches out to snag my waist, and the warmth of his hands seems to ignite the flames already building in me. I reach up to press my hands flat against his chest, feeling the strength of the muscles there. We've both been getting more in shape since we started playing this game, and it shows in both our bodies. I trace the ridges of his pecs, down to the outline of his abs, which I can feel if I press on the fabric of his shirt. "We're a bit short on showers up here," he says, with an exaggerated glance around.

I stifle a laugh, rolling my eyes. "Not that part."

"Ahh. I see." His smile deepens. "So it was the public aspect you liked. The thrill of getting caught. No?" His hands slip beneath my shirt, press flat against my skin.

I sweated a little on the hike up here, and so did he. But somehow, that makes it all the hotter, when his hands glide over me easily, as if we're both covered in grease.

It makes me realize what else is slick. Soaked, in fact. I grab the hem of his shirt in one fist and drag him closer. He obeys, grinning, until his mouth hovers mere centimeters from mine. "Maybe I liked that aspect, yes."

He chuckles under his breath. "And what else?" His hands roam lower, toy with the hem of my hiking pants.

"I liked that you didn't hesitate," I murmur, gaze darting from his mouth to his eyes and back. "You just took what you wanted."

"If that's what you want, then I'm happy to oblige." His grip shifts. Without warning, he picks me up and twirls us both around, stepping forward until my back is pressed flat against a broad tree trunk, the bark lightly scratching at my back where my shirt has gotten hiked up.

I open my mouth, either to gasp or cry out, but his mouth is on mine already, tongue parting my lips. I moan into the kiss, hands fisted tight in his shirt. We break apart long enough for me to rip it over his head and drop it into the leaf pile beside us. Then he kisses me again, harder this time, more desperately. One of my hands slides around to the small of his back for support, bracing myself. The other flattens across his abs, delving down to where the little cut of muscles has formed over his hip muscles.

I'm about to slide a hand under the hem of his shorts, when he catches my wrist, a playful look on his face.

"Ah, ah. You said you wanted me to take what I want," he says. "Which means, it's my lead."

Laughing, I drop my hand. "Yours, then, Sebastian."

He bends to kiss me again, a white hot, searing kiss that makes my knees go weak—especially when he slips one hand beneath my pants and underwear in one go, his fingers splayed flat on my mound. "Yes," he whispers against my mouth, breath hot and tingling. "Mine."

His hand glides lower, which is easy to do, since I've waxed everything. He catches my eye with a questioning look.

"You like it?" I manage, only slightly distracted by his fingertips finally reaching my nether lips, his forefinger and thumb gently spreading them. "Figured I'd... try something new. Perks of owning a... spa." The last comes out more of a gasp, as he lets a single fingertip gently inch inside me.

"I like," he murmurs, bending to kiss my jawline, the edge of my neck. "But then, I always like you. In every way."

I laugh breathily as his fingers continue their ministrations, crooked at just the right angle to coax a hot rush of liquid between my thighs. "Even... like this?" I glance around at the wilderness around us. "Sweaty and mid-hike?"

"Especially like this," he replies. Then, without warning, he drops to his knees in the leaves before me.

"Bash," I hiss.

He grins and pushes my shirt up, bending to kiss my stomach. His tongue finds my navel and flits into the hollow there, like he's tasting me.

I can feel my muscles tense, fresh worries mounting. Maybe this was a bad idea. Someone might come along, see us, and then what? Would this count as public indecency? Could we be arrested?

"Jen." His voice calls me back to reality. "Stay here," he orders, one hand pressed to my belly again. Gently, he forces me back against the tree. I lean my weight into it, let the bark hold me up. "I want you here and now." He bends to kiss me again, lower this time. He follows the line directly below my navel, one fingertip gently circling inside me, not yet deep enough to make me cry out.

"God, that feels good," I murmur, my head falling back against the tree trunk now. Without even realizing I'm doing it, I reach down, my hands winding into his hair for support.

"Good," Bash murmurs, lips barely leaving my skin as his free hand works my pants down over my hips. He pushes them to puddle at my ankles. "Because I am about to make you cum so hard you forget your own name."

I tense, and he knows it—with that finger inside me, he can feel the sudden, startled clench of my walls. He chuckles knowingly. "Bash…"

"No use protesting." He leans forward to catch my underwear in his teeth—his teeth, fuck—and jerks them down. I gasp as the bare air hits my wet pussy, drawing a shiver from me, in spite of the relative warmth. "You told me to take what I wanted, right?" He pauses to grin up at me, one brow quirked questioningly.

He'd stop if I asked him, I know that. If it turns out this whole public sex thing is more than I bargained for, and I'm having second thoughts. But right now, all I can think about his fingertip inside me, the tantalizingly close heat of his breath against my bare mound. I don't usually wax, so I'm not used to how smooth everything feels, how close the contact when he leans in to drag his tongue along my mound, all the way down to where my slit begins.

Because he knows every inch of my body, he stops right before he reaches my clit. It makes me throb with heat—with naked, wanton desire.

"Don't stop," I gasp. What the hell else am I going to say? I'm already half gone.

Bash's grin widens and he uses his free hand to flatten my hips against the trunk. At the same time, he moves lower, his tongue circling my clit. He laps at me in wide circles at first, tongue flattened and broad. But with each stroke, he narrows in closer, closer.

"You taste so fucking good," he stops to murmur, just when I'm about to crawl out of my skin with want.

I keep one hand fisted in his hair and reach back with the other for balance, my legs already shaky. "You are… so bad," I manage.

"Me?" He clicks his tongue, but he does it right against my skin, the very tip flicking along the sheaf of my clit. I gasp, arching at the motion, but he uses his single broad hand to force me back against the tree, pinning me there. "You're the one with the naughty imagination. Want to know what naughty girls get for such dirty thoughts?"

He nudges my legs farther apart, then without warning, removes his fingertip from inside me. In its place, he drags his tongue along the length of my slit, all the way from back to front, then slowly back again.

I moan, low and throaty. The sound makes him laugh softly.

"That's my naughty girl. More of that, please." He licks me again, and again—slow, patient strokes, his tongue broad and flat like a blade.

I already knew I was soaked, but now I'm positively dripping. My juices glisten on his chin when he pauses to look up at me, their shine almost as bright as the spark in his eyes.

"Louder," he orders, then laps at me again.

It's not hard to obey him. The next moan I make startles me in its intensity, so deep it barely sounds like me at all. Fuck me. We've barely gotten started and I'm already out of control.

But I don't care. This is exactly what I've been craving ever since that desperate, grasping fuck. I want to let go of control; I want to take risks, ride this adrenaline high. I've missed this.

Bash pushes his tongue between the folds of my lips, inside of me, and I cry out again shakily. He moans, too, the vibration passing straight from his lips and over my pussy, making me clench again, this time around his tongue rather than his finger.

At the same time, he reaches up with one hand to grab a fistful of my ass. He peels my hips up and off the tree, angling me perfectly for his tongue to have the best access. It's all I can do to remain on my feet, standing, as he begins to thrust his tongue into me, out again.

My eyelids droop to half-mast. Everything around us

fades—I forget where we are, who we are. There's just the spikes of pleasure radiating through me, climbing higher with every firm thrust of that tongue.

When he's had enough of teasing me, he pulls out to drag his tongue over my clit in a long, slow slide.

I gasp, shaking. But he won't let me fall, I know that—he's got both hands holding my hips now, bracing me as he sucks my clit, then licks again, slower. The sounds he makes would make anybody blush, all wet and slick and hungry. My face—hell, my whole body—feels beet red, flushed with want.

He starts moving faster, lapping at me, and I know I won't last long. Quaking, I cry out, my voice a ragged moan. I can't even form words; can't tell him I'm about to cum, but he knows it anyway.

He keeps going, tonguing me until stars glitter at the edges of my vision. The orgasm hits me with such force I actually feel out of body. My hips buck off the tree, my one hand fisted tight in his hair, pressing his face to my crotch. At the same time, my vision goes dark, the sound that emerges from my throat almost a growl.

Sebastian keeps going, his tongue going flat and broad again, dragging over me. I can barely stand I'm shaking so hard, and oh, God, if he makes me cum again I might fall.

I grip the tree for balance, just as a sudden, sharp sound breaks our concentration.

Gasping, I straighten, just as Bash pulls back from me, whipping around. So he heard it too—it wasn't just me. We both stare, eyes wide, as a young woman gripping a pair of hiking sticks trudges into view on the trail. She stops dead at the same moment we turn, her eyes wide.

For a moment, none of us move. The only sound is the breeze rustling the trees overhead. All my earlier panic comes rushing back in one fell swoop—are we about to be arrested?

Then, to all of our shock, the woman starts cackling. "I'll have what she's having," she calls, giving us a one-armed salute before she sets her hiking poles in the opposite direction and starts clomping away, boots crashing through the underbrush.

I take one look at Bash and dissolve into laughter. So does he, sitting back onto his heels. I slide down the tree trunk until I'm splayed opposite him, both of us full-belly laughing like we're teens again. He grabs me by the waist and drags me over, until I'm lying flat on top of him, both of us covered in leaves and forest floor grime. He kisses me hard and deep, and I taste myself on his mouth, the slick flavor of my juices mingled with his steady, musk smell.

When we break apart, gazing into one another's eyes, I feel lighter than I have in years. "I love you," I murmur, running a hand through his hair.

He grins. "Love you too, my wild woman." Then he slaps my naked ass for emphasis, and sets us both off all over again.

Chapter Nineteen

Sebastian

After the hiking trail, Jen and I cannot keep our hands off one another. We manage to control ourselves enough to eat dinner back at the hotel, but halfway through dessert, her foot starts sliding up my leg under the table. She's always been dexterous with her feet, but this is a new level. She gets her foot onto my lap, her toes toying with the crotch of my jeans until I have an erection so enormous there's no way I can stand up from this table and go anywhere.

As soon as we finish eating, I drag her upstairs. We don't even wait until the room. I catch her waist and pin her to the wall down the hall from our suite, my tongue in her mouth, my fist in her hair, the memory of her taste all over my lips.

I want her again. Right here, preferably. But we both have at least a little latent sense of propriety, so in the end, I drag her into the bedroom, slam the door, and then pin her against that instead. We get all the way down to our underwear before Jen decides that I already had my turn, and now it's hers. She pushes me onto the bed instead, straddling me, and who the hell am I to complain?

Dimly, some part of my brain is aware that we're going to be exhausted tomorrow. But I couldn't care less. We've needed this—we've needed each other. It's been too long since we let ourselves truly drink our fill.

We wake the next morning, bleary-eyed, aching all over, but somehow reenergized. Like in draining ourselves, we filled each other up.

We are on fire at the tournament. There's no other description for it. If I thought Raleigh and silver was good, we're on track to breeze right past that. In the back of my mind—the back of both our minds, no doubt—that golden ticket dangles, tantalizing.

Just one gold. That's all we need to cinch a spot in the Atlanta finals. Winning those to secure the golden ticket to Palm Springs will be a whole other ball game—a problem for future Jen and Bash. Right now, I just want us to stay in the running.

We steamroll our first five matches. 11-3, 11-2, 11-4, and so on. By the sixth match, we're starting to feel unbeatable. Even a match against C+C Non-Music Factory doesn't feel like it would shake me now—though thankfully, we're not up against them. I pity anyone who gets their tournament rained on by those assholes.

Our last two matches are against teams who have lost several of their first games. I'm feeling confident—that gold medal is within our reach. Just two more games and we'll cinch it.

But then Jennifer's phone rings, during a break before our final rounds. "It's Mia," she says, picking up right away. We have a rule—always answer for the kids. But when we're away on weekends like this, they usually only call us for emergencies anyway.

I frown. That frown deepens the longer Jen talks, her face angled away from me, a notch in her brow appearing. When she finally disconnects, I can tell it's bad news before she says a word.

"It's Mom," Jen says, and guilt immediately rushes through me.

Geraldine flew in for another visit, ostensibly to check out the spa. Deep down, I have a feeling she's trying to maximize family time while travel is still relatively easy for her. I've kept my promise, not saying a word to Jen about her mother's condition. But Geraldine hasn't held up her end of the bargain. She was supposed to have come clean about the situation by now. The longer this drags on... "What about her?" I ask.

"Mia says she was really out of it this morning. Groggy, confused. They're at the walk-in clinic now, but Mom keeps trying to insist she's fine."

I stand. "Maybe we should go back."

Jen stands too, looking confused. "It's okay. I talked to Mom, convinced her to speak to the docs. She probably just picked up a bug on the plane."

The guilt worsens. If Jen knew what was really wrong, she would want to turn around and go home right now. That, or she wouldn't have agreed to come to this tournament in the first place. But... Geraldine promised she would break the news to Jen herself soon. She's right—it is her secret to tell. She ought to be able to decide how and when to tell her only daughter.

Would she want us sprinting back to town frantically now? Or would she want us to stay here, enjoy the trip, and get more time with the grandkids before she breaks the news to Jennifer?

I hesitate, torn.

As if reading my mind, my phone pings. I glance down at a new message from Geraldine. Everything in hand here. Don't you two ruin your big trip worrying about me.

A knot forms at the base of my throat. Fuck. I need to be able to talk to Jen about this. She's put me in such a terrible position. But that's Geraldine for you—she's as stubborn as they come, and impossible to defy.

"Who's that?" Jen asks.

"Your mom." I pocket the phone again. "She must be a mind-reader. She said she doesn't want us ruining our trip over her."

"There you go." Jen brightens, smiling at me. "Dilemma solved; we'll stay through the weekend."

But for all her smiles, the news must worry Jen more than she lets on. The next game, all our invincible star power begins to collapse. We miss a few easy put-aways that go wide, and struggle to return some hits that should've been right up our alley. Before long, we're trailing behind.

We lose game seven, but that's alright. I check the

standings and give Jen a pep talk—we can still pull out a win, so long as we win our eighth game handily.

Right off the bat, it becomes clear that's not going to happen. If game seven was a mess, game eight is a wreck. We completely fall apart, losing not just our chance at gold, but our chance at silver, too. To make matters worse, C+C Non-Music Factory coast to victory in the wake of our train wreck.

They spend the whole medal ceremony posing for obnoxious photos with what looks like an actual paid photographer—did they seriously hire someone to follow them around and take pictures? In the meantime, we trade irritated glances with the silver medalists.

"Well," Jen whispers on our way out of the tournament, "That's one silver lining." She taps the bronze medal around her neck. "If we don't make it to Atlanta, at least we won't have to see their smug faces for another year."

I snort under my breath, then quickly compose my expression as C+C breeze past us, trailing expensive perfume and cologne in their wake.

"Shame about your last couple of matches," Crys calls over her shoulder as they go. "Better luck next time." But her eyes stray to mine and only mine, as if Jen doesn't even exist.

I can feel Jennifer bristling with a retort, but I get there first. "See you two in Atlanta," I reply, my smile wide and easy. Take the high road. That's what Jen always taught me. And I must admit, it is a little satisfying to see Crys's smug smile falter, like she's startled by my confidence.

Then she turns away, and I turn to Jen, ready to fry bigger fish than this tournament. "Let's go home tonight," I say.

"You don't want to spend our last vacation day here?" she asks. I can tell that she's torn, by the way she picks at her thumbnail. Nervous habit she's never been able to break.

I shake my head. "Your mom is more important. And I can tell your mind is back home."

I don't mention the last couple games, or the balls she let by, but Jen flinches anyway as if I had. I grimace. That's not what I meant, I'm about to add, but she's already squaring her shoulders and marching past me toward the room. "You're right. Let's get going," is all she says.

Chapter Twenty
Jennifer

By the time we get home, Mom's flitting around the house cooking and claiming she's never felt better in her life. Bash and I trade eyerolls behind her back, but I'm happy to let her fix us both plates of dinner, after that long drive.

"How'd the tournament go?" she asks.

I don't have the heart to tell her. How can we be so on fire one minute and in such shambles the next? "Fine, I guess." I shrug, eager for a change of subject. "What did the doctor say?"

"Oh, he said I'm fine. No need for all the fuss. But I told your daughter that right off the bat. Didn't I, Miss Mia?" she calls over my shoulder. We both glance at the living room, where Mia's "watching TV," aka scrolling on her phone. Probably texting the boyfriend I still haven't met.

"She did the right thing," I say firmly. "You, on the other hand, apparently can't be left unsupervised to look after yourself." Tsking, I stand up to take over the washing duties. "Go relax; I'll do these."

"I'm almost done anyway," Mom replies, snapping the towel at me. So we wind up doing the dishes together, her washing and me drying and stacking them away. "How's that boy of yours doing? Not gotten his nose into any more trouble, has he?"

"He's been a huge help this summer," I admit. But something in her tone makes me glance at her sideways. "Why? How did he seem this weekend?"

Mom bobs her head side-to-side. "Helpful enough at chore time. But he seems… moody."

"He's a fifteen-year-old boy," I point out.

"Moodier than usual," she amends. "I can't help wondering if there's something more to it all. I know Mia explained about the bullies, but…" She shakes her head. "I don't know. Can't quite place my finger on it, but he seems different than usual. Slower, more distracted."

I sigh. I've noticed that too, I have to admit. "I wish I could talk them into coming on one of these trips with us," I say, remembering how good it felt to be with Sebastian on that mountain trail. Even before… well. My cheeks turn bright red, and I talk quickly in order to keep my mother from asking any untoward questions. "It can be really relaxing just to get away from everything for a bit. See somewhere new."

"Let me guess," Mom says. "They have no interest in going on a family trip to some mountain town so they can hike or play Ping-Pong or whatnot—"

"Pickleball, Mom," I correct, elbowing her.

She smirks. "Whatever the kids are calling it these days." She finishes the last dish and wipes her hands on the dishtowel. "Aren't any of your tournaments somewhere fun? Somewhere they might actually want to go?"

I blink, remembering back when Sebastian and I first learned about the Southern Pickleball Championships. There was one trip that I'd thought they might jump on. "There's one in Orlando at the start of August," I murmur.

"There you go." Mom beams. "Perfect family outing. As long as they're not too cool for Disney these days—at what age does Disney go from being cool to being dorky?"

"Never," says Mia from the kitchen doorway as she pads inside, tea mug in hand. "Why?"

Mom wiggles her eyebrows at me and I stifle a grin. But it's as good an opening as any. "Because," I say slowly. "Your father and I have an idea."

* * *

As our plane glides down onto the tarmac at Orlando International Airport, I realize I didn't actually expect this to work. Shockingly, even Logan decided he wasn't too cool for the mouse—probably because he's always been the more fanatic fan, between the two of them. Back when he was little and we visited, we got him an autograph book to ask characters to sign. Logan had refused to stop until he collected every single signature.

As for Mia, she's mainly in it for Universal Studios. "There's this new ride that's supposed to be insane," she explains, showing us videos of it the whole plane ride.

It looks nausea-inducing to me, but her and Sebastian can knock their socks off.

We book a whole week for the trip, with the tournament right smack in the middle. We figure we can all do some family stuff at the parks early in the week, then Mia and Logan can have a day at the resort pool while Bash and I play. But to our surprise, when the tournament day dawns, our kids wake up with us and lace their shoes.

"What did you two decide to do today?" I ask.

They trade looks. "We're gonna come watch you," Mia says.

My eyebrows shoot up. "Really?"

Logan shrugs. "You and Dad have been playing so much of this game. Figured we should check it out. Make sure you haven't joined a cult for old people or something."

I snort. Mia elbows him. Bash just laughs, stepping back out of the bathroom in his usual game day outfit. "If anything, it's a cult for people of all ages," Sebastian says, winking at me. I glare daggers back while the kids dissolve into laughter.

The trip has been great so far. We visited the Disney parks already, and we have plans to check out Universal Studios after the tournament ends. Mia has been chattier than usual the whole time—in between making us take all sorts of ridiculous videos of her for her social media pages.

As for Logan, even he has poked his head out of his shell. He made us stop to watch a few performances of the mascots last night, making me wonder if he regrets quitting theater, or misses his drama club. But otherwise, he's been sociable, friendly, upbeat—a Logan I haven't seen in a long time.

We're all feeling optimistic going into the tournament. But once we get there…

"Holy crap," I murmur.

Mia and Logan gawk around, mouths open. "Are all the places you go like this?" Mia asks.

"Definitely not," Bash says. Because this place is massive. If I thought the clubhouses we've been playing in were big, they have nothing on an Orlando city-sized club. The courts here stretch as far as the eye can see, and the registration tables for the tournament look more like the kind of registration tables you'd see at a city marathon starting line.

I try to count how many people are waiting in line, and lose count after a couple hundred. "Wow." We join the line, my heart a tight fist in my chest.

"Scott warned us this would be the biggest tournament," Sebastian reminds me.

I nod. "But I didn't think it would be this…" I shake my head, glancing at the courts nearby. A few people are warming up, firing the kind of shots at one another that remind me of C+C, or our coach June. "Intimidating," I finally finish.

That, it turns out, is a good word to sum up the Orlando branch of this tournament series. The competition is tougher than anything we've encountered in North Carolina. Despite the energy boost we both get from seeing our kids cheering us on in the stands, we struggle to keep up. We lose our first match 11-9, and our second 11-8.

"You've got this, Mom!" Logan shouts after I just barely lose a return, the ball skipping off the edge of my paddle instead of sailing back over the net.

"Go, Dad!" Mia hollers when Bash hits a particularly Bash-esque shot straight down the center at our opponents.

Maybe it's wishful thinking, but the kids seem genuinely into the game. Especially our third match, which we win 11-6. They go wild when the last shot gets called in our favor, both screaming and jumping up and down, hugging each other like lunatics.

It reminds me of when they were little and we used to take them to baseball games. Mia now declares baseball "the most boring sport ever," and Logan only wants to go with his friends anymore, but I still remember those early days when we could all get into the competitive spirit together.

It warms my heart, watching them now. Bash is affected too, I can tell, though he tries to hide it with some gruff comments and slaps on the shoulder. But there's a moment, when neither kid is looking our way, when Bash catches my eye. He winks, and I feel a rush of warmth flood my system.

This is what it's all about. Not the win itself, but the togetherness. The sense of belonging, right here, having fun with my family.

Although the tournament isn't our worst performance—in the end, we win 5 of our 8 matches—we still don't place anywhere near the medal stand. But that doesn't even really bother us. Because after the tournament, the clubhouse staff announce that anyone can stay to play open games, including the spectators.

At once, Mia and Logan bound to our sides. "What are we doing now?" Mia asks.

My eyebrows rise. "Nothing, why?"

"Well…" Mia glances past me at Logan, who's walking close enough to be within earshot. He gives her a small nod, and Mia looks back at me. "We were thinking maybe we could try a game. Play doubles against you and Dad?"

I have, in fact, tried to talk both of our children into coming to the Riverbend Country Club with us for practice games several dozen times. Based on their complete lack of reactions, I didn't think either of them had any interest, though.

"Yeah," Logan adds. "It looks kind of fun."

Bash glances at me, and my smile is so wide it actually hurts. "We'd love that, honey."

We didn't bring any spare paddles, but luckily the organizers have plenty. We get one for each of the kids, then find ourselves a free court. There are a few open ones, but I'm surprised how many other people are staying behind for friendly matches. Some people have kids with them, others are just playing for fun against one another. Even the gold medalists, I notice, square up against the silver medal winners for a friendly rematch.

We talk the kids through the basic rules: the kitchen, the baseline, how to score points and where to keep your feet for the best chance at hitting the ball back at your opponents.

Mia is quick on the uptake—and on her feet—but Logan's a little slower. It takes him a couple rounds to get the hang of it. Once he does, though, he and Mia get a kick out of imitating me and Sebastian with our communication.

"Mine!" Logan loves to shout, for almost every ball that sails back over the net toward them.

But Mia starts calling them too, until they remind me of those seagulls in the one cartoon movie, both yelling mine as they chase balls on opposite ends of the courts.

Bash dissolves in laughter as I march up to the net, shaking my head, to retrieve the ball they let escape yet again. "You need to work together," I admonish them. "You're a team; we're your competition, not one another."

"Can we switch partners?" Mia asks. "He's the worst."

I snort and glance over at Bash, who shrugs. "Alright, come here." I beckon her, grinning. "Boys against girls. Let's show them how it's done."

Mia and I win one and lose one to Bash and Logan. Bash wants to go for a tiebreaker, but Logan complains that he wants to be on my team. So we swap again. Logan and I lose miserably both times to Mia and her dad, who invent a whole dance to rub this fact in our faces.

"That's not very sportsmanlike conduct," I remind them after their third victory in a row, while Mia shakes her tush in Logan's general direction.

"True, true." Sebastian gestures at his daughter, reining her in. "We should be gracious in our victory. Congratulations to all." He catches my eye and winks, and I flash one back, my heart fluttering.

He's right. Congratulations to the four of us really are in order. As it turns out, we had a victorious trip to Florida after all—it's just, some victories don't come in the form of medals or trophies.

Chapter Twenty-One
Sebastian

After Orlando, the kids are happy to tag along with us to the clubhouse. We spend most of August playing pickup games on the weekends. Once, Mia's boyfriend even joins us. Jaxon seems like a good kid, if a little quiet. Maybe he'll warm up over time—or maybe he was put off by all the loud shouting Logan and Mia were doing, their latest attempt to throw me and Jen off our game long enough for them to catch up.

It didn't work, of course. But points for effort.

The kids clamor to come along on our next tournament, in Greenville, but unfortunately school has started back up, and we don't think it'd be a good idea to pull them away already. Logan's finally off of house arrest, and at our urging, he signed up for a new club this year. Maybe trying his hand at lacrosse will take his mind off all that drama with the drama club last spring.

As for Mia, jazz band has a lot of rehearsals right at the start of the semester, so we leave the kids for a sleepover with Ellen and drive down to Greenville just for a quick overnight trip. The facilities seem nice enough—ten courts set right in the middle of the city, in a public park full of trees, the leaves just beginning to turn golden with the barest hint of fall.

The tournament has drawn a big crowd, too. At least a couple hundred people, maybe more. Surprisingly, our first match winds up being against Ryan and Maria. We trade a lot of good-natured barbs, but in the end, we both agree that we're happy if either one of us take home the win at this tournament.

Pretty quickly, though, it becomes obvious that the game belongs to Jen and me. We sneak a couple past Ryan, then trick Maria into swinging at an out-of-bounds ball. Before long, we're finishing them off, 11-7. As we walk up to tap paddles, Ryan grins at me. "Look, I want to lose to the champs, okay? So you'd better bring home that gold."

We laugh it off. But there's something in the next look Jen shoots my direction, a fire that tells me she's taken his words to heart.

Our next game goes even better. 11-2. And the next is similar again. Every time we step off court for breaks between matches, there's a spark in the air, a heat that flares with every look we cast one another. After our fourth straight win, I catch Jen around the waist, pull her in close enough that only she'll hear me. "You are so hot, I could devour you right here, babygirl," I whisper.

She casts me a sly grin over one shoulder. "Promises, promises. Bring me a win and we'll talk, big boy." With that, she skips off to the sidelines, leaving me to take several deep breaths before I calm the blood racing southward enough to follow her.

You'd think the sexual tension would be distracting, but in reality, it's the opposite. The taut energy between us seems to spur us both on to bigger and better swings. We both hit banger after banger, until a decent sized crowd gathers around our match, chanting our names. Bashifer, Bashifer. Bash used to just be me, but lately, Jen's showing a pretty decent bashing arm too.

I try not to watch her too closely as she lunges for a return hit. But the arch of her arm is distracting, the graceful tension of the muscles in her calves—not to mention the flex of her ass. Fuck, my wife is sexy.

Thankfully, I'm able to pull my attention back to the game long enough to fire back a few shots of my own. We win our fifth game, then our sixth. Going into the seventh, the crowd around our court is bigger than ever. Word's gotten around, I guess, about our perfect streak. One more win and we'll be 7 and 0, with a shot at the medal stand.

I try not to think about that, as I draw Jen aside for a pre-match pep talk. "Remember June's rule?" I ask her softly. "We just have fun. That's all."

But Jennifer's answering smile is all fire and mischief. "Agreed," she murmurs. "We're gonna have fun cinching that gold." I laugh. She doesn't. Instead, she reaches up to snag my shirt in one fist. She drags me down and I have just enough time to brace myself on her hips, one hand on each, before our mouths collide.

Her tongue tastes hot and bittersweet, like adrenaline

and sweat and the perfume she likes to wear, mingled with the same soap brand she's used since we were young. The kind of taste a man could get addicted to. I slide my arms around her hips, one hand flattened against the small of her back, every muscle in my body screaming for more.

If we were alone right now, I would bend her right over that net in the center of the court. But we've got an audience, alas—as evidenced by the cheers that erupt when we pull apart, both of our chests heaving. We trade one last grin, then stride onto the court for our final match.

With every point we gain, my pulse ratchets higher. Soon we're up 4-2, then 6-2. They come back for a few rounds, bringing the score up to 6-4, but I don't even feel worried. Not with Jennifer beside me, as on her game as I've ever seen her. And not with all the confidence I've built up over the past months buoying me. From the sidelines, Ryan and Maria chant our names, along with a mob of people—some friends and acquaintances we've met at the clubhouse or other tournaments, others newcomers drawn by the crowd to watch what might be the most interesting match of this particular tournament.

The word comes down the grapevine at our next water break—most of the other matches have been played out already. The gold hinges on this match. We win, and it's ours.

Jennifer grins at me over a swig of her water bottle. "Atlanta, here we come, baby."

From her mouth to God's ear. We stride back onto the

court, lining ourselves up at the edge of the kitchen for our next serve. The volley goes long—our opponents are good, I've got to give that to them. Every time we send the ball their way, they knock it back over. But they've had a long day already—we both have. For some reason, though, the day has buoyed me and Jen's energy levels, whereas it seems to have drained our opponents'.

They miss one shot, then another. We pull ahead 8-4, then score a ninth point. Before we know it, it's game point.

I can taste everything we've been working for. Practically feel victory in my bones already. Jennifer serves this time, and I'm ready to back her up the moment they return it. We volley for what feels like eternity before I spot a gap in their movements, a weak point down the center line. The next time the ball comes my way, I send it straight there, the way June taught us with her dot shots.

It works. The crowd goes wild almost before Jen or I realize what's happened. And then it dawns on us, both at the same instant—we did it.

We're going to Atlanta.

Jen pumps her fist in the air. I don't wait for her to turn. I catch her shoulders, spin her around to face me, lifting her bodily into the air at the same time that my lips find hers. She laughs against my mouth, arms reaching up to latch around my neck for balance as we spin across the court.

The long press of her body against mine is in danger of making me too hard to stand on a medal podium, though, so

I'm forced to set her back on her feet, stepping far enough away to keep my wits about me.

We congratulate our opponents, who will almost certainly take silver, then head over for the medal presentation. The whole while, my hand lingers at Jen's hip, her waist, her lower back. Hers does the same, drifting to my thigh, my arm, the center of my back. I know we're both thinking the exact same thing.

But when I start toward our hotel room, Jen stops me, one hand around my wrist. "We should help clean up," she says, confusing me. Maybe we aren't thinking the same thing after all?

I frown, studying her backside as we both pick up towels to join the groups wiping down the courts outside. Jen moves slower than the others out here, though—a lot slower. I keep one eye on her and the rest of my attention on the others out here, lingering around the court.

Before long, we're the only people still left outside, as the sun drops toward the horizon in the distance, lighting the empty courts around us with a golden hue.

Jen catches my eye where she's holding the towel, one hip cocked, a fist resting on it, near the farthest court from the clubhouse. I walk toward her slowly, my pulse picking up. Surely she can't be thinking what I think she is…

But there's no mistaking the wicked glint in her eye when she grins at me. As I reach her, my eyebrows rise, a smirk creasing my mouth. "Someone's been having wicked thoughts, haven't they, babygirl?"

Her eyes flash. She reaches up to grasp the medal around her neck, but I catch her wrist, grinning. "Leave it on."

She leaves the gold medal in place, and doesn't protest when I turn her around, both of us facing the clubhouse, no doubt scanning for an audience. At the same time, I run my hands over her curves, her hips, the line of her ass. "God, you are so fucking sexy," I murmur, eyes trained on her gorgeous figure.

I cannot get enough of this woman, even after all these years. My hands itch for their favorite places, but I hold myself back, bask in watching her for now. Even that alone is making me hard, all the blood rushing straight from my head to my cock.

Jen must notice the pressure against the curve of her ass, even facing away from me, because she smirks and shifts her weight back against me. "Someone's eager, huh big boy?" Even through the fabric of her athletic shorts and my own, I can feel how soft she is, her thighs parting just where the hard jut of my cock rests.

"For you, babygirl?" I lower my voice to a husky whisper. "Always."

She catches my hands and folds them around her waist. No sign of movement from the clubhouse. Everyone's probably upstairs at the reception party, drinking and toasting to their various successes. But there's nowhere else I'd rather be than right here.

Jen runs my hands over the arches of her hips, down to the tops of her thighs. "My big strong Bash. You were incredible today." She lifts my hands up to her chest next, and I gently massage her, my fingers swirling around each of her areolae in turn, pressing just enough to make them harden through the fabric of her shirt.

"Nothing compared to you, firecracker." I pause in my ministrations to tweak the gold medal. Then, getting an idea, I pick up the medal itself and slip the cool metal underneath her shirt. I trail the gold along her stiff, hard nipples, one after the next. She gasps, her back arching, and I grin. "You like how that victory feels, baby?" Slowly, I reach up to slip the medal from around her neck, then trace it down her body, over the arch of her hips.

Jennifer groans and rolls against me, her ass grinding into my crotch hard enough to draw a guttural grunt out of me. My cock pulses, rock hard and trapped between her thighs, separated only by the thin fabric of both of our athletic shorts. "Oh, yes," she murmurs, hips wriggling side to side now, the motion making my cock jump again. "There he is..." She flashes me a sly, hooded look over her shoulder.

Unable to wait any longer, I grasp both of her hips in my fists and rotate sideways. We're standing in the middle of the court, right next to the net, which makes for a handy target. I bend her over it, pinning her beneath me. "Here I am," I reply, as I bend down to kiss the back of her neck, trace my tongue along the arch of her spine. She moans, breathy and hot, a soft surrendering sound that makes me—how is that possible?—even fucking harder.

As she does, I reach down to push off her shorts. She peels mine down at the same time, exposing my bare ass to anyone who might wander out onto these courts. I couldn't care less.

I whip her panties off next, shove them down around her ankles aside. Before I can touch her again, her hands find me, both of them, cupping the thick shaft of my cock.

"My big boy." Jennifer's eyes dart to mine, snag and hold my gaze, even bent double in this position. "Are you ready to take what's yours?" As she speaks, her hands stroke my length, from the base of my shaft to the tip and back. Her fingers trace the ridges of the veins expertly, wind around to grip the underside, along the seam.

I groan at the sensation of her soft fingers against my hard length. But two can play at this game. Reaching down, I flatten one palm against her mound, my fingertips searching lower, spreading her nether lips. I don't even have to press a fingertip inside her slit to feel the damp—she's practically gushing, wet and fragrant. My lips curl into a smirk. "Seems like someone's more than ready for me, aren't you, dirty girl?" I slide my fingertip lower, spread her lips and stroke along her slit. "Be honest. Have you been having naughty thoughts?"

She bites her lower lip, a motion that nearly kills me, it's so fucking hot. "All damn day, Bash. You drive me wild sometimes, you know that?"

"Not nearly as crazy as you make me," I murmur, gently pressing one finger inside her. Her pussy tightens around me at once, a hard clench that sends a fresh pulse of blood rushing southward. I curl my fingertip inside her, run the pad of my fingertip along her front inner wall, as I press deeper into her. "I am so addicted to you."

Jen winds a hand through my hair. "Bash…"

I slide my finger out, in, out again. "Go on, babygirl. Say my name again."

"Bash," she repeats, her voice quivering slightly on the vowel as I thrust inside her faster. She tries to keep moving her hands along my cock, but I add a second finger and she gets too distracted, her hips bucking. "Bash."

"Tell me what you want," I breathe, right against her neck.

"You," she gasps, and I grin.

"Hmm." I withdraw my fingertip, dripping with her juices. Eyes locked on hers, I lift it to my mouth and slowly lick it clean. Heat flares in her eyes, as she tracks the motion of my tongue. "What do you want me to do, exactly?"

Her chest heaves. At the same time, her hands tighten around my length. "I want you… inside me."

I reach down to gently peel her hands free. Using one hand, I pin them behind her back, her shoulders arched so her whole glorious body is spread beneath me, her plump ass just begging to be used as cushioning while I drive into her again and again.

"Fuck me," she gasps, and I can't hold myself back any

longer. Pressing into her feels like a live electric wire and sweet release all at the same time. Relief floods my body, because this, right here, with her, is what home feels like.

I wrap my fists around both of her hips, while she reaches down to brace herself against the net. I pull back, slow and sweet, savoring every inch of her pussy fisted around my thick steel shaft. As if reading my mind, she clenches, and I groan. "Just like that, dirty girl."

I thrust inside her again, until her ass lies flush against my crotch. She wriggles against me, moaning with pleasure, and I tense up, drawing back to thrust into her again until we're fucking with abandon. Maybe we should try to stay quiet, in case anyone else comes out to the courts. But we're too far gone for that. She screams my name as I reach down to stroke her clit, making her spasm underneath me with the force of her orgasm. I keep going, fucking her hard and fast, the wet slick noises driving me up a wall, until there's no more willpower left in my body.

I cum hard inside her, growling at the sensation, the sheer ecstasy she drives me to.

It's not enough. It never is. We barely make it back to our hotel room before we're on each other again, and I pin her against the door, trapping us both inside. By the time we check out the next morning, every muscle in our bodies screaming. But our hearts, for once, are at ease.

Chapter Twenty-Two

Jennifer

Even though we already have our ticket to Atlanta cinched, we still need to compete in one last tournament to make the full six. We sign up for the Pawley's Island tournament in October, a pretty island in South Carolina. The facility is right on the beach—not quite in view of the ocean, but close enough to hear the waves and taste salt on the breeze. The courts are nestled between heaps of sand dunes, twelve outdoor courts, six of which are covered in case of heat or rain. With the grassy knolls of sand on every side, we could be in some tropical paradise, if not for the hum of activity around the courts.

This tournament seems smaller than the last couple we've been to. Maybe only a hundred people. But it's kind of a nice break from the crowds and the noise. With less matches, we have more downtime to watch the other games and appreciate our potential competition in Atlanta.

The night before the tournament, we grab dinner at a beautiful little Italian restaurant in town, then stumble onto a live band playing at an outdoor venue—still possible in October this far south.

Since we don't need to place this time, we're free to enjoy ourselves, rather than staying laser focused on the gold. It leads to fun games, a lighthearted atmosphere that's partly us and partly all the other people we're meeting here. None of our usual friends came to this tournament, but we make new ones easily. Everyone seems so open and eager to make new acquaintances.

Well. Everyone except a certain duo. We haven't seen C+C Non-Music Factory since Asheville. They show up late, after missing an earlier match, and they don't even bother to apologize. They just stride right onto the court for their following match like nothing happened.

Luckily, we don't play them directly. I'd hate for something like that to sour our otherwise pleasant weekend.

Still, it's hard to ignore them entirely once they're here. They're loud, both with their snide comments masquerading as encouragement, and with their disdain as they sneer at other people's matches. Thankfully, due to their late arrival and the fact that they don't seem to be giving this tournament their usual all, they only wind up taking silver overall.

The gold medal goes to a local rock star duo, best friends who tell us they've been playing pickleball for years now at the Litchfield facility. We congratulate them on a well-deserved win, then hang around for post-tournament drinks, not ready to leave yet. This has to be our favorite location we've played so far, even after all of the other stunning locations.

Unfortunately, during the cocktail hour after the tournament, I lose Sebastian in the rush. As soon as I do, Chris of C+C makes a beeline in my direction. I spin around, hoping to evade him. He and I have never spoken one-on-one, and I have no desire to start now.

But he corners me before I make it more than a few steps, stepping into my path, a gin martini in one hand and the usual sneer on his face. "I hear you cinched yourselves a gold," he says, without bothering with pleasantries.

"We did." I raise my chin at that, look him dead in the eyes. I dare him to second-guess me or try to talk us down now. We've proved we can be every bit as good at this game as him and his worse half.

"Congratulations," he says, though his fake smile doesn't reach his eyes. "I actually wanted to pass along a warning."

My eyes narrow. "Thanks, but we know what we'll be getting into in Atlanta." I'm about to turn away, when he steps into my path once again, stopping me. Something about his expression throws me off—his brows are drawn tight, his mouth pinched. He looks... well, not sympathetic. But actually concerned, maybe. I have no idea about what. Is he actually threatened by us?

"It's not about Atlanta," he says, voice dropping an octave. "I felt like I should warn you about your son."

An electric shock jolts through my nervous system. "What the hell did you just say?" I spit, before I can stop myself. But then... fuck it. I let the anger that's been building all day—hell, all year, every time we run across these assholes—burst out of me. "How dare you talk about my children. You don't know me. You don't know the first damn thing about my family, either."

Chris raises both hands, spilling a little gin onto the floor as he does. "Never claimed to. Just trying to be neighborly. Your boy's name is Logan, right? I heard he's been running with a rough crowd lately, that's all. It's the sort of thing I'd want to know, if a friend overheard it."

My eyes flash. "We are not friends," I spit, fists balled. Hopefully that hides the way they're trembling. Because in the back of my mind, alarm bells are flashing. Logan. How does he know Logan's name? I tell myself it's nothing. That Chris just wants to get inside my head, and he's figured this will be the best way.

But deep down, I can't help wondering… what if there's some truth to what he's saying?

* * *

Back home, I ask Logan about how school's been going. His grades have been back up so far—not great, certainly not at the levels they used to be at the start of last year, but much better than the near-failing grades he ended last semester with. He's been coming home earlier too, except on the nights when he has lacrosse practice. We make him text us photos every afternoon from practice—something he complains about, but, as we pointed out, he's on the right path to earning our trust back. Just a little longer should do it.

There's nothing in his responses to indicate that I should

be worried. But I can't help it—Chris got inside my head. I feel like I need to keep digging. "Any new friends you've been hanging out with lately?" I ask.

Logan frowns at me over the kitchen table, where he's doing homework while I prep dinner. "Uh… not really? Why?"

"Just curious." And then, unable to get those words out of my head… "I just heard something, is all."

My son blinks at me. "Heard what?"

"That you started hanging out with some new people."

His frown deepens. "Who said that? Are you asking teachers about me?"

"No," I reply evenly. Then I arch an eyebrow. "Why, should I?"

He groans and pushes back from the counter. "I thought you said I was doing everything right. That you were going to start trusting me again soon."

I wince. "We did say that, honey—"

"So then why are you talking to random people about me? Why are you still making me send photos from practice every day?"

"Trust takes time to build."

"I spent the whole summer with you. That wasn't enough?" He grabs his homework and shoves it into his backpack. "Is this just what the rest of high school is gonna be like? I made one mistake and you're going to punish me for it forever?"

"You have to admit, it was a pretty big mistake," I say softly.

"And for the millionth time, I'm sorry. But I don't have

a time machine, so can you just lay off?" With that, he shoulders his bag and storms toward the staircase.

Groaning, I sink onto the stool where he was just sitting, burying my face in my hands. I can't help but feel like this is exactly what that asshole Chris wanted. To make me question my son, poke cracks in my family. Why would I take his word over my own child's?

Shaking myself, I shove back to my feet and circle back around to the oven. I'll apologize over dinner. And right there and then, I make a silent promise to myself: that's the last time I listen to anything C+C tell me.

Chapter Twenty-Three
Sebastian

Geraldine's next visit lines up perfectly with Atlanta. She arrives a few days before we need to leave, so she can visit with Jen and check out the spa, and then she'll hang out in town with the kids while we go to the tournament. I'm excited to see her, but also dreading the visit, because she still has not told Jennifer about the cancer.

The longer the secret drags on, the worse I feel about it. At night, lying in bed with Jen cradled in my arms, or in the mornings when she rolls over to kiss me awake, it hovers at the back of my mind, a constant reminder that as good as things feel between us right now, I'm not being fully honest with my wife.

And, of course, there's the worry for Geraldine herself. The sooner she begins treatment, the better her chances. I understand being afraid of what treatment will entail, or nervous about how her life will change, but ignoring the problem won't fix anything.

Geraldine helps us load up the Jeep as we get ready to leave. While we're doing that, Jen heads inside to pack some car snacks, and I draw Geraldine aside. It's my first chance to catch her alone since she arrived this trip. "You need to tell her," I say, my voice pitched low in case Jen comes out of the house.

Geraldine startles, then glances over my shoulder, no doubt worrying the same thing. "I said I would. And I will."

"When?" I grimace. I don't want to be unsympathetic, but I also don't want Geraldine to face this problem alone just because she's too stubborn to worry anyone else. "It's been months. Did you get any more test results yet? What have the doctors said?"

Geraldine avoids my eye. "I'm doing all the tests the doctors want me to, don't worry."

"Okay. But what do the results say?"

"Let me worry about that." She pats my arm.

I groan and shake her off. "Geraldine. Jennifer loves you. She will want to help you. Not just for your sake, but for hers too. And I can't keep lying to her like this. Please, you need to talk to her."

She bites her lip. Up close, there are new worry lines I didn't notice before around her mouth and accentuating her already deep crow's feet. Her eyes are bloodshot, baggy underneath. Clearly, she hasn't been sleeping well. "I know, Sebastian. I will. It's just complicated."

"What's complicated about the truth?"

Her eyes flash with sudden intensity. "The truth can hurt people. Jen's been through so much already, and this year has been so stressful for her. The last thing I want to do is add to her burdens—"

"Lying won't help anyone. Least of all Jennifer."

Geraldine's cheeks flush red. "It's not a lie. It's kindness.

I'm protecting her."

"You're coddling her. But Jen isn't a little girl anymore. She can handle this." I straighten, my expression shifting to a pensive one. "She's a hell of a lot stronger than you think." Stronger than I knew, too, though only because I wasn't paying attention properly.

Now I am.

Geraldine's expression softens. "When you get back," she says softly. "I'll tell her then. Is that good enough, Mr. Nosy?" She tries for a playful smile, but I keep my expression stern.

"You promise, this time?" I study her closely. She nods, apologetic now, and I relent, shaking my head. "Look, whatever the results say, we'll read them over and face them together, alright? As a family."

"What are you two whispering about?" interrupts a familiar voice, close enough to make us both leap apart guiltily, as though scalded. I whirl around to find Jennifer beside us, wearing a bright smile, two snack baggies tucked under one arm. She offers me one, head cocked, and glances at her mother.

Geraldine pats my shoulder, slightly harder than strictly necessary. "I was just warning this one to take good care of my little girl."

Jennifer snorts. "More like the other way around."

"That, too." Geraldine glances from Jen to me and back, her expression softening, turning nostalgic. "Take good care of each other. Both of you. Life can be a long, hard road, but with the right partner beside you, it's an adventure, too."

Jennifer frowns, shooting me a bemused look. "What's gotten into you? You sound like a fortune cookie all of a sudden."

"Someone's been watching too many Hallmark movies," I tease, reaching over to slam the trunk, after double-checking that we both have all of our pickleball gear stacked on top, where it won't get damaged if the Jeep jostles around on the highway.

Geraldine inhales sharply. It only sounds the tiniest bit stuffy. "That's right. With Christmas coming up, I've been binging way too many of those." She extends her arms for a hug, grabbing me first. Her arms squeeze me tight, and I can hear all the things she's silently communicating—keep quiet, I promise I will tell her soon. She lets me go, and then seizes Jennifer next. This hug looks, if anything, even more desperate.

Swallowing hard, I look away, my chest tight. I don't want to think about what it will mean, if her test results are bad. And they can't be good, right? Or she would have eagerly told me about them already.

We're not ready to lose her, I think. Especially not Jen.

But I can't concentrate on that right now, because Jennifer is breaking away from her mother's overly tight embrace, still smiling, but a little confused now, like she's not sure what's going on. I turn away, pulling out my phone to scan the traffic report, so she won't notice my expression. "Well, we should get going," I call, giving Geraldine one last wave.

"What was that all about?" Jen asks under her breath as

we climb into the Jeep and buckle up.

I take a deep breath, suppressing my frustration. I want to tell her. I wish I could. But Geraldine and I both have different promises to keep. "No idea," I say. "Can't be anything important, though."

She shrugs. "I suppose not." Then together, we pull out of the driveway. She leans over to switch on the radio, changing the subject, and my shoulders sag with no small amount of relief.

I find myself grateful for Atlanta for more reasons than one. At least it gives me a much-needed break from needing to focus on reality just yet.

* * *

If I thought the Orlando tournament was big, it has nothing on Atlanta. Fully eight hundred people are here, from all over the South. Everyone is competing for the same thing—those coveted golden tickets to Palm Springs, and a whole new league of pickleball.

"I can't believe we're actually here," Jen murmurs, as if reading my mind. She hooks one arm through mine as we explore the tournament grounds. The complex is nestled in an idyllic copse of trees, which have fully shifted into autumnal colors now—brilliant yellows, fiery reds and glowing oranges provide the perfect backdrop to the courts themselves. Rows upon rows of courts are lined up, some beneath temporary tents in case of weather, other exposed to the open air.

It's a beautiful day today. Crisp, with a hint of November chill, but not so cold that we're uncomfortable in our light jackets. The sun shines on the early players, warming up before the first round of matches begin.

We won't play until Sunday, the last day of the tournament. Usually, we'd arrive right before our games, but this time we wanted to experience the full tournament. Besides, it will give us some time to study the other games, examine the other players here, and make any last-minute changes to our own strategy before we have to play.

Jennifer frowns at the courts, nestling a little closer to my side as we watch a couple whip the ball back and forth at high speed. "What if we're not up to everyone else's level?" she murmurs. "This is only our first year playing; some people have been at this for ages already. What if—"

I silence her by leaning down to kiss her gently, a move that makes her chuckle, before she rises up on her toes and deepens the kiss. When we draw apart, I catch her eye, smiling. "We made it this far, which means we deserve to be here. Every bit as much as any of these other players." I gesture broadly at the courts, and she nods, turning back to squint at the ongoing games.

When she doesn't speak again, I exhale, resting my chin on top of her head. "Remember what June always says?"

"Just have fun," Jen says. She tips her head back, until I'm forced to lower mine and meet her gaze. "But winning is fun, too."

I laugh. "And that's exactly the spirit we need to be bringing into the tournament this Sunday. So you see?" I jostle her side, laughing. "We'll be fine."

Nodding slowly, Jen faces the field again. Pressed as close to my body as she is, I feel it when her muscles suddenly tense. "Shit. Don't look now."

"Where?" I ask, immediately disobeying that command. I crane my neck to follow her gaze, and she elbows my side, looking put out.

"I said don't look." Still, she inclines her head in the opposite direction I'd been looking. I keep my head facing another direction, and swivel my eyes around to peer from the corner of them.

Fuck. Immediately, I realize what she was looking at—or rather, who. C+C Non-Music Factory stride through the same doors we just entered, a veritable fan club trailing in their wake. They're dressed, as usual, to the nines—though I wonder how either of them can move, their expensive athleisurewear clings so tightly to every inch of their toned bodies.

Chris's nose wrinkles as he studies the tournament grounds. As for Crys, she barely even glances at the rest of the courts. She just tosses her hair and taps one of the people following them on the shoulder. The guy pulls out a camera—not a phone, but an expensive high-resolution lens contraption. Did she actually hire a photographer?

Forgetting Jen's advice, I openly gape at them now,

unable to tear my eyes away. To be fair, though, half of the rest of the attendees are doing the same, while Crys strikes her best influencer poses for the camera, not caring if the flashes distract the people playing their matches behind her.

"Unbelievable," Jen mutters. "After all her bitching about people so much as breathing around her when she's playing."

"Somehow, I'm not surprised," I reply, teeth gritted. Then I give myself a hard shake and turn away from the show. "Come on. Let's go find a spot to watch today's matches. Preferably far away from the Non-Music Factory crowd."

Jennifer snickers under her breath at our private nickname, then points with her chin across the courts. "I saw a refreshment stand over that way. Since we're not playing today…"

"Cheeky afternoon beer while we watch?" I finish for her, grinning.

She flashes me a smile. "You read my mind. But only a couple," she adds quickly. "We can't throw ourselves too far off our game."

"Definitely not," I agree, with one last sideways glance over at C+C. They've finished the photoshoot, and now they seem to be loudly offering pointers to the nearest duo playing their singles' match. From the looks on the players' faces, the input is very much not wanted. "We have a pair of tickets to win. Because I'll be damned if they're going to Palm Springs in our place."

Jennifer laughs. "That's the spirit. We'll win through sheer spite if we need to."

Chapter Twenty-Four

Jennifer

Some of the adrenaline of the tournament is wearing off as we get to our rooms. I've been having a ton of fun watching all the other matches today, but I can't deny that it's also wearing on me. I'm used to walking into a tournament, playing our games, and then being able to relax and watch how everyone else does. I'm not used to getting here early, and being the last to play.

It gives me way too much time to get into my own head.

I was expecting tough competition, but these players seem even more intense than those in any of the previous tournaments we've played in. We've only played a couple of warm-up matches before the actual tournament starts, and already, every muscle in my body feels ready to explode from anticipatory tension. At the same time, my head buzzes, unable to rest, because I'm anxiously composing every single possible play-through—every way our matches could go tomorrow.

It's like if I game-play out all the possible scenarios, I'll be able to prevent all the bad ones from happening. In reality, though, there's nothing I can do about tomorrow until we get there, and that fact alone is exhausting.

I collapse face-first onto the mattress of our bed—

surprisingly comfy for a hotel mattress. I make a mental note to thank the organizers for getting everyone to book this hotel in particular.

Sebastian is in the shower, steam pouring out from under the door. I shift my head to one side to watch it, too tired to even lift my chin off the mattress.

Something dings, loud and right next to my ear, making me startle. Groaning, I reach up to grab my phone and silence it, just as it dings again, louder and more insistently.

It's a mark of how tired I am that I don't process right away why my phone looks weird. The case feels the same— same shape and weight—but the background screen is all wrong. Mine's a photo of the four of us on the last Halloween that our kids let us dress them in a family costume, a million years ago. Sebastian and I are Morticia and Gomez Addams, while Mia's in a dark braided wig as Wednesday, and Logan is dressed as Pugsley, complete with a bodiless hand on his shoulder as Thing.

This screen, on the other hand, is a much more recent photo. It's the four of us at the Disney parks, posing in front of the Cinderella castle. Mia is rolling her eyes, while Logan strikes his usual ridiculous pose, tongue out, mouth open wide. I'm laughing, while Sebastian stares deadpan at the camera, as if to lament his ridiculous family.

I'm still staring at his expression, a smile tugging on my lips, when the phone dings again. I glance at the three most recent notifications, and frown, confused. They're all from my mother. I skim them in reverse chronological order.

Geraldine: And here's the last one. Inconclusive. So you can see why I don't want to say anything yet.

Geraldine: Bloodwork, which the doctor said looks okay, but that doesn't mean I'm in the clear.

Geraldine: As promised, I'm sharing my results. Here's the first test. Seems pretty certain that it is cancerous, and the prognosis for this type isn't good, but...

The text preview cuts off there. My pulse picks up, hammering at my throat, my temples. What the hell is this? Sitting up straight, my earlier exhaustion forgotten, I swipe open the screen. But, of course, it requests Sebastian's pin. I grimace, trying to remember it. For a while, we both had the same one—Mia's birthday—but Sebastian changed his a couple years ago. He's told me the new one a dozen times since, but my short-term memory isn't what it once was.

I try our wedding anniversary, then the anniversary of our first kiss. After attempting Logan's birthday, the phone warns me that any more tries and I'll be locked out.

I toss it onto the covers, both frustrated and terrified. Then, unable to let it lie, I snatch it back up and skim the texts again.

Cancerous. Prognosis. Inconclusive.

My temples pound, joining in the angry protest. Why would she send these to him? Maybe she sent them to both of us? Dropping his phone, I launch myself across the room to the spot where I dropped my bag the minute we got back to the hotel. I root through it until I find my phone, and turn it back on. I had it off for the tournament, just in case anyone called. I didn't want to disrupt anybody's game—God forbid someone like Crys claim I was attempting to sabotage them, for example.

It takes a minute to power up, during which I pace around the hotel room in circles, those words wearing the same holes into my brain. Cancerous. Prognosis. Inconclusive.

Finally, my phone turns on. I scan through the recent texts—nothing. Then I check my voicemail. Also nothing. Just for shits and giggles, I check my email too, even though the last time my mother sent me an email she needed the librarian at her local branch to help her do it right.

Nothing, again.

I drop back onto the bed heavily, losing all control over my legs. Cancer. Does my mother have cancer? If so, why didn't she tell me? How long has this been going on?

My gaze drifts to his phone again, a fist tightening inside my chest where my heart ought to be. There's no preface to those text messages. No by the way, I might have cancer. Whatever my mother is texting Sebastian, he already knew about.

He knew, and he hid it from me.

The scene outside of our house as we were leaving returns to me in full force. I knew Mom was acting funny. Her and Sebastian were talking about something, and they both jumped when I interrupted. I asked him about it and he said he didn't know, so I thought nothing of it. But now...

White hot fury seizes me, just as the shower squeaks off. I raise my gaze, scowling at the door. A minute later, Sebastian emerges, towel around his waist. "—hope we get to watch a few of the games tomorrow," he's saying. "Did you see that one guy from Raleigh with the…" He trails off, finally registering the expression on my face.

I grab his phone and thrust it at him. "Care to explain this?"

His brow furrows. "My phone?" But he takes a step forward, accepting it. One glance, and I can see the moment it registers. He tenses, inhaling quickly, and then just as quickly tries to smooth his expression, contorting it into one of false surprise. "Oh. Your mother texted me?"

"I noticed." My voice comes out flat, emotionless. "What's going on, Sebastian?"

He opens the phone, skims the messages. With each one, his frown deepens. "I-I don't know. It seems like… um…"

"Do not bullshit me," I say, hardening my jaw. "She's sick, obviously. How long have you known? More importantly, how long have you been keeping this from me?" Did she tell him earlier this visit? Maybe he didn't want her to tell me because of the tournament—because he thought it would throw me off my game.

Well, I'm certainly off it now.

"I wanted to tell you," he says, voice much softer now. "But your mother asked me not to, and I couldn't betray her confidence—"

"Not even to be honest with your wife?" I interject, fury

swelling my chest, making it hard to see straight. I storm forward, practically vibrating with anger. After everything we've been through—all the progress I thought we were making this year. We'd come so far in trusting one another, in communicating. And all the while, he was lying to me. "How long have you known?" I repeat, louder now.

"Only a few months," he says, pleading.

I freeze, shocked all over again. I'd expected him to say a few days. "Months? How sick is she? Why is she hiding it? Give me the results." I make a grab for the phone, but he moves it behind his back.

"We should talk about this after we've both calmed down."

"Don't you dare tell me to calm down." My eyes flash, fists clenching at my sides. When I speak again, my voice breaks, an unexpected sting hitting the backs of my eyes. "I thought we were a team." With that, I brush past him, starting for the door.

"Jennifer, wait!"

I slam it after me, viciously pleased by how the sound echoes in the empty hallway. I storm up the hall, not sure where I'm headed or why. At the same time, I pull my phone from my pocket and dial my mother's number.

It rings twice, then goes to voicemail. I try again—straight to voicemail this time. Great. Now she's screening my calls. Anger swells all over again—at him, but also at her. Why would she tell Sebastian and not me? Doesn't she trust me? Doesn't she want me to help her?

All at once, I realize what's really behind all this fury. I stop dead in the middle of the hallway, hunching over my midsection as tears pour down my cheeks.

I'm afraid.

I can't lose her. Not yet. I'm not ready. Losing my father was hard enough, but Mom… she's been such a stalwart presence in my life—in all of our lives. She's supposed to be here to keep watching Mia and Logan grow up. We're supposed to find her a scenic cottage near our house to buy in her old age, so she'll be within easy walking distance of us. She's supposed to torment us with chores and to-do lists as she gets older, just like my grandmother once did to her.

I don't know how long I remain frozen there, tears streaming, in the middle of the hotel hallway, before a soft, warm hand comes to rest in between my shoulder blades. "Jennifer."

I don't move. Don't make a sound except for a sharp inhale, which comes out much snifflier than I'd like.

"I'm sorry," Sebastian says softly. "I never meant to hurt you. Neither did your mom—that's why she didn't want to tell you about this. I tried to tell her that was the wrong decision, but…"

I take another deep breath, somewhat less shaky. "Was it… did you not want to tell me because of the tournament?"

For a moment, he doesn't reply. The silence stretches on long enough to make me look up, straight at Sebastian's wounded expression. "Jennifer." He takes my hands, squeezing tight. "How could you ask me that?"

"Well…" I swallow hard. Lower my gaze to our joined hands. "I mean, this all seems so important to you. And I've enjoyed it, too, it's really helped our relationship, but…" I squeeze my eyes shut, embarrassed to feel a tear slip out and track down my cheek. "I don't know. I can't help but think, if we didn't have pickleball in our lives, would this… would we still work? Or…"

Sebastian's warm hand cups my cheek. His thumb swipes the tear away, then keeps tracing along my cheekbone, to the edge of my jaw. "You matter more to me than any game. Any tournament." His hand drops, and he jostles my hands until I open my eyes again, raising my gaze to meet his. "If you want to leave, tell me. We'll go pack right now."

I study his expression. Look deep into those familiar, handsome brown eyes. "You mean it?"

He flinches. Barely perceptible, but it's there—a slight tightening around his eyes, a pressure at his mouth. But then he nods, and drops my hands to turn back to the hotel room. "Come on. Let's get our things."

I watch him go, heart rising into my throat. "Wait."

I don't know what I want right now. For none of this to have happened? For my mother not to be sick, and my husband not to have known and concealed it from me. But I don't want to just give up, either. Not after all the hard work we've put in to get here. I swallow again, harder this time, around the lump that's formed solid in the middle of my throat. "I don't want to go home. Not yet," I clarify.

Sebastian studies me closely, his brow creased. "Are you sure? Because it's no problem, Jen. There will always be other tournaments, other years. But right now…"

I lift my chin and ball my fists. "Right now, we have a pair of tickets to win," I say. "Whatever else is going on, it'll keep for a couple of days."

He nods solemnly, gaze fixed on mine. "It's your call."

"I know," I reply. "And I've made it."

Chapter Twenty-Five
Sebastian

Neither of us sleep well that night, which is exactly what we don't need going into this tournament. Jen tosses and turns beside me all evening, and I lie on my back, gaze fixed on the ceiling, running through every one of the tests Geraldine texted me.

She's right: it doesn't look good. The doctors have a couple of treatments they'd like to try, but honestly, she should have started them months ago. All this procrastinating will only lower her chances at beating this thing. With every passing day, the clock keeps ticking, and Geraldine remains frozen, indecisive.

I finally drop off sometime around three, but my dreams are restless too. They're filled with all the usual anxiety markers—teeth falling out, missing the winning shot in a college soccer game, waking up and forgetting I'm still in high school and I have a huge test today, one I didn't study for.

It's funny, how we revert to younger versions of ourselves whenever we're stressed out or anxious about something. Like teenage Sebastian never totally grew up—he just learned how to disguise himself as an adult.

When our alarms go off bright and early, we both wake up cursing. "I feel like I just got run over by a truck," Jen mutters on her way into the bathroom.

"At least you look great," I try, but that only earns me a middle finger before she shuts the door and turns on the shower.

I roll back over on the bed, staring at the ceiling once more. This is the worst possible headspace for us right now. We'll need to be at the top of our game today—communicating perfectly, reading one another's minds on the court. Instead, we feel like two halves that have just been forcibly pulled apart.

All through our morning routine, we dance around one another, hesitant, uncertain. Before we head out the door to our first match, however, I stop her. "Are we okay?" I ask gently.

She holds my gaze, unflinching. "Not completely. But we will be."

A small smile touches the corner of my mouth, and she answers with one of her own. A year ago, she would've just said yes. We would've just told each other whatever we wanted to hear. But this sign of confidence—the honesty— buoys my spirits. "Alright. Love you."

"Love you, too." Her smile widens. "Now let's go kick some ass."

We both laugh. And I realize she's right. We have a lot to work through, but in the end, we're going to be okay.

* * *

Thankfully, C+C Non-Music Factory aren't in our bracket. We find that out when they hand out the list of the matches we'll be playing. We don't recognize any of the names on the list, but given the size of this tournament—and the caliber of all the players in it—that's not surprising.

As we step onto the court for our first match at 10AM sharp, breakfast churns in my gut. "Remember," I call to Jennifer, before we greet the other team to determine who will serve first. "Just have fun."

"Right." She winks. "Have fun winning."

I'd been worried about all the pressure getting to us. Not to mention our lack of sleep last night, and the argument looming over our heads. But if anything, all that added adrenaline seems to help. The other team wins the first serve, but the moment they send the ball over the net, my fuzzy head clears.

"Yours," I call, because it's headed straight for Jen. She's already on it, volleying the ball back over the net, and we fall into our familiar stances. "Mine," I tell her at the next one, just to keep up the consistent flow of communication.

We move like that for the next few rounds, in easy synchronicity. A few points slip through our fingers, but for the most part, we lead the game. It's 6-4, then 7-5, then 8-6. Around the seventh point, we begin to pull more decisively ahead—scoring several in a row, until we hover at 10-7, closing in on the win.

Jen flashes me a confident smile before her last serve.

And she's right to be confident. The ball sails off her paddle and over the net, and the moment it comes back to her, she's right there to catch it again. We send volley after volley back, until finally she sneaks one past our opponent in the right service area.

The other team groans as we cheer and slap palms.

One down, six more matches to go.

Matches two and three go even faster. If we thought the other tournaments were difficult, the competition there was nothing compared to this. Everyone here in Atlanta is at the top of their games. Some of the players I recognize from videos June showed us back when we were still learning, when we never dreamed we would ever compete at this level.

Part of me can't believe we're playing among these people. But another part of me—the competitive part from college that never quite died—knows we've earned it. Jen and I have worked so hard this year, not just on our game, but on us. We've learned how to communicate better, how to read one another's bodies—and appreciate them again.

Even with our argument last night—a year ago, a fight like that would've thrown us out of whack for weeks. We would've tiptoed around one another, neither of us wanting to admit wrongdoing or back down, both of us wanting to work past the problem but neither quite sure how to even approach it.

Now, even though we haven't resolved the issue, we know how to communicate. We've discussed what we need to do, and both of us trust each other enough to know we will figure it out, one way or another.

I suppose at the end of the day, that's all you can really ask for in a partner: someone who's willing to figure out the solution to all of your problems, together. Even when we don't agree, or when both of us need to take different approaches, we understand intrinsically now that we're on the same team.

Hopefully that team spirit will carry us through our toughest challenge yet, right here on this court. Because as the day progresses, and our morning matches bleed into the afternoon ones, the going only gets tougher.

We're standing at four wins and three games left to play when we hit our first stumble. Match five, against a pair from South Carolina with a wicked backhand game. For the first time all day, we start to fall behind—they pull ahead 5-4, then 6-4.

We pause for a water break, and I draw Jen aside. "He seems like he's stronger on his backhand than his forehand, for some reason," I murmur.

She nods, squinting back at the court. "And I've been watching; she keeps neglecting that back corner, near the baseline."

We trade smiles and nod at each other. We have our game plan now.

Back on the court, we seize control of the ball, slowing down our return hits, just the way June taught us. You don't win every game with bangers, as she likes to say. Once the ball is within our control, we both start to aim for that rear corner Jen spotted, making sure to hit it whenever the guy on our opposing team is distracted or too far out to help.

We sneak one past them to regain the serve, and then manage another one to bring the score up to 5-6. Before long, we've tied it, and then we're back on top again, playing tighter than ever.

They steal control back and gain again, but once we've figured out our play, we're unstoppable. We finish the game 11-9, grinning as we tap paddles and compliment our opponents. They fought like hell, I'll give them that.

Going into game six, the energy on the court is palpable. By this time of day, several other matches have already finished, so ours is attracting a crowd. A couple people at first, then a couple dozen. I try my best to tune them out— even the supportive cheers can be distracting when you need to concentrate.

Still, it's heartening to hear a couple people pick up the familiar call. Bashifer, Bashifer! There must be some players from the other tournaments we played in here. I stifle a grin as Jen flashes me a wink.

Neither of us check the other courts, or the overall standings. I'd rather not know how close we are to the medal podium until we're in tasting distance. Otherwise, it will just throw me out of the game and into my head.

Our game six opponents put up the toughest fight yet. We wind up with a score of 11-10 us, which means we have to go into overtime, because you need to win by at least two points. We eke out another point, winning 12-10, amid cheers from the gathering crowd.

One last game. The winner of this one will determine the winner of our overall bracket. I'm pretty sure if we cinch this, we'll take the lead, but I don't want to jinx us.

We toast our water bottles courtside as we prepare ourselves for this final match. "Here's to having fun," Jen says, raising her water bottle. "Whatever happens... I'm glad we're here."

I laugh and clink mine against hers. "Nobody else I'd rather do this with."

Back on the court, we size up our opponents. He's tall, with a long reach and an athletic stance. His partner is a bit shorter, but from the way she bounces on the balls of her feet, she seems quick and eager.

My initial assessment proves correct, once we start to play. She's fast, and he's like a brick wall, nearly impossible to get around. But we didn't come all this way for nothing.

They start out ahead, 1-0. We tie, they inch ahead again. And so on, and so on, until we're hovering around 6-5 with them in the lead. But opposition has always motivated us, competition even more so. Jen and I feed off one another's energy, calling out shots, seamlessly returning the ball from her area and mine. Wherever we need to be, we're already there five steps ahead of ourselves.

Before long, we tie it 6-6, and this time, we're the ones

to pull ahead. 7-6 now. Our opponents tie it, and we inch ahead again, until we're both hovering at 9-9. Jen gives me what's become our signal of the tournament—a determined nod, both of our jaws set, ready for action. Then I serve one, spinning sideways, a tricky angle to hit. They manage to return it, but wildly, and Jen takes full advantage of that, sending it right back over on a tricky backhand.

They return this one even less confidently, and I snap it back to them, sneaking it under their guard. 10-9. Game point. More people have joined the crowd around us—from murmurs, I catch the drift that the other bracket has already finished. Since there are so many people here at Atlanta, the tournament is structured so that after the round robin eliminations—where all teams play at least eight games—the top winners of each bracket face off against one another in a best of three.

This match will determine whether we go to that finals round. And we're so close I can already taste it.

Then I overhear someone mention the name Chris. I don't even know which one they're talking about, but a sinking sensation hits my gut. I'd bet anything I already know who won the other bracket.

That's a later problem. Focus on now, I remind myself, just as our opponents line up a serve.

Jen returns it, and then the ball flies at me. It's high, but that's the perfect setup for a Bash special. I return it with a slam, and it rockets down the center of their court. One of them nearly gets a paddle on it, but instead, they just tip the ball out of bounds, sailing free.

Then it's our serve. I give as good as we've gotten, a tricky serve they strain to return. Jen answers them, and the ball comes my way again. I fire it back, but they lunge just in time to return it. Doesn't matter. Jen is way ahead of them. She flips the ball over the net, real close, and they have no chance. One of them fully dives for it, knees skidding on the asphalt, but it's too late. The ball dribbles twice, and that's it.

Game point. Match to us.

Jen screams and launches herself at me. I catch her in a bear hug, swinging her up off her feet and around in a circle. The crowd around us goes wild too, and for a moment, all I can hear is the roar, the chanting. More people have caught on to our nickname, and it echoes from the rafters. "Bashifer, Bashifer!"

I place Jen back on her feet, grabbing her wrist, and raise it up over both our heads. The crowd roars in response.

We step off the court, wiping our foreheads, only to freeze. Sure enough, just as I'd feared, the winners of the other bracket stand nearby, surrounded by their own little fan club. Chris looks like a Greek god, posing with one fist on his hip as he tosses back a mouthful of electrolytes. Crys, on the other hand, looks like a model—or at least, a wannabe model. She poses with one leg up on a bench, calves flexed, and pretends to not be paying attention while a photographer snaps images of her.

"You've got to be kidding me," Jennifer murmurs under her breath.

I exhale hard through my nose. "Of course. Who else would we need to fight for those tickets?"

Chapter Twenty-Six
Sebastian

As an announcer calls out the next steps of the tournament, we glance past C+C Non-Music Factory, over the heads of the crowd to the distant billboard at the head of the tournament grounds. A pair of stylized golden tickets are emblazoned on the sign like a taunt.

We're so damn close. I refuse to let these assholes, of all people, snatch victory away now. "Just one last series," I say softly. We know the format: us against C+C, best of three games. "We only need two wins. We can do that."

No doubt both of our minds go to the same place. To the last time we played C+C, when we only managed to eke out a single win to their two trouncing victories.

Jennifer bites her lip, and I rest a hand on her shoulder, lowering my voice still further. "Last time we played them was a long time ago. We're better now. A whole different team than we were back then."

The uncertain little frown remains etched into her forehead, but she nods slowly. "You're right. We've got this."

There's a short break for both of us to recover before the finale begins. During it, workers come out to prep the court where we'll be playing, while other employees of the club set up makeshift chairs along all the other courts, creating space for all the other players to watch this showdown.

I catch more than a few people shooting us commiserating glances. I'm not sure whether that should buoy my spirits or sink them further. Everyone knows C+C are good. I've no doubt they've also experienced some of the fuckery C+C Non-Music Factory are notorious for in these circuits.

But can we beat them? That's the question, at the end of the day. One that nobody—least of all us—knows the answer to… yet.

Chris and Crys spend the break peacocking as per usual. At one point, Jen nudges my side. "Don't look now, but they're actually offering to sign autographs for people."

I snort. "Any takers?"

She peers around my shoulder and wrinkles her nose. "A few, alas."

We trade another eyeroll, but it doesn't quell either of our nerves any. When it's time for the first match to begin, we both stride onto the court with our shoulders back and heads held high, despite the absolute haywire going on internally.

I want this more than I can put into words. It's not even about Palm Springs anymore, or those tickets. It's about proving to ourselves that this whole journey has been a success. It's about showing each other that we've both learned from this, and grown, and improved more than just our pickleball game.

This game is about us, as much as it's about vanquishing

our nemeses. And that makes the stakes sky-high, for me.

Several hundred people cluster around our court—a bigger audience than we've ever had for any one game before. It feels like all 796 other people at this tournament have gathered here to watch us either sink or swim.

Across the net, Crys shoots us a vicious sneer, disguised as a sugar-sweet smile. Chris doesn't even bother—he just narrows his eyes, sizing up me and then Jennifer, upper lip curled back. Their fan club spreads out at their back, a couple dozen other dyed-blonds in expensive-looking gear. They squint critically at the field, shooting disdainful glances toward our side of the court.

As for the people clustered behind us...

"Bashifer, Bashifer!" Someone takes up the chant again, and several dozen more people join in, until it feels like half the audience is chanting.

I stifle a grin. Chris and Crys might have the elites, but we've got numbers on our side.

Crys gets the first serve, which she accepts with a disdainful little sniff. As she lines up on her usual side of the court, opposite Jen in their left service area, she narrows her eyes at us both. "Could you tell your fan club to tone it down?" she calls. "Some of us need to concentrate here."

The yelling does die down, though it's no thanks to me. Someone nearer to Crys must have passed the word along, because a hush falls over the crowd.

Crys lifts the ball. "Zero, zero, two," she says, her tone

clipped and precise, like someone who would rather be anywhere else. Then she tosses it up and swings.

For all of my pent-up nerves coming into this, it's almost a relief when the actual match begins. There's no more wondering how it will go or anticipating all of the ways we might fumble. Instead there's just here and now, the actual doing.

The first volley winds up sneaking past me and Jen. 1-0-2 as Crys serves again.

"It's okay," I call to Jen, not caring who else hears. "It's just one point. Don't let it throw you."

Then another one slips by. And another. 3-0-2, and we haven't even won the serve back yet. Finally, I manage to sneak one under Chris's guard, and we get our first chance. I serve, 0-3-2, and after an interminably long volley that has both of my feet aching already, Jen manages to hit one in the far corner, just outside Crys's reach. It's with some satisfaction that I serve the next ball.

"One, three, two," I call and swing my paddle. From there, we creep back up to 2-3, and then 3-3. Determined not to be outdone, Chris slams one past me, and regains his serve. They gain another point, and then another. 5-3. But even if we go down, it won't be without a fight.

We come back, then tie it at five. But we've barely gotten to celebrate that win, when Crys puts one into Jen's far corner, and Jen misses by centimeters.

The crowd remains silent, though whether it's at Crys's

behest, or just because everyone is so intent on studying this game, I don't know. It's a nail-biter for sure. We tie it again, and they pull ahead once more. Before we know it, they're ahead at 9-8, then 10-8.

"Ignore the score," I tell Jen. "Just focus on enjoying ourselves. Right?"

"Right," she answers. Though judging by her gritted teeth, I'm not entirely sure she's hearing me.

Still, we manage to win back the serve, and then sneak another point in. 10-9 now. They're on the verge of a game point, but if we can get one more, tie it up, then we'll go into overtime and we could pull ahead.

We lose the serve, and I reach over to clasp Jen's shoulder briefly. "We're not giving up."

She flashes me a brief, hard grin. "Never."

But the next ball sails right between us, after an embarrassingly short volley. We both groan, as the announcement comes through. 11-9. First match goes to Chris and Crys.

My stomach sinks. C+C Non-Music Factory's fan club goes wild. As for our half—or slightly more than half—of the stadium, everyone goes silent. Someone in the distance even boos, which surprises a laugh out of me. "It's not over yet," I murmur.

Jen shakes her head. "That was the warmup. Now we really show 'em what we're made of."

We stretch and shake our legs out, fueling with some

water before we head back onto the asphalt. I bounce on my toes experimentally, testing it. Beside me, Jen goes through her usual pre-game motions: stretching her arms, her torso, then swaying side-to-side. It's a series she learned from one of the massage specialists at her spa, and she insists it helps her game by relaxing her, getting her into the right mindset.

I do my best to imitate her lead, hoping for the same. We need clearer heads going forward, if we want to turn this one around.

But game two starts out even rockier than game one. Chris fires a hard shot right past me, and then Crys sneaks one by Jennifer too. We muscle our way back into the running, but they race ahead again, both of us neck and neck, until we're trailing 7-6.

The crowd around us is growing antsy. I hear more chants mixed in with the Bashifer so many have been shouting all match. Now more "Chris, Chris, Chris" chants take over from their side. Crys tosses her hair with a smug smile, giving her fans one of those pearl-touching waves like she's a British monarch.

As for Chris, his lip curls as he prepares for his next serve. "Don't worry," he calls across the net to us. "We'll go easy on you."

I grind my molars. Beside me, Jen purses her lips. "Ignore him," she mutters under her breath. "They just want to get under our skin."

Crys must really have supersonic hearing, because she

leans closer suddenly, calling over the net. "Remind me to talk to you both about my sunscreen line later. All this outdoor activity has not been friendly to your skin, I must say. Those burns have got to be distracting."

The only burn here is the one we're about to put on the two of them. But I bite my tongue, refusing to stoop to their level with a comeback. The only thing that matters is the game. Nothing more.

Chris serves, and I send it back easily. Crys picks it up, and Jen answers her. Back and forth we go, our volleys getting harder and faster each time. Jen and I communicate easily, almost without thinking about it. But I notice that Chris and Crys take their spaces for granted. They don't speak much, unless the ball is right down the center line. That interests me.

The next shot, I send just off center, slightly on Crys's side. She gets the edge of her paddle on it, but not fast enough. It goes wide, and beside her, Chris curses.

"The hell was that?" he barks, as someone in the crowd catches the ball and passes it to me. Our serve now.

"Like you were any help," Crys snaps back, and a few mutters pass through the onlookers.

I resist the urge to grin at Jen. This is what we need. We just have to find the cracks. I serve, and we fall back into position. Jen's and my confidence grows as their sinks. Soon we're climbing again, with C+C playing catch-up instead. We get ahead 8-7, then 9-8. But at our next water break,

Non-Music Factory pauses for a conference. When they return, they must have ironed out some of the kinks in their discrepancies, because they're on fire again. They tie it up at 9-9, then sneak ahead. 10-9.

Game point.

No way we're going down like this. The next volley seems interminable. For every fiery shot we send over the net, they have a retort. The balls of my feet throb, and my hand aches where I clutch the paddle. The entire day worth of matches is catching up to me, and beside me, I sense Jen flagging too.

Meanwhile, across the net, Chris and Crys get cockier with every shot. They seem to flounce across the court, rather than running. It's like they're showing off now, peacocking for their fan base in anticipation of the win. Crys keeps shooting flirty little winks at the crowd near their side of the net, and Chris barks out a laugh every time Jen lunges for the ball, like he's trying on purpose to distract her.

It pisses me off.

My next overhead shot I catch, I return with a wicked hard slam, right at Chris's feet, for a side out. The majority of the crowd goes wild, while his lip curls again. Beside him, Crys snaps something that makes his face flush. The two of them bicker, voices pitched low, while I pass the ball to Jen for her serve.

She winks at me. "Nine, ten, one," she calls, and serves.

This volley, if anything, is even more frantic than the

previous ones. But Crys's movements are sharp and irritated now, and Chris keeps lunging for balls he doesn't need to try that hard to reach. They're getting anxious, whether they'll admit it or not. I sneak one past Crys, and the crowd goes wild as we tie the match. 10-10.

On Jen's next serve, Chris makes an uncharacteristic mistake. It was an easy return shot, but he aims too low. The ball hits the net for an unforced error, and suddenly, we're ahead.

The entire audience goes wild. Even a few people on the Non-Music Factory side of the net snicker behind their hands, casting one another sly looks. "What the hell was that?" Crys snaps.

"Oh, like you haven't missed a shot before," Chris calls back. "Two games ago—"

"Two games ago didn't matter," she hisses.

To judge by the tension around Jen's mouth, she's trying hard not to snicker. We line up on the baseline, and Jennifer calls out, in a perfectly even voice, "Eleven, ten, one." Game point, if we can sink it. The atmosphere goes tense around us, people holding their breaths in anticipation.

Jen serves, and holy shit. It's her best of the day, a deep shot on Crys's backhand side. Crys lunges for it anyway, managing to get her paddle on it barely. It sails back in our direction, but too high, too fast.

"Let it go," I say, both Jen and I watching it go. Sure enough, it lands a foot past the baseline, and the entire crowd goes wild. Jen whoops and leaps at me, and I catch her, spinning her in a wide circle. Twelve points—we win.

Now for the tiebreaker. Setting Jen back on her feet, we pause for a long, searing kiss. That earns us a few whoops from the onlookers, and I hear Chris mutter, "Case in point."

"Oh, step off," his wife replies stiffly.

As the next game begins, our spirits remain high. Jennifer and I keep up a constant stream of communication, commiserating anytime we miss and uniting anytime we succeed. Chris and Crys don't fully choke—they keep up with us, the game neck and neck the whole way through. First we're ahead, 3-2, then they pull in front 4-3, then we catch up and surpass them again. Back and forth we go, yo-yoing with the lead.

But the whole time, Chris and Crys snipe at one another. Anytime one or the other messes up, the other goes in on them. Chris misses a shot and Crys nearly bites his head off. Then Crys hits one out of bounds, and Chris actually screams in frustration.

So it's not really surprising when we pull ahead at the tail end, 10-9. It's my serve, and it's all I can do not to grin as I send a rocket over the net.

Chris gets his paddle on it for a backhand return. Jen answers, and Crys flicks it back, her lips pursed, her hair falling out of its usual neat ponytail to tangle around her face.

Then a volley comes flying at us that nearly stops my heart. It's aimed for Jen's side, a searing shot on her lefthand side. But just when I think there's no way she can possible return this, Jen tosses her paddle into her off-hand, and fires a lefthanded bullet shot straight down the line toward Crys.

My jaw nearly hits the asphalt. The whole crowd goes silent as the ball flies. To her credit, Crys does her all. She scrambles backward, paddle high, and manages to tip the ball. But it's not enough. The ball flies off at an odd angle, missing the net and the boundary. It cracks onto the asphalt, and there's a beat of dead silence before the whole place erupts.

I shout, not quite believing my own eyes. Jen does too, whipping around with tears in her eyes. I reach for her, but before I get there, shouts break through the general din.

We glance across the net to see Crys throw her paddle down, so hard it cracks. Beside her, Chris is yelling, and Crys storms up into his face, shouting right back. "My fault?" she bellows. "If you weren't such a loser, we would've had them five points ago."

"Oh really? You wouldn't have choked yet again?" he scoffs.

Jen tugs my arm until I face her. Then she reaches up to cup my cheek and draws me down to her level, pressing her lips to mine. I sink into her kiss, and all the cheers and shouts fade into background. When we break apart, I cradle her face between my palms. "We did it," I whisper, mouths inches apart.

She tips forward, stealing another light kiss, eyes bright with mischief. "Palm Springs, here we come."

Chapter Twenty-Seven

Jennifer

The post-tournament celebrations last well into the wee hours. We stay for one drink each, but even watching C+C Non-Music Factory implode, both snapping at each other and storming away in opposite directions, doesn't feel quite celebratory enough. The party's still going strong when Sebastian leans into my side, his breath searing hot against my neck. "How about we play hooky and go for a ride?"

I grin, turning to meet him, my lips catching the edge of his jawline. "You read my mind."

We leave our half-finished cocktails on a side table and abscond out the door. If anyone notices the triumphant victors slipping away, they don't comment. My mind is all over the place—reliving that final shot, the absolute high of vanquishing our nemeses once and for all; daydreaming about Palm Springs and the national level tournament— but the moment we exit the hotel complex into the cool November night air, everything else falls away. It's just me and Sebastian, on our own private team.

He drives aimlessly at first, until we notice signs for one of the big state parks outside the city. Then I notice him shifting in that direction, a smile playing around the edges of his mouth.

I reach over to graze a fingertip along his cheekbone. "What are you plotting?"

The smile widens. "You'll see." He reaches out, palm up, to take my hand. On the radio, one of our favorite songs plays, and we both croon along—me in tune, and Sebastian very much not. We dissolve into laughter, rolling down the windows. For November, the weather isn't bad—crisp, but not cold yet. Just enough of a bite in the air to refresh you, without overwhelming you yet.

After a while, we turn off the highway and onto a smaller road. From there, we weave onto smaller and smaller streets, until we're trundling along a gravel road under arching canopies of trees.

"Where are we?" I ask, my voice hushed. Something about the remote area and the wilderness outside makes me feel like I should keep quiet.

Sebastian grins. "I came here with some friends after a game in college. After we won the regional championships."

"I remember that," I say. He and I had only just started dating. "I wanted to go to the game, but I was so swamped with homework and mid-terms coming up, I couldn't make a whole trip like that work."

"I know." Sebastian glances over at me, eyes bright in the dim night air. "The whole time, I kept wishing you were there."

My chest tightens unexpectedly. "Can you believe how long it's been?"

"Hell no." He turns off the gravel onto a packed earth area, clearly made for parking. He pulls into a spot, shuts the Jeep, and turns to face me. "But I wouldn't trade a minute of it." He holds my gaze just long enough to make my heart skip, and I'm so grateful for that—for the fact that after all this time, he still has such an effect on me.

I feel my body tipping forward, leaning into his gravity. But for some reason, the moment I do, Sebastian leans back.

"Hold that thought," he murmurs. Then he pops the door and steps out of the Jeep. For a moment, I just stare, unsure if he wants me to follow him outside. But when I realize what he's doing, I laugh and undo my belt to help.

Together, we roll back the top of the Jeep, folding it up and opening the whole car to the clear night sky. Instead of getting back into the front seat, Sebastian opens the door to the backseat and climbs inside, tilting the seats back to give us both the best view.

I climb in beside him, eyes on the stars. It's been a while since I've gone stargazing, and out here, there are so many visible. Everywhere you look between the treetops, they're laid above us like a glittering blanket. I rest my cheek against Sebastian's chest, and his hand strokes absently through my hair, tangling gently in the waves.

"I wanted to show you this," he says, voice a low purr against my cheek. "Back then. I wanted to share everything I saw with you, in fact."

I smile, my eyes half-closed. He feels so warm against the

chill in the night air, like a perfect contrast. "I know what you mean. I felt the same way, right from day one."

"And we have." He rests his chin on the top of my head, and there's a sense of full-body warmth, of being completely enveloped and protected here. "Whatever other mistakes we've made, we did that one right."

I laugh softly, turning to press my face against his chest. "We did," I murmur, voice muffled by his shirt. When I look up again, Sebastian runs his fingers through my hair, then gently draws my face up to his. Our lips meet, and it's softer, sweeter than usual.

Sebastian shifts underneath me, pulling me more firmly on top of him. I swing one leg over to straddle his lap, my hair falling around us like a curtain as our lips remain locked. He lets out a soft sound, almost a moan, low in his throat, and it sends a pulse of heat through me, tightening the muscles behind my navel.

I shift against him, lower myself until my hips are poised above his. When I roll forward, I feel the hard jut of him, growing with every second.

On the radio behind us, classic rock plays, filling the car and the air around us. We break apart, and I tip my head back to look back up at the stars. When I glance down again, Sebastian's gazing at me with hooded eyes, hungry and intent. "You are so fucking incredible. How did I get so lucky?"

I laugh, running a hand through his hair, nails extended to drag against his scalp the way he likes. His eyes fall all the way shut, like a contented cat. "I ask myself the same question a lot," I murmur.

He reaches up to cup the back of my head and draws me in for another kiss. Harder this time, more frantic. My hands slip from his hair and down his shoulders, tracing along his chest and over his abs. He draws back from the kiss, watching me closely. "Last time I came here, you know what I was daydreaming about?" he asks quietly.

I shake my head, even though at this point, I think I have some idea.

He reaches between us to undo the clasp of my jeans. I lift one leg to let him push them down, wriggling out of them in the backseat, while his free hand roams across my belly, the backs of my thighs. "I wanted to bring you out here under the stars…" He leans up to kiss along my collarbone, flicking his tongue into the divot at the base of my neck. "And worship every inch of your body." His mouth shifts lower, even as I reach down to help him, dragging my shirt off over my head.

He cups my breasts through my bra, his tongue sliding into the space between them, making me shiver.

At the same time, I reach down for his jeans clasp, my hands fumbling with the button. It's even harder to concentrate when he nudges my bra off, his tongue licking and circling around my nipples, one after the other. When he pulls away, the night air turns them hard at once, and he reaches up to roll them between his fingertips, sending little shockwaves of pleasure down my spine.

I arch against him, groaning, and his smile widens. "I love how responsive you are," he says. To demonstrate, he leans back in and flicks his tongue over my nipple, his free hand still massaging my other breast. He rests his teeth gently on either side of my nipple, his tongue flicking back and forth over the tip until I moan again. "See?" he breathes, hot against my chest. "Everything I do, you respond to. So fucking sexy…"

"What can I say?" I reply, my voice only a little breathy, which I'm proud of. "You know all the right spots to hit."

He pushes his hips up against me, sending a pulse of heat through my core. As he does, he wriggles out of his jeans, pushing them over his thighs and letting them puddle at the floor of the Jeep. Only my panties and his boxers separate us now, thin slips of fabric that feel barely-there. The slick fabric of my panties adds a little extra slide as I lower myself onto him again, rolling my hips to grind against his hard, thick shaft.

"You like that, big boy?" I murmur, leaning in close to his ear. My hair grazes his bare chest, his cheek, his neck.

"Oh, you have no idea." He slides a hand up to wrap it into my hair, using it to draw me in close, tilting my head to the side until his lips find my neck. He kisses me hard and long, sucking gently. It'll leave a mark, but I don't care. It feels right—we feel like teenagers again. Hooking up in the backseat of our parents' car on a drive after we snuck off together.

"Mmm." I roll my hips along his length again, sending

shivers down both our spines. "I think I have some ideas…"

With a wicked grin, Bash reaches down to dip a hand beneath the hem of my panties. His fingers skim along my mound, then lower, at the same time as he wraps his other hand around the back of my neck to hold me in place above him. "Do you now?" His fingers slide lower, lower.

I squirm, letting out a faint sigh as his fingertip parts my lower lips, sliding along the slick path of my slit.

"Certainly feels like you've been having naughty thoughts." He runs that fingertip along me again, then circles my entrance, teasing. "I love how wet you get for me, babygirl."

I roll my hips forward and closer to him, bucking when he slides that finger inside me. "Fuck, Bash."

"That's right." He crooks his finger inside me, curls along my front wall, even as his thumb finds my clit, gently rolling back and forth across the tiny bud. "God, I love the sounds you make."

This, because a low keening sound has started in the back of my throat, almost without my realizing it. I swallow hard, trying to get myself under control enough to reach down and work my own palm beneath his boxers. My hands are cold, so I press them flat against his stomach first, letting them warm. "You drive me so wild," I murmur.

He shivers, and drops his free hand to cup mine, sharing his body heat. "Here's hoping I never stop." His eyes flash when they meet mine, and at the same time, he adds a second finger, making me gasp at the sensation, my pussy stretched a little fuller. His fingers move in an easy rhythm—but not fast enough.

I arch against him, trying to ride him. But he grips my hip, pulling me back down.

"Ah, ah. Not so fast." His eyes find mine again, drinking me in. "I want to savor this."

I bite my lower lip. It takes all of my concentration not to grind against his palm, driving myself closer and faster to orgasm. "Do you… plan to torture me first?" I manage to ask.

He chuckles. "Maybe a bit." His fingers stroke a little deeper, a little faster. "I must admit, I enjoy watching you squirm."

As if in answer, I wriggle against him, slowly losing control over my own body. "Bash…" His thumb circles my clit, moving faster, and I gasp. "Oh, yes. Right there, fuck…"

His grin widens. "Right here?" He moves his finger faster, and my hips buck out of control up off his lap.

"Oh God. Yes…"

"That's it." He buries his face in my chest, tongue lapping at my hard nipple as his hand moves faster, deeper. "Cum for me, babygirl. Right here."

My breath is hard and fast, any sense of control I had left quickly fleeing my body. "So… close," I manage to pant.

Suddenly, his hand draws away, dropping out of me, and I cry out in frustration and protest. But I shouldn't have questioned. I barely register the absence before his hard cock lines up with my entrance, and he pushes inside of me in one fluid motion.

"Fuck," I cry out, as he grabs my hips in both hands and starts driving up and into me. "Bash…"

One hand still bracing my hip, he slips the other between us. All it takes is a single, barely-there graze of his thumb over my clit, and I'm gone. Stars spark behind my eyes as I scream, the orgasm hitting me like a tidal wave.

"God I love how much noise you make," Bash says, somewhere in the distance. I'm still working on regaining control of my vision, and he's already returning his hand to my hip, pulling me up and back down onto him, his cock thick inside me, stretching my pussy to its limits.

I arch my back, tipping my head up to stare at the trees above, the gap between the canopy revealing more stars than I ever notice back home. Sebastian keeps going, hands roaming all over my body, from my hips up the curves of my sides to my breasts and back. He drives into me over and over, my already sensitive clit tingling again, still recovering from my first orgasm and well on the way to another.

We feel like the only people in the world out here, maybe in the whole universe. "Bash," I whisper, and then, gaining confidence, I stretch higher above him, call out louder. "Bash."

"Yes." His hands tighten on my hips, and he thrusts into me harder, faster. "Say my name, babygirl."

I shout it again, loud enough to echo through the trees. He sits up, pulling me flush against his chest, so our bodies are pressed fully together now, his hands still guiding me as

I rise off his lap and thrust back down against him, giving every inch as good as I get.

Bash curls his hand through my hair, tightens it into a fist to drag my mouth to his. I sink into his kiss, savor the muffled groans he lets out, as his thrusts grow wilder, less controlled.

I run both hands through his hair, digging my nails in lightly, then draw him back just far enough to meet his gaze. "Your turn," I whisper, breathy and confident. "I want you to cum inside me." I feel his cock jump inside me at those words, can sense how close he is to the edge.

I run my nails down his bare back, trail them along the arches of his hips. At the same time, I tighten my thighs, clamping them around his, and buck above him, driving his thick shaft deep into my tight pussy with every movement.

"God, Jen." His voice is a low, guttural growl, on the very edge of losing control. "You are so fucking... hot."

I grin as I bend to kiss his neck, lips parted. I drag my teeth lightly over the sensitive skin there, and feel more than hear him gasp an inhale.

"I'm so close," he pants, and I smile against his neck.

"Cum for me, baby." I rise up, so far only his tip remains inside me. Then I thrust back down again, letting him fill me once more. At the apex of his thrust, his hands suddenly grip both of my hips, his body jerking as he groans.

"Baby Jen, Baby Jen," he grits out, as a hot rush fills me up, flooding my insides. Our commingled juices spill out around us, over his lap. At the same time, I keep moving, tightening my muscles around his shaft, savoring every twitch and jerk, milking every last drop from him.

When we finally collapse back against the leather seats, we're both laughing, sticky, our skin cooling fast in the night air. But neither of us move to cover up. Sebastian rolls onto his side, tucks me against his chest, and our eyes find the stars overhead. Still there, quiet and sedate. Watching everything down here like they've seen it a million times before. Probably they have.

"Yep," Sebastian says after a while, prompting me to glance over my shoulder up at him. He flashes me a grin, and leans down to capture my mouth in a quick kiss again. "Exactly as great as I always imagined it would be."

Laughing, I roll my eyes, but arch up to return the kiss. "Hmm," I murmur, as we break apart once more. "And here I hoped it would be better than your imagination."

Laughing, he slaps my bare ass lightly. "Careful, or I'll be tempted to demand a redo."

Grinning right back, I arch my back to press my ass against his crotch, wriggling lightly. "Watch out, cowboy, or I'll take you up on that offer."

Eyes bright, we both roll over, and I drag him on top of me this time, one leg hooked around the back of his thighs as we lose ourselves once more.

Chapter Twenty-Eight

Jennifer

My body is still singing with leftover adrenaline and serotonin when we get back to the hotel later that night. I'm so ready for sleep. The only thing I'm thinking about as we pull into a spot out front and park, is collapsing face-first into our comfy, enormous hotel bed. We climb out of the Jeep, and I cast one last fond glance into the backseat. Already, I know I'll return to this night over and over in my memories.

You can always tell when something is going to become a core memory. And it doesn't get much better than this.

I hook my arm through Sebastian's arm as we strut through the hotel sliding doors. "What do you think Palm Springs will be like?"

Sebastian chuckles. "Can't rest on your laurels, huh? Already got to be planning the next victory?"

I smirk. "What can I say? The thrill is pretty addictive."

Inside, we head up to our room, passing clusters of late celebrants still awake here and there in the lobbies. Everyone who sees us shouts out congratulations or raises nearly empty glasses to our victories. We wave back, laughing, and stop to chat with a couple of people who want tips on imitating Bash's hard slams or my hand-switching trick.

"How did you even do that?" one woman gushes, and I feel my cheeks warming, even as Bash tucks a proud hand around my lower back. "I don't think I could be that coordinated."

"Neither did I," I admit. "I'm not really sure how it happened; it was just an instinctive reaction, in the moment."

"She's being modest," Sebastian says. "She's a hard worker, and she practices every day."

The woman chuckles. "I'll have to up my game next year." Then she gives me another little tip of her cocktail. "Good luck to you both in Palm Springs. We'll all be rooting for you."

My chest swells with another burst of pride. Together, Bash and I head for the elevators, hips brushing, arms around one another's waists. "I can't wait to do all this over again," I murmur. "With even higher stakes next time."

He laughs softly. "I wouldn't charge back into battle with anyone else on my right."

I roll my eyes, but I'm grinning. "You're so cheesy, you know that?"

He bends to kiss the top of my head. "I try."

Upstairs in our room, I let Sebastian take the first shower while I get my things ready. I dig my toiletries out of my suitcase and lay them on the bed, then strip down to my underthings and wrap a towel around myself, leaning back on the bed to wait.

My cell phone, which I left up in the room all throughout

the tournament, lights up, catching my eye. I put it on silent, so the ringer wouldn't disturb other hotel guests in neighboring rooms. But now I brighten, realizing I should update the kids on our results.

I lean across the bed to snatch it up. The moment I check the screen, however, my heart freezes.

There are dozens of missed calls and texts. I skim the list, bile creeping up the back of my throat. They're all from my mother. Fuck. Memories of our fight last night flood through me again, and I remember everything I've tried so hard all day to forget. I hope nothing happened.

Pulse racing, I open the phone and skim the messages first. They're not helpful. Call me, says the most recent one, and before that, We need to talk ASAP.

I tap her number, taking deep breaths as I wait for the phone to connect. My pulse continues to race, only slowing somewhat when my mother finally picks up.

"Jennifer? Where have you been?"

The sound of her voice sends a spike of relief through my veins. At least she's well enough to answer the phone. "Mom. We were on the courts; I left my phone in the room. What's wrong?" I can't believe you lied to me, I want to shout. But whatever this emergency is needs to come first.

"It's Mia," she says, and my stomach drops out entirely.

Whatever I expected this to be about, it wasn't my daughter. "What do you mean? What happened?"

Mom exhales angrily. Even through the phone, I can

picture her expression—furrowed brow, pinched lips. The expression she gets when she's furious. "She told me she was going to the mall with friends, but she's two hours late getting home. She's not answering her phone. I got worried and I went to check through her things, and... I found condoms in her dresser drawer."

It takes me a second to process those words. And then a longer second to put them together. Jaxon. He seemed like such a nice kid, but... "Shit. Did you ask Logan where she'd go?"

"He's not here either," my mother says, and I curse internally. "He's been at a sleepover all weekend."

"A sleepover?" I repeat, bewildered. "With who?"

"I don't know. He said you knew about it."

I groan. "I most certainly did not. Why didn't you ask me first? Ugh, never mind! You keep trying Logan," I say. "I'll call Mia now." I hang up and dial my daughter's number straight away, pulse ratcheting, if possible, even higher than it's already been racing. Mia's phone goes straight to voicemail, and I curse. "Mia. Call me, now." Then I hang up and type out a text instead. You're giving your grandmother a heart attack. Where are you?

Inspiration strikes a moment later, and I call the school directory to find Jaxon's home number. While I'm dialing, Sebastian steps out of the shower. He's wearing a huge grin, but it falls the moment he spots my expression. "What is it?"

"The kids," I manage to say, before tears spill over, and my throat chokes up. I drop the phone and bury my face in my hands. The worst part is, we should have seen this coming. We knew something was going on with Logan. Now Mia's gone off the rails too. And where have we been? Running all over the country like a couple with no kids playing a fucking game.

"Slow down. Deep breaths." Sebastian perches beside me on the bed, rubbing my back. "Start from the beginning."

In fits and starts, I tell him about Mia's absence, Logan's too. The condoms in Mia's bedroom. Sebastian's expression darkens with every new detail. He snatches up his phone. As he does, my expression drifts away, a sudden memory springing up.

Chris, at the Pawley's Island tournament, wearing his usual smug smile. I felt like I should warn you about your son… Your boy's name is Logan, right? I heard he's been running with a rough crowd lately…

I shove to my feet, heart pounding in my temples now. "I know who might be able to help us."

✢ ✢ ✢

I leave Sebastian calling around to Logan's school friends and parents, and hurry down to the lobby. The after-party has mostly broken up, but a few stragglers happen to know where the room I'm looking for is. Naturally, they booked the honeymoon suite—no doubt planning to peremptorily celebrate their victory.

But any joy or smugness I might have felt about snatching that away has long since melted in the face of this anxiety. Our win doesn't matter now—nothing matters more than our kids' safety.

I swallow my reservations and pound on the door of the honeymoon suite. Judging by the loud music playing inside, they're here, and still awake, which is a relief. I just hope they're willing to open the door once they see who it is.

I press my ear to the wood, knocking a second time. On the far side, I catch shuffling footsteps, and I straighten just in time for the door to swing open on a bleary-eyed Chris.

He takes one narrowed glance at me and groans. "I thought you were Crys."

I frown, momentarily distracted. "Why, isn't she here?"

He pushes the door wider and retreats back inside. I follow him a couple of steps, pausing at the sight of the hotel room. The bed is unmade, clothes strewn around it. A single pickleball paddle rests against the screen door out onto the patio, as if it had been thrown there. "Obviously not," he drawls.

"Didn't mean to intrude," I say, because I really didn't. I cross my arms, ignoring the chaos around me. I came here for a reason. "Back at Pawley's Island, you told me you'd heard some rumors about my son. Was that true, or were you just trying to get inside my head?"

"Little from column A, little from column B..." Chris plops backward onto the bed, shrugging.

"What exactly did you hear?"

Something in my tone must tip him off, because he looks up again, a spark flaring in his eyes. "Uh oh. Trouble in paradise?"

"Don't be an asshole, Chris. This is my son we're talking about."

He relents a little at that, sinking back onto the bed. "It's probably nothing. Our son is in the same grade, just goes to a different school. I overheard him talking about a Logan Hayward getting into trouble with the Bryce twins and their good-for-nothing friends…"

"Who?" I demand. I've never heard about any Bryce twins before.

Chris heaves a sigh. "Delinquents. They've been arrested a couple times; I made our son promise to stay away from them years ago. Lately they've started selling drugs to some of the kids at his school."

My heart drops all the way into my gut. A buzzing sound starts in my eardrums, far away at first, but growing louder with every passing second. Logan. We need to find him.

"Jennifer?" Chris's voice sounds distant, hazy. "Are you alright?"

Without bothering to answer, I whirl around and race toward our hotel room. Bash and I need to get home. Now.

Chapter Twenty-Nine
Crys

Those bastards did not deserve the win. I pace back and forth across the now-empty courts, the asphalt clicking under my high heels every time I whirl around to stomp in another direction. No matter how many times I mentally replay the match, the outcome remains the same.

Infuriating.

All our hard work, all our talent, and we lose to a couple of amateurs. My lip curls, and I grab a stray martini glass someone left outside—the cleaners haven't gotten out here to deal with the aftermath of the afterparty yet—and hurl it at the nearest net. It lands with a satisfying crash. But then I'm just standing there, empty-handed and still radiating anger.

Fuck Jennifer. Fuck Sebastian. Fuck the whole Hayward family and their stupid unfounded confidence. We're so much better than them. We've worked harder for much longer. Those tickets should've been ours.

I squeeze my eyes shut. I can still see that last ball sailing past me. I can still see my husband immediately after it went wide, screaming in my face.

Well, fuck him, too. If it weren't for his shitty communication skills—not to mention his cockiness that made him miss half of Bash's shots—we wouldn't be in this mess.

If only I could pass some of our problems on to so-called "Bashifer," then maybe they wouldn't waltz to an unfair win at Palm Springs, too.

Suddenly, I straighten, as inspiration strikes. That's it. Their communication, their lovey-dovey perfect-couple bullshit. That was the only reason they won here today. If I can undermine that, they won't stand a chance at nationals.

And I know just the seed of doubt to plant. Smirking, I straighten my outfit and stride back across the courts, with purpose this time. I dance around the post-party refuse, sail through the empty lobby, and out the sliding glass doors to the front parking lot.

Sure enough, their obnoxiously pedestrian Jeep is parked right where I last saw it. There's no mistaking whose car it is, given the Riverbend Country Club parking sticker on the windshield and the Lake Heather Fire Department license plate frame on the back. I step up to the vehicle, surveying it, rolling my eyes as I see a saccharine "perfect little family" photo dangling from the driver's sun visor. The top is down, which will make my job that much easier.

Casting one last glance at the hotel lobby, I reach up under my mini skirt and hook a thumb under my red silk panties. This two-piece set cost more than Jennifer's entire wardrobe, most likely, but it's worth it. Sacrifices must be made, in the pursuit of ultimate victory.

I nudge my panties down over my hips, until they puddle at my ankles. Carefully, I step out of them one high-heeled shoe at a time, kicking them up into my hand. It's easy enough to step up onto the running board of the Jeep, and even simpler to aim them at the backseat. I toss the bright red, obviously used panties onto the floor behind the driver's seat, where they'll be easily visible from anyone sitting in the passenger side, the moment they glance behind themselves.

Snickering under my breath, I hop back off the Jeep and step back, dusting off my hands. Mission accomplished, I stride back into the hotel lobby with a wide smile, feeling lighter than I have all day.

* * *

Jen and Sebastian's story continues in book 2... coming soon.

Part of the ♀-♂-2♥ *series*

JOHAN MIDDELTHON

StoryTerrace

Chapter One

Jennifer

My skin feels ready to combust when I finally step off the plane. It was the worst, longest-feeling flight of my life, despite actually being one of the shortest I've ever taken.

I launch myself through the airport, bag slung over one shoulder. I don't let myself slow down, because if I do, everything will catch up to me.

My muscles are still sore all over from last night. Not just the tournament win, but everything that followed—the Jeep, Sebastian, deep inside me, hands gripping my hips.

Was everything a lie? Or just that? Just us?

I don't know what to think anymore. Who to believe. Mom offered to meet me at the airport, but I declined, too in my head about everything to open that particular can of worms just yet.

On the far side of security, I call a shared car to our address. Just typing it in sends a knot of anxiety looping around my throat. Is he home yet? Theoretically, my flight should've been a hell of a lot quicker than the drive, but there's airport security lines to factor in, plus the trip to and from the airports on each end.

I'm not sure what I'll do if he's there. The last words we

said to one another before I left are still ringing in my ears.

I shake myself, cram into the backseat of the miniature-sized car I had the misfortune of lucking into, and open the window, hanging halfway out of it despite the November bite in the air.

I need to forget about my husband. I have bigger problems.

On my cell phone, under recent calls, are half a dozen unanswered calls each to my children. Mia, in particular, stings. I know how addicted she is to her cell. It hardly ever leaves her hand, let alone her sight. She's screening my calls on purpose, which means she knows how much trouble she's in.

Condoms. My god. Are we at that age already?

Of course, if she is going to get intimate with this boy, I'd prefer that she be safe about it. But she's so young still, barely sixteen, and while he seems nice enough, he's a teenage boy. Have they had all the discussions they need to before they take a step like this? Has she truly considered all the risks? Does she trust him, and how will she react, if he fails to live up to that trust?

My chest tightens. I wouldn't trust any man right about now. But that is my own concern. Something I need to compartmentalize when I confront my daughter, or she'll see right through me.

As for Logan... Christ. Where to even begin. I pray that what Chris told me back at the tournament, about the bad crowd Logan's fallen in with, is bullshit. Knowing the Non-

Music Factory, he was probably trying to psych me out. Get into my head, and exact whatever kind of revenge he could manage for our victory.

But I can't help feeling that some of his warning rung true. Logan has been hanging with a new crowd—kids I don't know much about. And he's certainly been demonstrating a willingness to lie to our faces, and sneak away from the house for long periods of time to God knows where.

The car pulls up outside our house after what feels like an interminable amount of driving, and my blood runs cold. Not because it looks any different, but because it doesn't—from the outside, you'd never know anything was wrong in our lives. Everything looks exactly the way I left it just three days ago.

How much can a person's world change in three days?

Apparently, it can turn all the way upside-down. I tip the driver and head inside, feet feeling heavy as lead on our walkway. At the door, I pause for a second, then pull out my key.

Inside, the vestibule is silent. I pause for a moment, holding my breath. Tears sting the backs of my eyes. I remember the first time we crossed this threshold as owners. The way Sebastian was so excited, bottle of cheap bubbles under one arm, his eyes alight with possibility.

He walked me through the foyer pointing out all the work we could do. He had big visions for the kitchen, the dining room. And we've followed through on most of them. We updated the outdated old kitchen into the modern one of our dreams. We opened up the old boarded-over windows in the dining room, tore out the stupid drop ceilings from the 80s and restored the original, beautiful crown molding.

We built a life here. Now, it feels like it's all crashing down.

The floor creaks underfoot as I take another step. "Logan?" calls a voice from the living room opposite the stairwell, suddenly. "Logan, thank god—"

My mother bursts through the door, then freezes at the sight of me.

Now that I know, it's impossible not to see it. The bags under her eyes, the sallow note underlying her skin tone. How old and tiny her hands look, like bird's claws. How tired she keeps telling us she is.

"Where's Sebastian?" my mother asks.

I open my mouth—to do what, I'm not sure. Yell at her for lying to me? Demand to know why she hid her cancer diagnosis? Shout about where Sebastian is and what that bastard did to me, to us?

Instead, I burst into sobs. My mother hurries to my side, wrapping her arms around me. Normally, her embrace comforts any ailment, soothes me the way nothing else can.

Now, I stand stiff and tense in her arms, wondering how much longer she'll be around to hold onto.

Also by Johan Middelthon

Don't Shark the Dolphins
A Guide to Pickleball and the P3 Way of Life

Avaliable on Audible,
iTunes, Kindle,
Amazon, and Barnes
and Noble

Let go of "the old way" of playing pickleball and let the "P3 way" guide you to the most fun and satisfaction you have ever experienced in the game. This book is for everyone, from those just beginning their journey with the game to those looking to master the sport.

Don't Shark the Dolphins teaches you tips and techniques with easy-to-understand terminology to help you improve your game. On-court lessons are extended off the court with the P3 Pickleball lifestyle, a philosophy taught through inspirational stories and perspectives on how we should consider carrying ourselves throughout our daily life. Finally, it introduces "Turbo", the revolutionary new doubles strategy that is going to change the world of pickleball forever.